Forever in Good Hope

C

Also by Cynthia Rutledge/Cindy Kirk

Forever *in* Good Hope

——·——

CINDY KIRK

Montlake
Romance

Text copyright © 2017 Cynthia Rutledge

Published by Montlake Romance, Seattle

www.apub.com

Amazon, the Amazon logo, and Montlake Romance are trademarks of Amazon.com, Inc., or its affiliates.

ISBN-13: 9781477848777
ISBN-10: 1477848770

Cover design by Janet Perr

Printed in the United States of America

To my daughter, Wendy. I can't imagine my life without you in it. Thanks for all your support and love.

ChapterOne

"Will your boyfriend be upset when he hears you've had breakfast with me?"

When Jeremy Rakes's bold blue eyes met hers, God help her, Delphinium Bloom felt the pull. Which didn't make sense, considering what they'd once shared had been a lifetime ago.

She'd moved on from him and from Good Hope. Xander Tillman, her current main man, was big city all the way. With his smartly styled dark hair, piercing brown eyes, and tailored Tom Ford suits, Xander was the perfect fit for her LA lifestyle.

Still, she had to admit there was something about Jeremy with his tousled blond hair, vivid blue eyes, and ready smile. If he lived in California, she could easily see him on a board, riding the waves off Oceanside Pier.

But he was far from an aimless surfer dude. He'd rocked a tux at her sister Marigold's wedding, and at the recent meeting of the town board, wearing a tailored suit and a serious expression, he'd radiated power and authority.

"Why should Xander care? It's just breakfast. It's not like we're getting naked together." Fin brought the mug to her lips, which curved slightly at the flash of heat in his eyes.

Instead of jerking his chain further, Fin took a moment to glance around the interior of Muddy Boots. She liked the changes her brother-in-law had made since buying the restaurant several years earlier.

Gone was the wallpaper, a hideous coffeepot pattern in harvest gold and mud brown. In its place, cobalt-blue paint splattered like rain on the now-white walls. The mural of a young girl in a bright red jacket with shiny red boots on the far wall, painted by a local artist, drew the eye and never failed to make Fin smile.

The pleasant scent of yeast and cinnamon from the monkey bread she knew had been baked early that morning teased her nostrils. Warmth eased around her shoulders like a comfortable old sweater. It was all so nice. So familiar.

Even the stares from other customers were familiar. A single woman sharing a meal with the unattached mayor was always news. Fin wouldn't be surprised to find the fact mentioned in tomorrow's gossip column of the *Open Door*, a daily e-newsletter.

Only when she refocused her gaze on Jeremy did she realize he was also staring at her.

She lifted a brow.

"Why shouldn't he care? You're my ex-girlfriend. You and I were . . ." Jeremy paused, inclined his head. "He does know about us."

Though it was phrased as a statement, she heard the question.

"Xander is aware we got naked in high school." Fin waved a hand, showing off her glossy, red-tipped fingers. "Ancient history."

She said it with just the right amount of casualness, even added a little smile. It was the truth. What she didn't say and didn't want to admit—not even to herself—was the history she and this man shared was something forever woven through the fabric of her life.

"I'm surprised you didn't leave with him." Leaning back against the cherry-red vinyl, Jeremy's hands cupped the mug as if he needed to warm his fingers. Which was laughable, considering it was mid-August with today's temperature projected to reach the lower eighties.

"Xander understands I don't get back to Good Hope as often as I'd like." Fin lifted one thin shoulder, let it fall. "He didn't need me to take another look at the alternate sites. He has Liam, his cinematographer, to offer input."

"Will he finalize a contract with one of the towns while he's there?"

"Maybe. From what he's said, both towns are eager to move forward." Fin recalled the hard edge to Xander's jaw when Jeremy had cast the tiebreaking vote against the proposal. "But Xander is accustomed to getting what he wants. He wants, ah, wanted, Good Hope."

"That was obvious." Jeremy's voice remained nonchalant, his expression giving nothing away.

Fin kept her tone casual. "It appeared to me a lot of people in town wanted the proposition accepted."

"Xander was confident we'd vote to approve." Without taking his eyes off her, Jeremy took a sip of the strong chicory blend.

"Confident is his middle name." Fin added a dollop of cream to her cup, wondering how anyone could love coffee this strong. "The money he offered for any inconvenience to Good Hope was substantial."

"Closing down the town for the month of December so he could film here was a substantial request." Jeremy's blue eyes darkened as he placed his cup on the table. "It's not as if the community simply

3

celebrates a few days around Christmas. When you include the Twelve Nights events, the entire month of December is celebration."

After taking a testing sip, Fin grimaced and set the mug aside. She leaned forward, resting her forearms on the table. "I understand that, I really do. But it's only for one season. And the money—"

Before she could say more, Dakota Lohmeier appeared, platters of food balanced on her forearms. With her dark hair pulled up and back, she looked more like the college girl she was instead of the child Fin remembered.

Dakota hummed as she served the daily special, a crisp parmesan omelet with a slice of banana bread and a grilled tomato.

Fin cocked her head, attempting to place the tune. "Is that 'It's the Hard-Knock Life'?"

Dakota grinned. "*Annie* opened last night at the playhouse. I can't get the songs out of my head."

"There are so many good ones." When she'd been young and actively involved in Good Hope Community Theater, Fin had happily imagined a life spent singing, dancing, and being onstage. "Is Gladys still playing Miss Hannigan?"

The girl nodded. "Word is she's retiring from performing once this show closes."

"Good Hope Community Theater won't be the same without her." For as long as Fin could remember, Gladys had been a mainstay of local stage productions. "She was Miss Hannigan years ago when I played an orphan, and later when I played Annie."

Dakota's hazel eyes went wide. "*You* were Annie?"

From the girl's look of awe, Fin might have been an A-list Hollywood actress.

Fin waved a hand. "It was no big deal."

"Fin has a beautiful voice." Jeremy's eyes were as warm as the hand he settled over hers. As if realizing the inappropriateness of the gesture, he pulled back.

"You could take over for Mrs. Bertholf." An eagerness filled Dakota's voice as the words spilled out. "I mean, you're not old like she is, but they can do a lot with makeup, and if you can sing and act you—"

"I don't sing anymore." Though it was true, Fin discovered simply saying the words brought a pang. "And I don't live here."

"That's right. You live in Los Angeles." Dakota supplied the information as if eager to show that, despite now attending college in La Crosse, she kept up with local news. "My grandmother says you'll never come back to Good Hope to live."

Dakota's grandmother, Anita Fishback, had once dated Fin's father. The woman wasn't particularly fond of any of the Bloom sisters, and the feeling was mutual. The happiest day of Fin's life had been when her dad had finally seen Anita for who she really was and broken it off.

"Miss, could I get a refill?" A man at a nearby table held up his cup. "And more cream, too."

"Right away, sir." Dakota flashed an apologetic smile at Fin and Jeremy. "Duty calls. Enjoy your breakfast. Let me know if I can get you anything else."

Dakota hummed as she hurried off.

"Gladys has been onstage since the 1950s. Her retirement will leave a void in the core troupe." Jeremy picked up his fork, shot her a curious stare. "Did you mean it? You don't sing anymore?"

Fin thought back to the show choir competition in Milwaukee the spring of her junior year in high school. Thinking of that day and what had happened in the motel room during that trip forever linked those two events in her head. She hadn't sung since.

"It's different now." She forked off a bite of the omelet. "I live in a city with zillions of talented singers. My talent is business."

Pride rang in Fin's voice. After years of work in PR and marketing, she'd finally found her dream job. She'd recently joined Entertainment Quest—a production and development company—as a development executive. The company focused on book-to-screen adaptations. The film Xander would direct in December was based on a book written by one of their authors.

As Xander was a rising star in the film industry, Fin's boss, the company's CEO, was determined to do whatever it took to cultivate his favor.

Fin smiled, remembering how Shirleen had practically pushed her out of the office when Xander mentioned he'd like Fin to accompany him on this trip to Wisconsin.

Jeremy lifted his mug in a salute. "You've done well, Finley."

Hearing his pet name for her roll off his lips was bittersweet.

So much stood between them now. So much Jeremy didn't know.

Fin was relieved when a man in work boots and a ball cap stopped by the table. Tall, with broad shoulders and a workingman's body, the guy had a roll of blueprints under one arm. His dark hair held the merest hint of a wave, and his eyes were nearly as blue as Jeremy's.

"Fin Bloom, I'd like you to meet Kyle Kendrick. Kyle is in charge of the Living Center construction." Despite the food growing cold on his plate, Jeremy gave Kyle his full attention. "Last I heard, Chapin Enterprises was anticipating a September twenty-ninth grand opening."

"That's the plan." Kyle slanted a glance at Fin. "Did he tell you his grandmother has already picked out her apartment in Independent Living?"

"She'll keep everyone on their toes." Fin adored Jeremy's grandmother. Heck, everyone in Good Hope loved the petite firecracker.

"Ruby had been coming down every day to inspect the progress." Kyle's dark brows pulled together. "I haven't seen her since the heart attack. How's she getting along?"

"There may be surgery in the future. Nothing definite." Jeremy cleared his throat, then took a sip of coffee. "Do you think you'll be ready for her to move in at the end of next month?"

"Lynn Chapin is wanting a few changes to the interior, but we should have everything wrapped on schedule." Kyle's gaze returned to Fin. "You're Ami Cross's sister."

Fin returned his smile. "I'm here from California visiting family."

"Fin is an old friend of mine." Jeremy's voice held a warning even the deaf could hear.

"Well, it was a pleasure meeting you." Kyle spoke easily and gave a little nod. "Mayor."

Fin watched Kyle walk away. She was certain they'd never met before, but there was something familiar about him. "I bet the single women in town are spending a lot of time visiting his job site."

Jeremy's gaze sharpened. "You have a boyfriend."

"I wasn't speaking about me. Though I like to window-shop as much as any woman." Xander certainly didn't mind her looking at other men, even when she was with him. He did the same when she was on his arm.

Jeremy's gaze met hers. "I'd hope my girlfriend wouldn't have the desire to window-shop."

Fin shrugged. "Things are different in California."

Jeremy's blue eyes turned stormy, as if waging an inner battle. Then he smiled. "Got big plans for tonight, California Girl?"

"Not really." Fin took another bite of omelet, chewed. "Ami goes to bed early, so I'll probably head straight back to the motel after dinner. Those morning hours at the bakery are taking their toll on her, especially now that she's eight months pregnant. She and Beck are firmly in baby-waiting mode. That's why I'm not staying with them. They need this alone time. They certainly won't have it once the baby arrives."

Fin realized with sudden horror she was rambling and clamped her lips shut.

"I've got an alternative to a quiet evening at the Sweet Dreams Motel." A twinkle replaced the storm clouds in Jeremy's baby blues. "Want to come to a party?"

A party.

Jeremy's invitation had Fin smiling as she left the café. She found the stroll down Main Street nearly as pleasant as her morning breakfast. The sunny summer day had tourists crowding the streets of Good Hope's business district.

It was really, Fin thought, very similar to the busy foot traffic on Rodeo Drive. Except instead of Jimmy Choo or Louboutin, most women wore sandals or running shoes. And while there were plenty of quaint storefronts, there wasn't a single designer store or shop.

The weather reminded her of California, with sun warming her bare shoulders and a light breeze ruffling her hair. Over the past six months Fin had let her sleek brown strands interspersed with blonde highlights grow longer.

At work, she'd taken to wearing her hair pulled back in a low knot or a tuck and roll. Now the silky strands she'd left hanging loose wafted in the breeze. The hint of moisture in the air reminded her Green Bay was a mere block away.

Fin was relieved Xander hadn't wanted—or rather hadn't asked—her to accompany him and his cinematographer to the other two sites. Remaining in Good Hope while the two men traveled gave her a chance to finally spend time with friends and family. When they'd first arrived, Fin had been excited, seeing this as Xander's opportunity to meet her family and get acquainted.

While Xander *had* agreed to one family dinner, anytime she'd suggested further contact with her sisters or father, he'd pulled the "We're here on business" card.

Fin wondered if allowing her to stay in Good Hope while he traveled was an apology of sorts.

She was still mulling over that possibility when a small boy appeared and cut in front of her. To avoid slamming into the child, Fin sidestepped. The kid's mother zipped past, hot in pursuit.

Fin may have avoided a collision with the boy, but the zigzagging movement had her teetering on her heels. As she fought to regain her balance, strong hands gripped her shoulders, steadying her.

"Thank you. I'm so sorry—" Fin stopped when she saw who'd saved her from a fall. "Eliza. Hi."

Eliza Shaw, executive director of the Cherries and owner of the Good Hope General Store, dropped her hands as if Fin's shoulders had turned red-hot.

"I heard you were still in town." The polite smile that graced Eliza's red lips didn't quite reach her eyes.

Wearing Louboutins and dressed in a Max Mara jacquard shift dress of contrasting geometric patterns, Eliza would be at home on Rodeo Drive or Fifth Avenue. In her early thirties with dark hair cut in a sleek bob and cool gray eyes, she was even more stunning than she'd been in high school.

Knowing Ami and this woman had recently renewed their friendship had Fin responding more cordially than she might have in the past. While she still didn't like how Eliza had treated her sister after that long-ago accident, if Ami could forgive and forget, she'd try. "I didn't mean to jump in front of you. The boy came out of nowhere. Thanks for the steadying hand."

Eliza dismissed the thanks with a careless flick of her wrist. Then her eyes narrowed. "Since you've been back, you've been seeing a lot of Jeremy. I heard you had breakfast with him today."

For a second Fin almost explained she had a boyfriend—a serious one—but while Ami may have forgiven Eliza, Fin still hadn't.

Let her wonder, Fin thought. *Let her worry I'm going to take her precious Jeremy away from her.* Not that Eliza and Jeremy were a couple. But they were *something.* Fin wasn't sure exactly what was between them, wasn't sure she wanted to know. "It's been nice to . . . reconnect."

She added her best feline smile.

Eliza stiffened. She didn't appear to notice—or care—that people were having to step around them. "You didn't leave with the others."

"I'm enjoying my time in Good Hope too much." Fin gave a low chuckle. "Reconnecting with an old lover can be oh so enjoyable."

Then, because she'd exhausted everything she had to say to Eliza, Fin stepped back into the flow of foot traffic and sauntered off.

Chapter Two

"I had no intention of coming tonight." Marigold Rallis, her golden mane a curly cloud around her shoulders, stepped from Fin's rented BMW Roadster.

"I'm glad you changed your mind." When Jeremy had invited her to attend a barbecue he was hosting for Good Hope's business owners, Fin's initial response had been to politely decline. Then she realized this was an opportunity to get a feel for what the movers and shakers of Good Hope thought of the town board vote.

It wouldn't change anything, but having more information might make Xander feel better about the outcome. She knew he hoped for a revote, although in her opinion that seemed highly unlikely. At least not without a groundswell of support for the project.

"The fact that you readily agreed to come with me tells me you didn't have anything better to do." Fin kept her tone even, knowing she and her youngest sister could get into a sparring match with little effort.

As Marigold was the youngest, Fin thought it was because her baby sister had been spoiled. Ami said it was because she and Marigold were so much alike.

"Well, there is that." Marigold expelled a dramatic sigh. "Cade is on duty tonight, so my choices were extremely limited."

Fin had known that Marigold, the owner of an up-and-coming hair salon, had been invited. "Since you were obviously at loose ends, why hadn't you planned to attend?"

Marigold lifted a shoulder, let it drop. "I guess I didn't feel like going alone."

The crushed gravel of the lot, which sat down the hill from Jeremy's impressive home, crunched beneath their feet. His house, a massive structure with leaded glass above each window and a turret topped in copper, stood three stories tall. The porch that wrapped halfway around the front added balance and beauty.

Fin had always loved not only the Victorian house painted in shades of salmon, green, and yellow, but the land surrounding the home. Though known as Rakes Farm, it was really more of an orchard, with five hundred acres of tart cherries and thirty acres of apples and pears. It was likely even more acres had been added in the years since she and Jeremy had dated.

In addition to fruit trees, the estate held a converted barn and an elegant Victorian home, both popular venues for parties and wedding receptions. Although the peak of the lavender season was several weeks past, the heady aroma from the nearby fields wafted in the air.

Marigold tugged at the bodice of her strapless short dress festooned with flowers and topped with a sleeveless denim jacket. She looked big-city chic from the tips of her gladiator sandals to the small turquoise bag holding beauty essentials.

Fin had opted for russet-colored cropped pants, a tropical-print one-shoulder shirt, and bejeweled T-strapped sandals. Once again, she'd let her hair hang loose.

"I wasn't keen on showing up alone, either." Fin smiled at her sister. "I'm glad we could come together."

"We certainly can't count on Ami for any activity after supper." Marigold grinned at Fin's look of surprise. "Hey, I got the bulletin about not calling after eight. Prim and Max aren't much better. They have the boys in bed by seven thirty."

"Two nephews and a niece or nephew on the way." Fin shook her head. "It's hard to believe."

"Ami and Beck are certainly excited about the baby."

Fin slowed her steps as she and Marigold traveled up the paved wide walkway leading up to the house. She wondered what it would be like to feel a baby move inside you. To eagerly anticipate its birth instead of being filled with fear and dread.

Marigold touched her shoulder. "Are you okay?"

Fin blinked and forced her thoughts back to the present. Seeing the worry in her sister's eyes, she flashed a smile. "I'm exceptional. Why do you ask?"

"You went sheet white." Marigold studied her face. While Prim and Ami were always likely to take her word as gospel, suspicion lurked in Marigold's eyes.

"I haven't eaten much today." Impulsively, Fin looped her arm through Marigold's. "I may embarrass you by pigging out tonight."

"It'll take you dancing on a table with a greasy chicken leg in one hand and a big ol' hunk of cake in the other to embarrass me." Marigold chuckled. "But I say go for it. Let's liven up this group."

A half hour into the barbecue, Fin decided Marigold was right. The group could use some livening up. She'd already grown bored. Part of the problem may have been that, other than greeting her at the door, Jeremy had been occupied with other guests.

Marigold struck up a conversation with Charlotte McCray, owner of the Golden Door Salon and Spa. When talk turned to product lines and discounts, Fin excused herself.

As she crossed the yard, Fin was reminded of all the events she'd attended here. Tonight, Chinese lanterns in a variety of vibrant colors had been strung across the endless manicured patch of green.

Blue-and-white-striped cloths covered strategically placed rectangular tables. The tables held side dishes ranging from sweet and spicy coleslaw to corn salad with red bell peppers and jalapeños to cowboy beans. Instead of burgers and brats, attendees had their choice of smoked brisket or tangy pulled pork.

Scattered picnic tables covered in the same striped cloths were there for guests who preferred to eat sitting down. Though galvanized tubs filled with ice, beer, and an assortment of soft drink bottles offered a variety of options, when Fin realized she was thirsty, she headed to the terrace, where a margarita machine whirred happily.

Fin smiled when she saw that Ruby Rakes manned the machine. Tiny as a sprite, the older woman's perfectly coiffed, champagne-colored hair curled softly around a too-thin face. Still, the smile she shot Fin was as bright as ever.

"I saw you talking to Charlotte and wondered when you'd come and give me a hug." Jeremy's grandmother stepped from behind the table holding the machine, her arms open wide.

Ruby was smaller than even Marigold's diminutive five-foot-three-inch frame. Fin had to bend over to wrap her arms around the woman. Though she had to be close to eighty, Ruby had always been so . . . vital. Now she was thin as a willow branch. Fin squeezed gently, afraid of shattering bones.

When she released her hold, Ruby clasped Fin's arms and studied her. "Still pretty as a picture."

"Always generous with the compliments. Is it any wonder I love you?" The sentiment came easily because it was the truth. From the time she'd first become acquainted with the woman at fifteen, Fin had adored the feisty head of the Rakes family.

"You're a sweet talker, Delphinium Bloom."

"What are you two girls up to?" Jeremy appeared from the back of the house. Though his tone was light, Fin saw the concern in his eyes when his gaze landed on his grandmother.

"Ruby is going to make me a margarita." Fin spoke lightly, confused by the sudden tension in the air.

Jeremy frowned at his grandmother. "We have staff for that duty. I don't want you taxing yourself."

Ruby stiffened. "This may be your home now, but it was mine long before. I told you. I won't stand around and do nothing."

"You can talk with me." Fin's voice portrayed none of the distress that had her heart racing. One look at Jeremy's face told her Ruby's condition was more serious than she'd imagined. "I'm the odd one out here tonight."

Ruby's expression softened. "You belong here, Delphinium. I knew that from the moment my grandson first brought you over to meet Eddie and me."

It was apparent Jeremy hadn't told Ruby she had a boyfriend. It was equally apparent that his grandmother had misconstrued the reason behind her invitation this evening. It wasn't that Jeremy was personally interested in her. He was merely being kind.

When Fin opened her mouth to make that point clear, Jeremy took her hand. His fingers laced with hers, and she forgot what she'd been about to say.

"I don't think you or my grandmother will have a chance to say much." Jeremy gestured with his head. "Gladys is headed this way. She came representing the community theater."

"She came," Ruby reminded her grandson, "because she's one of my oldest and dearest friends."

"They don't get much older than Gladys." Jeremy's quip earned him a warning look from his grandmother. He grinned.

Purple caftan fluttering, Gladys Bertholf swept onto the terrace. Tall and whippet thin with pale blue eyes and a shock of dark black hair highlighted by a bold swath of silver resembling a skunk stripe, the woman cut an imposing figure.

For as long as Fin could remember, Gladys had been a larger-than-life presence in Good Hope. A whiz with numbers, she'd served as treasurer of the Cherries for decades until Fin's sister, Prim, had taken over the task a couple of years earlier.

Most in Good Hope knew her as a stage actress. Fin had been cast in several productions as a child and had enjoyed playing opposite Gladys. A talented actress with a booming voice that could reach the rafters, at ninety-six, Gladys showed no signs of slowing down.

"It's been far too long, my dear." The older woman's voice held a throaty richness.

Before Fin could respond, she found her shoulders grasped firmly in bony fingers bedecked in jewels, then her cheeks air-kissed.

Over the years, Fin had grown used to the eccentricities displayed by many Hollywood actors. Often all the craziness made it difficult to discern what they were really like. With Gladys, Fin didn't have to wonder. She knew beneath the woman's flamboyance was genuine caring and a warm heart.

Gladys had lit up the stage at the Good Hope Playhouse as far back as Fin could remember. If what Dakota had said was true . . . Fin experienced a pang at the thought of never hearing that booming voice reach the back row again.

"It's absolutely marvelous having so many of my favorite people together in one place." Gladys flung out one hand in a dramatic gesture. "I told my son, Frank, when he dropped me off that I knew this was going to be a fabulous soiree."

Fin wasn't sure a backyard barbecue qualified as a soiree, but the term, spoken with such dramatic license, made her smile. "It's good to see you, Gladys."

The sentiment had barely left Fin's lips when she found herself enfolded in another hug. The woman's arms were like bands of steel.

Fin heard Ruby's delighted laugh. "That's exactly how I felt when I saw her. Our girl is finally back home where she belongs."

"It's about time." Gladys shifted her focus to Jeremy. "Your mother may have thought it should be you and Eliza, but the first time I saw you with this one, I knew you'd end up together."

Ruby nodded agreement. "Rakes always marry their first loves."

Jeremy didn't give Fin a chance to respond as he took her hand again and angled her toward the French doors. "If you ladies will excuse me, there's someone I'd like Fin to meet."

The two older women exchanged glances and tittered.

"If that's your excuse for snatching a little alone time with your sweetheart, go for it." Ruby glanced at Gladys, who nodded. "You have our blessing."

Gladys patted Fin's bare shoulder. "It's good to see the two of you back together."

"We're not back together."

"If you say so, dear." The two women spoke as one, then looked at each other and giggled like a couple of teenagers.

"You behave." Jeremy's indulgent smile took any sting from the words.

Fin waited until they stepped into the empty kitchen to speak. "They think we're . . . together."

Jeremy pointed to her, then back to himself. "We are together."

Fin huffed out a breath. "You know what I mean. Your grandmother and Gladys think we're a couple."

"They also think Elvis is still alive," Jeremy teased, then his expression sobered. "I get what you're saying, but Grandma Ruby's condition is . . . delicate. I see no reason to push the fact that you'll soon be returning to LA."

"What about Gladys?"

"I believe she's simply playing along." The look in his eyes grew distant before he turned to open the refrigerator. "The crazy thing is I get the feeling Gladys wants you to stay even more than my grandmother."

Fin rested her back against the counter, took the bottle of water he offered. "Why?"

"Dakota isn't the only one who thinks you'd be a worthy successor." Jeremy smiled sheepishly. "I overheard Gladys telling my grandmother once she'd always hoped you'd take her place on the stage."

At her look of disbelief, he simply lifted his hands, one still holding the water bottle. "You've got the trifecta. Not only can you act, but you dance and sing, too."

"Well, I'm not staying. They need to understand that, and they need to know you and I aren't together."

"Let them have their dreams, Finley. Just for a little while." His light tone didn't match the somberness in his gaze. "Sometimes dreams are all a person has. Sometimes that has to be enough."

After the barbecue Friday night—which ended up being more fun than Fin had anticipated—she spent Saturday with family: the morning at the bakery with Ami and her second-in-command, Hadley; the afternoon at the community pool with her sister Prim, brother-in-law Max, and their twin boys, Connor and Callum; the evening with everyone gathered at the family home, her dad cooking steaks on the massive grill.

Xander laughed when she called that evening and told him how she'd spent the day.

"All I can say is I'm glad I was far, far away."

Even as the amused tone and cavalier dismissal set her teeth on edge, Fin told herself it was hard to convey just how enjoyable the day had been in a few succinct sentences. That had been all the time she'd used, sensing Xander had much to tell her. This was a business trip, after all.

She listened and murmured appropriate responses as he told her about the repeat site visits. According to him, both city administrators were ready to sign on the dotted line, but Xander had put them off.

Fin tried to summon some sympathy. She'd read the script, seen pictures of the other towns, and personally thought either alternative would work just fine.

Still, she reminded herself, she wasn't a director. Xander had a vision for this project, and Good Hope fit perfectly. She could understand not wanting to settle for second best, but in this instance he didn't have a choice. "You're not happy with either of the alternate sites."

"No, I'm not happy." He clipped the words. "I want Good Hope."

"I don't know if this will make you feel better or worse, but I went to a party at Jeremy's house last night." Fin chose her words carefully. "While a lot of the merchants there agreed with the vote, there appeared to be just as many who wished Jeremy had voted to approve."

There was a long pause. "That is interesting."

"The problem is, unless Jeremy brings the issue back to the board, how those merchants feel is a moot point."

"Did you bring up that possibility to the mayor?"

"I didn't," Fin admitted. "A party didn't seem the right time, and I didn't feel it was my place to stir things up again. The town board voted. Jeremy broke the tie. The decision has been made."

"You and the mayor are good friends." Xander paused. "And I believe one of the women on the board who voted against my proposition is dating your father."

"Jeremy and I were friends, but that was years ago." Fin kept her tone matter-of-fact. "As for Lynn Chapin, I can't tell you why she voted against it. She left on a short business trip right after the vote, and I haven't had a chance to speak with her since she's been back."

"I'd like you to try."

"I've done what I can." Fin heard an edge creep into her voice and took a calming breath. "Changing a person's mind takes time and can't be forced."

"You're right. It does take time." The understanding in Xander's voice had Fin relaxing her hold on the phone. Despite his severe disappointment, he understood her position.

"Will you and Liam be returning to Good Hope?" Fin couldn't believe they hadn't finalized their going-forward plans before Xander had left with his cinematographer.

"Liam flew back to LA tonight."

"What about you?"

"My flight leaves tomorrow, but not until late afternoon. I'd like you to come to Milwaukee tomorrow and have lunch with me."

Fin blinked. "You're flying back tomorrow? What about me? I mean, did you book me on the same flight?"

"I thought you were enjoying reconnecting with family and friends."

"I was. I mean, I am."

"That's good." He paused, shifted gears. "I'm staying at the Pfister. Do you know the hotel?"

"Of course. It's lovely." Fin had seen pictures of wedding receptions held in the hotel's Imperial Ballroom. "It's one of the finest in Milwaukee."

"My flight doesn't leave until four." Xander's voice remained warm. "I'm in the Presidential Suite. Plan to arrive at the hotel by eleven thirty. I'll ask the concierge for restaurant recommendations."

Fin had a couple of favorite restaurants in the city, but they were ultracasual, and she doubted they'd be up to his standards. "I'll leave

Good Hope around eight. That will give me plenty of time to drive and park the car."

"I'm looking forward to seeing you, Fin. We have a lot to discuss."

As Fin clicked off, excitement began to build. While eager to see Xander tomorrow, it was the possibility of being able to spend more time in Good Hope that had her pulling out her phone, hoping Ami hadn't already gone to bed so she could tell her sister the good news.

Chapter Three

Aware of Xander's lofty expectations, Fin dressed carefully for her lunch in Milwaukee. Thanks to its leather belt, the casual sheath dress emphasized her curves. Though black worked for almost any venue and any occasion, she coupled it with ankle boots with silver buckles, not wanting to overdress.

After pulling her hair back into a sleek, low knot, she added a thin silver ring to each ear, then gave a satisfied nod.

Traffic moved fast, and the magnificent hotel, located in downtown Milwaukee, was easy to find. Seeing the imposing twenty-some-story Pfister brought back memories. She recalled all the times she'd begged her mom to let them stay here—just once—during their annual back-to-school shopping trip.

Now she was finally here. Not for a shopping trip but for lunch with a handsome, accomplished man. Fin had barely stepped out of the Roadster and handed her keys to the valet when Xander appeared and crossed to her. She didn't know what to think when he wrapped his arms around her and gave her a kiss.

Surprised at the display of open affection, she didn't have a chance to respond before he stepped back, studied her. "Beautiful as always."

Fin flushed with pleasure. Compliments from Xander had recently been few and far between. While she'd blamed his lack of interest on the stress of this new film, she'd begun to wonder if he'd found someone else.

Their relationship, which had started out like fireworks exploding over Green Bay during the Fourth of July, had started to fizzle. For months she'd been considering ending it and moving on.

Xander nodded his thanks to the bellman who hurried to open the door for them. Fin was surprised Xander continued to hold her hand. Had she underestimated the depths of his feelings for her?

When they stepped into the lobby, Fin paused for a moment, not sure where to look first. At the priceless Victorian art collection on the walls? At the ceiling mural with its cherubs and gold leaf?

Xander seemed amused by her awe but said nothing as she soaked it all in.

"I've never been inside." Fin gave a little laugh. "I've seen pictures, of course, but they don't do this justice."

She swept the area with her hand.

"It's surprisingly nice," Xander conceded. "There's a club lounge on the twenty-third floor that rivals other hotels where I've stayed."

Since he had a four o'clock flight, she doubted he'd have a chance to show it to her. "Did the concierge have any recommendations for lunch?"

"A few, but I decided we'd have lunch in my suite. It's more private."

Fin hid her disappointment behind an agreeable smile, reminding herself this was probably her only chance to see the Presidential Suite.

Everything about the expanse of rooms amazed and delighted, from the marble entry to the gold-plated chandelier over the table where a waiter stood at rigid attention, dressed in perfectly creased black pants and a crisp white shirt.

"I hope you don't mind, but I took the liberty of ordering." He lifted her purse from her shoulder and placed it on the seat of a white brocade chair. "We don't have much time together today, and I want to make the most of it."

"We haven't had a lot of time the past three months."

"I know, and that's my fault." With one easy movement, he stepped to a side table and picked up a white florist box. "I'm sorry."

Pleasure ran through her at the sight of the pretty red ribbon wrapped artfully around the box. "For me?"

"Do you see anyone else in the room?"

He'd obviously forgotten about the waiter, but Fin saw no need to mention the fact. Sliding off the ribbon, she carefully removed the lid to find two dozen long-stemmed red roses nestled inside.

Their sweet scent teased her nostrils. While she'd never been particularly fond of roses—she'd mentioned that fact to Xander on several occasions—the flowers were lovely.

She smiled at Xander, leaned forward, and kissed him on the lips. "Thank you. They're beautiful. I hope there's a vase around here."

"He'll take care of that." Xander motioned to the waiter, or maybe he was a butler.

Silently the man moved to Fin. "May I?"

She placed the box into his outstretched hands. "Thank you."

The flowers heralded the start of a perfect luncheon. The meal started with a Roquefort tart with caramelized onion before moving on to a black cod entrée with soba noodles and concluded with a blackberry clafouti with lemon sorbet.

Xander was witty, charming, and attentive. The waiter, quiet and adept at anticipating their every need, only added to the experience. But as soon as the dessert plates were removed, Xander dismissed the man.

"Alone at last." Instead of resuming his seat, Xander held out his hand. "Come with me."

Curious what he had planned next, Fin rose. With his palm against the flat of her back, he guided her to the parlor, with inviting sofas and large windows looking out over the city.

Fin sat, fully expecting him to sit beside her, or at least nearby. Instead he began to pace. He was nervous, she realized. Nervous enough that it showed, as it so rarely did.

"Is something wrong?" she asked, growing concerned.

"No. No. Nothing is wrong." He dropped down on the sofa beside her, took her hand, gazed into her eyes. "You and I have been seeing each other for almost a year now. We've had our ups and downs."

Fin stilled. Was all this his way of telling her they should start seeing other people? It was strange for such an announcement to come after a fabulous lunch, but Xander continually surprised her.

She searched her emotions, wondering how she felt about them going their separate ways. The fact that she'd considered breaking up with him many times in the past six months made the thought more palatable. Though it would be nice if they could remain friends . . .

"I'm in love with you, Fin." His brown eyes never left hers. "When I met you, I knew you were the one. It was only a matter of time until we arrived at this moment. My future happiness is in your hands."

Fin's mind reeled. She was still processing the unexpected declaration when he dropped to one knee and pulled a jeweler's box from his pocket. Her breath caught as she saw the *H* over *W* on top. *Harry Winston.*

"You're everything I want, everything I need. I can't imagine my life without you in it. Will you marry me?"

The sweet words, so unlike anything she'd heard come out of Xander's mouth, startled her. Despite knowing there were so many practical reasons she should say yes, Fin hesitated.

Without waiting for her response, Xander took her hand and slipped the ring on her finger.

Panic spurted. "Wait, I didn't say—"

"Leave it on." Still holding her hand in a firm grip, he leaned close and gently kissed her lips. "Try it out. Get used to how it feels. I'm betting, in time, you won't want to take it off."

Fin gazed down at the platinum-set pear-shaped diamond sparkling like fire on her left hand. "It's gorgeous. But I—"

He closed her lips with his finger. "Give it a chance. Give *us* a chance. Can you do that for me?"

They had so much in common. They were part of the same industry. Would she ever find a man better suited to her LA lifestyle?

"Okay." Fin blew out a breath. "Yes."

Now that the words had been spoken, Fin waited for the rush of excitement she'd always envisioned when she'd thought of this moment. When it didn't come, she told herself it was because she wasn't young like Prim or Marigold or romantic like Ami. "I know you planned to fly out today, but I'd love it if you could stay one more day. We could go back to Good Hope together, tell my family and—"

"I'm afraid that's not possible." His tone gentled, obviously sensing her disappointment. "I would stay if I could, but I have a meeting with Harvey first thing tomorrow."

Fin's hopes deflated like an untied balloon. Arguing would be pointless. Harvey Atherton was a brilliant director who Xander worshiped. Xander would never reschedule a meeting with him. Not even for her.

"I understand." She kept her voice light. "Business first. Once I get back to Good Hope, I'll pack and get an early flight to LA."

"Not so fast." He squeezed her hand. "I want you to stay in Good Hope awhile longer."

Genuinely puzzled, Fin furrowed her brow. "Why?"

"You have contacts in the community. I want you to stay and get Jeremy Rakes and the town board to reconsider my proposition. I want a revote. If that vote should once again end in a tie, I want your friend, Mayor Rakes, to vote in my favor. Keep in mind I need a site locked in by no later than the twentieth of September."

"It'd be very unusual for the board to revisit a topic so soon after a vote."

"I have every confidence in you and your connections." Xander cupped her cheek, gazed into her eyes. "You have my blessing to do whatever it takes to make this happen."

It was an odd thing to say. Fin let it go. She had more pressing matters on her mind. "Shirleen won't like me taking that much time away from the office."

"I'll handle Shirleen." A buzz sounded at his wrist and he glanced down. "The car service I ordered is here."

Fin frowned. "I can take you to the airport."

"Thank you for the thought." He leaned over and kissed her. "Everything is arranged."

Fin slowly rose to her feet. "Well, have a good flight."

He gave her a wink. "You drive safe."

"I'll grab my purse and walk out with you."

Xander waved a dismissive hand. "There's no need for you to rush off. I have the suite until three. Stay. Relax. Enjoy."

One more swift kiss and he was gone.

Restless and unsettled, Fin roamed the suite. In the kitchen area she discovered an ice bucket with an unopened bottle of Cristal.

Red roses.

A romantic meal.

A Harry Winston diamond.

Champagne.

He'd staged the scene perfectly.

Fin shoved the troubling thought aside. If Xander had staged the scene, it was because of what she meant to him. He said he loved her.

Only now, as she gazed down at the bottle of champagne with its distinctive gold label and clear, flat bottom, did Fin realize something else.

She'd accepted his proposal without ever saying the words back to him.

———

Bright and early Monday morning Fin drove the few blocks to the courthouse. She was going to be straight with Jeremy about what Xander wanted. She wouldn't use him or anyone else.

Still, she knew her boss would not be happy if she came back without getting the agreement Xander so desperately wanted from the town board. Especially after giving her this time off. From several things Shirleen had said, Fin knew her job might hang in the balance.

And then there was Xander. While she didn't appreciate him asking her to pressure Jeremy, Fin understood a successful adaptation of the best-selling book could be his ticket to the top.

She only hoped if the worst happened and she returned without the approval, both he and Shirleen would understand she'd done her best. A weight settled in Fin's chest, and she resisted the urge to sigh.

Stepping from the BMW, she gave herself a mental shake and lifted her face to the sun. As the rays warmed her face and she breathed in the clean, fresh air, Fin realized she'd been given a gift. The gift of time with her family and friends. What Xander asked, what Shirleen expected, was a small price to pay for such a gift.

Fin was nearly at Jeremy's office when she realized she was humming. Odd, she couldn't recall the last time she'd hummed a song, even one as catchy as "Tomorrow."

She pushed open the door marked "Office of the Mayor" and crossed the inside reception area with long, confident steps.

"I'm here to see Jeremy," she told the receptionist, not breaking stride. "We're old friends."

"Ma'am, wait. You can't go in there." Like a clown springing from an old-fashioned jack-in-the-box, the petite blonde popped up from behind the desk and scurried forward. "He's busy."

Fin wasn't sure what irritated her more: the attempt to deny her entry or being called *ma'am*.

Dear God, she was barely past thirty.

Ignoring the blonde's grasping hands, Fin pushed open the heavy oak door. Before she could step inside, the girl—she couldn't be more than eighteen—shoved through the doorway ahead of Fin.

"I'm sorry, sir." The girl's chin jutted up. "She wouldn't listen when I told her you were busy."

The way she said the words reminded Fin of her little sister Marigold and how she'd loved to tattle on her siblings.

"Not listening is a bad habit of Ms. Bloom's." As he rounded the massive wooden desk, Jeremy pocketed the phone in his hand. Shifting his gaze from Fin, he offered the blonde—who still appeared worried— a reassuring smile. "It's okay, Chelsea. You did your best. A seasoned bodyguard couldn't keep this woman out."

"I assured her you and I were old friends." Fin spoke in a breezy tone. "I don't think she believed me."

The girl opened her mouth, then shut it when Fin crossed the room in confident strides, hands outstretched.

Jeremy took her hands and gave them a squeeze. "This is a nice surprise on a Monday morning."

He turned toward the receptionist. "Thanks, Chelsea. I'll take it from here."

Casting one last curious glance at Fin, the girl slipped from the room.

"Do you have a moment?" The question was mostly for form. Fin had no doubt he'd make time for her.

"Actually, I don't." The regret in his voice was too real to be faked. "Ruby went for her checkup this morning and somehow ended up being admitted to the hospital. I was just speaking with the nurse."

Fin's heart rose to her throat. She gripped the sleeve of Jeremy's suit coat. "What's wrong? Is it serious?"

"I don't think so." He blew out a breath. "I hope not."

Fin found no comfort in the words. Her concern rose as Jeremy moved to the outer office.

"Cancel my three o'clock with Sheriff Rallis. See if he has any time free tomorrow morning." Jeremy tossed out instructions to Chelsea with each step. "Fit Ms. Bloom in . . . somewhere."

With that final directive, he strode out the office door, covering ground in long, determined strides.

He'd forgotten about her, Fin realized as she rushed after him, heels clicking on the marble flooring. Hoping to impress, she'd worn her favorite green jersey dress and a pair of Louboutin pumps. Fin couldn't help thinking a pair of sneakers would have been a better choice.

Jeremy moved swiftly, weaving through people in the crowded hall-way like a running back with a goalpost in sight. By the time she caught up to him, he'd reached the parking lot.

The expletive that burst from his lips as he skidded to an abrupt stop startled her.

"What's the matter?"

"I loaned my car to my receptionist." Jeremy blew out a breath and raked a hand through his hair. "Hers is in the shop and there was some business she needed to take care of for her mother."

"But she's back. I met her." At Jeremy's blank look, Fin continued. "The scrappy terrier guarding your office door? Blonde hair? Passionate Pink fingernails?"

Recognition dawned. A ghost of a smile briefly touched his lips.

"Chelsea is summer help. She was sent over from Public Records to fill in while Dee Ann is out of the office. I doubt she'd appreciate being compared to a dog." Jeremy spoke absently, his attention returning to the lot.

Fin could almost see his mind rapidly considering—and discarding—options.

Undoubtedly he had any number of friends who would happily lend him their vehicles, but those friends weren't here. Fin gestured to the red BMW sports car. "You need transportation. I have a car."

Without waiting for him to respond, Fin reached into her black leather satchel and located the fob. "Heads up."

He caught the keys with an effortless move that took her back to their high school days and his clever hands.

Jeremy, who'd already opened his door, raised an eyebrow when she slipped inside the vehicle. "What are you doing?"

"Coming with you, of course." Fin settled into the plush leather seat and fastened her seat belt. "You're not the only one worried about Grandma Ruby."

Not wanting to waste time arguing, Jeremy slid behind the wheel of the BMW and pulled out of the lot.

Despite what he'd said to Fin about the call likely being no big deal, he was concerned. There'd been an edge to the nurse's voice, and he knew they didn't admit anyone without a good reason.

As they reached the Good Hope city limits, he punched the accelerator. The vehicle leaped forward. "Thanks for the use of the car."

"Mi car-sa es su car-sa."

Jeremy laughed and some of his tension eased.

Reaching over, Fin hit a button that had the top of the convertible retracting. After settling a pair of oversize sunglasses on her nose, she leaned back, appearing not at all concerned about the wind blowing her hair.

He liked the way the thick blonde and brown pieces flowed together in no discernible pattern. At Marigold's wedding in June, her hair had been shorter and more jagged on the ends. The straight, blunt-cut strands now brushed her shoulders.

Even after all these years he remembered the feel of those soft tendrils against his bare chest. He shoved the memory aside. They'd been teenagers then, barely more than children. Neither had known what they'd wanted out of life.

If the thought didn't ring completely true, it was accurate enough. He'd moved on. She'd certainly moved on.

Then how, Jeremy wondered, could simply zipping down the road in a red convertible with her in the passenger seat so easily transport him back to a time when the sun shone brightly and life held endless possibilities?

Simple nostalgia, he told himself, *for a time when I was convinced the girl I desperately loved had loved me back.*

"What brought you by today, Fin?" His voice came out brisker than he'd intended.

Fin pulled her gaze from the sparkling waters of Green Bay and slowly turned to face him. Very deliberately, she lowered her oversize sunglasses, and he found himself pinned by unshaded emerald green eyes. "Did I say or do something to offend you, Jeremy?"

The tone might be pleasant, but those sea-green eyes were razor sharp and assessing.

"Of course not." He kept his voice neutral. "Why do you ask?"

"Something in your tone sounded . . . off." Fin shrugged, still not answering his question. The sunglasses were back up when she reached over and placed her hand on his arm. "Will Grandma Ruby be okay?"

Fin may have walked away from him without a backward glance, but he didn't doubt for a second that her concern for his grandmother was genuine.

"Will she?" Fin pressed.

"She had a mild heart attack last month."

"My dad said she recovered fully and was doing great."

"Tests at the time showed three vessels significantly blocked." Though his parents weren't overly worried, the doctors Jeremy had spoken with after the event had been very concerned. "She needs a triple bypass."

"Sounds serious."

"Any operation is serious, but another heart attack could be fatal." Jeremy tightened his grip on the steering wheel. "Grandma Ruby refused the operation, so they put her on medication and have been monitoring her."

Jeremy paused to get his emotions under control. He couldn't lose his grandmother. He'd do whatever necessary to get her to agree to the lifesaving operation. "She was at the clinic this morning for a routine follow-up. What they found had them admitting her."

"Ruby is smart and savvy." Fin's quiet voice soothed his raw nerves. "Why is she refusing the surgery?"

"Her father died after a similar procedure decades ago." Though they were the only two in the vehicle, he lowered his voice. "She's scared."

Fin cocked her head. "Do *you* think it's worth the risk?"

"Absolutely." When the doctor had mentioned the operation, Jeremy had combed reputable medical websites for information about the surgeon, the procedure, and the risks. Though his voice remained steady, his grip on the steering wheel tightened until his knuckles turned white. "The surgeon is experienced, the hospital in Milwaukee has a good success rate with these procedures, and my grandmother is in over-all excellent health. All these factors up the odds of a positive outcome."

"Then I hope you convince her." Fin was silent for several seconds. "If there's anything I can do, just ask."

"I appreciate the offer." Jeremy barely noticed the bright patches of wildflowers alongside the highway or the fields of corn giving way to groves of cherry trees, then to houses.

As the village of Egg Harbor came and went on the drive to Sturgeon Bay, Jeremy realized he still had no idea why Fin had come to see him. "Are you ever going to tell me what brought you by the office this morning?"

"It can wait. You have a lot on your mind right now."

"Did you come to tell me about your engagement?" Though what he and Fin had shared had been over years ago, the sight of the engagement ring on her left hand this morning had been a knife to the heart.

Before she could respond, the hospital came into view. Jeremy wheeled the car into the closest parking stall. Seconds later he was out and striding toward the state-of-the-art medical center.

Fin reached his side just as the automatic doors swooshed open and a faint medicinal scent replaced the cool outside air.

Jeremy paused at a circular counter at the end of the shiny hallway. A middle-aged nurse with bright red hair lifted her gaze from a monitor.

"I'm Jeremy Rakes. My grandmother, Ruby, was admitted to observation this morning."

"Ah, yes, Mr. Rakes." The RN cast a curious glance at Fin before refocusing on Jeremy. "As I said on the phone, your grandmother experienced some chest pain when she was in our clinic. The doctor was also concerned about a blood pressure spike, so he admitted her for observation. Once Dr. Passmore adjusted her medications, her BP returned to normal."

Jeremy glanced around. "I'd like to speak with him."

"He's with a patient right now but shouldn't be long. Your grandmother is in our VIP suite at the end of the hall." The nurse slanted a glance toward a long hall to her left. "I'll let him know you're here."

"I'd appreciate it." Jeremy offered a slight smile, his worry ratcheting up with each step down the corridor.

They'd nearly reached the VIP suite at the far end of the hall when Fin's steps stopped. "You go ahead."

"You're not going in?" Disappointment flooded him. He hadn't realized how much he was counting on having her beside him. "I thought you'd want to say hello. See for yourself she's okay."

"You have a lot to discuss with your grandmother and the doctor." She took a step back. "I shouldn't intrude."

"She'll want to see you." Without giving himself a chance to reconsider the wisdom of the action, Jeremy held out his hand. "And I'd like you with me."

A second later, her fingers curved around his.

Chapter Four

Fin knew taking Jeremy's hand was a mistake. Especially now that she was engaged. She should be putting more distance between them, not less. And regardless of what Jeremy said, this was family business. She didn't belong here.

"Fin." Just her name.

Jeremy wasn't Xander. He wouldn't push. If she insisted on remaining in the hall or returning to the car, he wouldn't stop her. Yet despite the confident set to his shoulders, a flicker of . . . something . . . in those liquid depths told her Jeremy was more rattled by all this than he was letting show.

"I suppose—" she began.

"Mr. Rakes."

The name, spoken in an imperious manner, had her and Jeremy turning as one.

The man marching toward them wore green scrubs and had the well-toned body of a dedicated gym rat. He stood around six feet and appeared to be close to Jeremy's age. That's where the similarities ended.

The guy, who Jeremy introduced as Dr. Nolan Passmore, wore his brown hair short. His polished look, coupled with the bold confidence in his hazel eyes, reminded Fin of Xander.

The surgeon's gaze lingered on Fin as Jeremy performed the introductions. "I've met your sister, Ami, at a function she and her husband attended. You could be her twin."

"That's not the first time I've heard that," Fin said with a smile.

Dr. Passmore's lips quirked. "I imagine not."

"Tell me about my grandmother's condition," Jeremy demanded.

While no one appreciated good manners more than Fin, she agreed with Jeremy. It was time to get down to business. This wasn't a cocktail party where small talk was de rigueur. The focus needed to be on Ruby.

"The nurse said her blood pressure spiked," Jeremy prompted.

The doctor glanced pointedly at Fin, lifted a brow.

"You may speak freely in front of Ms. Bloom."

"Your grandmother's condition has become more tenuous. Not only was she experiencing some chest pain while waiting for her appointment, her blood pressure rose to an unacceptable level."

A lump formed in Fin's throat. She slanted a sideways glance and saw lines had formed between Jeremy's sandy brows.

"Thankfully, she responded well to medication." The doctor continued to speak to Jeremy, ignoring Fin completely. "For now everything is stable."

For now.

A chill traveled up her spine. Just as she was sure it did Jeremy's. If the doctor hadn't been there, Fin would have reached over and looped her arm through Jeremy's. She'd have given it a supportive squeeze, offered him an encouraging word.

But this wasn't LA. Even though Sturgeon Bay was twenty miles from Good Hope, Jeremy was well known throughout the Door County peninsula.

And Fin, well, she was engaged. Not that anyone in LA—or Good Hope—was aware of the engagement.

"I suggest you revisit the benefits of bypass surgery with your grandmother." Dr. Passmore's eyes were solemn. It wasn't arrogance but concern reflected in the hazel depths. "If you think it'd add weight, I'll come in with you."

"Thanks, but I think it's better if Fin and I discuss this with her." Jeremy blew out a shaky breath. "The last thing I want is for her to think we're ganging up. Then she'll really dig in her heels."

Jeremy reached around Fin to open the door, and she found herself propelled into a bright and sunny area more suited to LA than Door County. The striated floor's mirror finish gleamed as if it had been hand waxed. Thick draperies in frosted emerald were open, and light streamed in through the floor-to-ceiling windows overlooking the hospital's rose garden.

Several paintings depicting pastoral scenes hung on moss-green walls in a sitting area. A modern work unit against one wall held a computer and printer. Two leather chairs and a sofa were grouped for conversation. A glass-topped coffee table held an enormous bouquet of spring flowers.

If not for the hospital bed in an adjacent room partially separated by a six-panel divider, this could be the interior of any upscale apartment.

"Isn't this a delightful surprise." Ruby lowered the newspaper she'd been reading and set it aside. She wore silk lounging pants and a matching tunic. Only when she rose did Fin notice the monitor wires peeking out from one of her pockets.

"Don't get up—"

Jeremy should have saved his breath. His grandmother was already on her feet and crossing the room.

"Delphinium." Ruby opened her arms, her deep whiskey voice at odds with her diminutive appearance. "What a delightful surprise."

Fin stepped forward and found herself enveloped in a warm hug. The jasmine-and-rose scent of Chanel N° 5, Ruby's signature scent, wrapped around her.

"When the nurse mentioned they'd called my grandson, I hoped you'd be with him. Come. Sit beside me." Ruby gestured to the sofa, then turned to Jeremy. "It's about time you came to your senses."

"Good to see you, too, Gram." Jeremy leaned over and brushed a kiss across Ruby's weathered cheek. "I came as soon as the nurse called. How are you feeling?"

"Lots of concern about a minor blip. Besides, we have more important things to discuss than my ticker." Ruby winked at Fin before refocusing on her grandson. "When were you planning to tell me?"

"That I'm concerned? That I'm worried about you? Well, I am." Jeremy expelled a frustrated breath. "Dr. Passmore is also concerned. He's—"

"Forget about Passmore." Ruby leaned forward, her blue eyes sparkling. "When's the wedding? I'm thinking spring would be nice. The church for the ceremony, then the reception in the barn."

Ruby patted Fin's hand. "Trust me. We'll do it up right."

Jeremy frowned. "What are you talking about?"

Ruby rolled her eyes before wrapping bony fingers around Fin's left hand. She lifted it high, where the overhead fluorescent lights caught the pear-shaped stone and sent prisms of color scattering.

"It's a lovely enough ring." Ruby scrutinized the diamond with the intensity of a pawn shop owner about to make an offer. "But I believe our Delphinium would have preferred something a little more personal, more tailored to her preferences."

Ruby released Fin's hand. "I assumed he picked out the ring without asking for your input?"

Fin dropped her gaze to the diamond. "He surprised me with it."

Ruby made a tsking sound and turned to Jeremy. "When's the date?"

Fin had no idea why Ruby would ask Jeremy. Then it hit her. The older woman obviously thought her grandson had known and withheld the news. Even she knew how much Ruby Rakes hated being out of the loop.

"We haven't set a date." Fin spoke before Jeremy could, knowing only she had the information Ruby sought. "The ring has been on my finger less than twenty-four hours. Even my family doesn't know about the engagement."

At Ruby's disbelieving look, Fin added, "But they will. As soon as I leave here, I'm heading over to tell them."

"I'm honored you told me first. And I am over the moon with happiness." Ruby's voice turned husky with emotion. "You've always been special to me, Delphinium."

Tears stung the backs of Fin's eyes. "You're special to me as well."

For the second time in less than ten minutes Ruby's arms stole around Fin. Once the hug ended, the older woman dabbed at her eyes with a delicate lace handkerchief before fixing her gaze on her grandson.

"Inform Passmore I'll have the operation." A determined look settled on the older woman's face. "Make it clear I want it scheduled as soon as possible."

Startled surprise mixed with relief stole across Jeremy's handsome face. He jumped to his feet and strode to the door. "That's wonderful news. I'll let—"

"It isn't every day there's a wedding in the Rakes family." Ruby smiled broadly. "I want to make sure I'm around to toast you and Delphinium."

Jeremy froze, his hand on the door latch. He turned in slow motion. "What did you say?"

"I said it isn't every day that a woman's favorite grandson gets married." Ruby rested a hand on Fin's arm. "I know you thought I was foolish and sentimental when I told you Rakes always marry their first love. Now you can see I was right."

"But Gram—"

"I've long dreamed of dancing at your wedding, Jeremy." Ruby's voice softened and her eyes held a sheen. Then her voice firmed and she was in control again. "Go. Tell the doctor I'll have the procedure as soon as he can get it scheduled. I'm ready to get this show on the road. We have a wedding to plan."

———

Over the years Jeremy had developed a stellar poker face. When a citizen said something outrageous at a town board meeting, he never let his shock show.

Just like now. He placed a smile on his lips and extended a hand to Fin. "Come with me, please."

Her manner equally calm, Fin smiled back. But the turmoil Jeremy saw reflected in those beautiful emerald depths confirmed he wasn't the only one reeling.

Even as his hand closed around hers, Fin's gaze drifted back to his grandmother.

"Go ahead, honey. He doesn't want to let you out of his sight." Ruby sighed. "My Eddie was the same way. Except he didn't want me out of his bed."

Jeremy stiffened. Yet when his grandmother cackled with laughter, he saw a light in her eyes he'd worried he might never see again.

With Fin's hand firmly clasped in his, they exited the room. Walking side by side, neither spoke until they veered into an empty waiting area down the hall.

Fin caught her bottom lip with her teeth. "She thinks I'm engaged to you."

"I'm aware." Jeremy blew out a breath. He couldn't believe he hadn't caught on when Ruby had begun to press for wedding details. He'd thought his grandmother was simply being polite.

Fool.

Jeremy began to pace, conscious of Fin's eyes following him.

When he stopped directly in front of her, she lifted her hands. "Once I realized she'd gone down the wrong path, I didn't know what to say."

"She said she'll have the operation." Jeremy breathed the words. Hearing his grandmother agree to the bypass had been an answer to his prayer.

He had tried numerous times to make his parents understand the seriousness of the situation, but they refused to intervene. What had his dad said when Jeremy had begged him to come to Good Hope and convince Ruby to have the procedure? Ah, yes. His mother was an intelligent woman who should be allowed to make her own decisions.

Fin rested a hand on his arm, her voice soft and low. "You know what Ruby means to me."

Jeremy's gaze searched her lovely face, made even more beautiful by the smattering of freckles lightly dusting the bridge of her nose. He thought back to the years they'd been together in high school. Her affection and kindness for his grandmother had been only one of the many things he'd loved about her.

But that, he reminded himself, had been a lifetime ago.

"It's just so . . . difficult. If she doesn't have the operation, she could die." Jeremy cleared his throat. "In fact, it's very likely."

Fin closed her eyes for a long moment.

"I've pushed hard to get her to agree. Dr. Passmore also tried, but you know how stubborn Gram can be when she gets something in her head."

"There's only one thing we can do." Fin's soft voice was resolute.

We.

Once he and Fin had been a team, so close he couldn't imagine anything—or anyone—coming between them.

"You're right. We tell her together." Jeremy squared his shoulders. "Then we'll revisit all the reasons surgery is the best option."

Fin shook her head. "Too risky."

"What?"

"It's too risky. She may still refuse the operation."

"It's our only option."

"It's not." Fin lifted her chin. "We can let her think you and I are engaged and planning a wedding. Once she's had the operation, we confess."

"You want us to lie?"

"I want your grandmother to live." Tears filled Fin's eyes before she blinked them back. "I'll do whatever is necessary to make that happen."

"You'll go so far as to pretend to be my fiancée?"

"If you have a better idea, one with the same likelihood of success," she hurriedly added when he opened his mouth to speak, "spit it out."

Jeremy took a breath, exhaled slowly. "You're engaged to Xander. He won't like it. Not even for a few days."

Fin waved a dismissive hand. "He won't care."

"He will care." Jeremy clenched and unclenched his hands. "This is my family. My problem. I'm not going to screw up your relationship—"

"Oh, for goodness' sake." Fin pulled out her phone, and after a couple of seconds a shade too brightly said, "Xander, hello. I'm with Jeremy. We have a situation here."

Jeremy listened to her explain what had transpired and what she was proposing.

Her brows pulled together. "No. I didn't have a chance. His grandmother—"

From where he stood, Jeremy heard Xander's deep voice cut her off. After a moment, she reluctantly handed her phone to him. "He wants to speak with you."

"Hello. Listen, Xander, I understand your—"

"Rakes, I only have a minute so I'll get to the point. You have my blessing to perpetuate this charade. I only ask one favor."

"What would that be?"

Out of the corner of his eye, Jeremy saw Fin intently watching him. As Xander laid out his terms, Jeremy found himself thinking his instincts had been on target.

Xander Tillman really was a Pompous Ass.

After working in LA for nearly a decade, Fin knew when deals were being forged. In the past few minutes, a simple question had morphed into a negotiation.

She recognized the determined glint in Jeremy's eyes. She'd seen that look in Ruby's eyes more times than she could count. Fin knew how much Jeremy's grandmother meant to him, but she also believed him to be a man of integrity. Not a politician whose vote could be bought.

When he handed the phone back to her, she simply stared at it.

"He had an important meeting." Jeremy hesitated, and she saw the lie even before he voiced it. "He said to tell you good-bye."

Fin didn't care about social niceties. Not with something far more important on the table.

"Did I just hear you agree to vote for the project?" Fin found herself holding her breath. She'd need the extra oxygen, because if Jeremy *had* agreed, she was going to kick his butt. If Xander had asked that of him, she would call him back and kick his.

"No." Jeremy met her gaze. "I only agreed to put the issue on the September agenda. That will give you time to make your case with the board members. Whether the outcome will change is impossible to say."

"What about if the vote ends in another tie? The deciding vote will be yours."

"I will look at the proposal with fresh eyes and an open mind." He smiled slightly. "It's what I do for anything that crosses my desk a second time."

"Why did you agree to put it on the agenda? There was no need." Fin couldn't hide her confusion. "My offer didn't carry strings."

"Based on feedback I received at the barbecue Friday night, I'd already decided to bring the issue back to the town board for a public hearing." A sardonic smile lifted Jeremy's lips. "This morning I instructed Dee Ann to make space on the September fifteenth town board agenda. I planned to call Xander today to confirm he hadn't already signed with one of the alternate sites. If he had, all this would be a moot point."

Fin narrowed her gaze.

"Always so suspicious." He chuckled. "I'm giving it to you straight, Finley. Many merchants I spoke with said they hadn't realized the testifying would be so skewed against the proposition. They want their chance to be heard."

"I heard the same rumblings." Fin recalled the comments she'd overheard. "Many seem to think they'll benefit more financially from the film crew and actors being in town than from the holiday events. Plus, they like the idea of the community getting the windfall of money to help with what they see as currently underfunded projects."

"While Xander might think he got a concession, he didn't."

"I can't believe he'd even ask. We're only talking a few days." The more Fin thought of Xander using Ruby's situation for his own benefit, the more her blood boiled. "I'm not his property. I only called to let him know what we planned as a courtesy, and yes, to show you that he couldn't care less what I do in Good Hope."

Fin ignored the odd look Jeremy shot her.

She clenched her teeth as a wave of heat washed over her. No one owned her. No one spoke for her. And no one, absolutely no one, put a squeeze play on one of her friends.

When her fingers threatened to crush the phone, Fin slung it into her purse. Her body vibrated with rage. "I am so angry with Xander right now. I'm going to—"

"What you're going to do," Jeremy's arms stole around her stiff body, "is take a breath."

Even when his arms tightened around her and he pulled her close, she didn't relax. After a moment, he dropped his head to rest against the top of hers. When he finally spoke, his voice was low and raspy. "It will be okay. Grandma Ruby will be up and dancing before we know it."

Fin closed her eyes and let herself relax against him. "I'm so worried. I didn't realize this was so serious."

His hand gently stroked her hair. "You're a good friend to her . . . and to me."

Locked in each other's arms, they stood together in the hallway. Soothed by the comforting embrace, Fin paid no mind to the kitchen worker bringing Ruby's lunch tray who stepped around them.

By the time she and Jeremy left the hospital, Ruby was on the surgery schedule for the next day. Fin's temper had dropped to a slow simmer, but she still planned to call Xander that evening and kick his ass.

Exhausted, neither of them spoke much during the drive back to Good Hope. They'd just passed Egg Harbor when Fin's phone dinged. She read the text from Ami twice.

Jeremy glanced sideways. "Problem?"

"Ami wants you and I to come to dinner this evening at six. She says it's important."

"Why is she inviting me?"

"I don't know." Instead of texting, Fin called her sister. "Hi, Ami. I got your text and—"

"Does Jeremy know about the invitation?" Ami interrupted.

Fin paused, glanced at the man in the driver's seat. "Yes, he's with me. We're driving back from the hospital to get some of Ruby's things together. Ruby is scheduled for surgery in Milwaukee tomorrow."

"That is good news. You can tell me all about it tonight. Will six work?"

"Yes, but I don't understand why—"

"I'd love to chat, Fin, but I'm at my OB appointment and," Ami called out a greeting, "she just walked in. See you both at six."

Fin stared at the phone for a second, then dropped it back into her bag.

"What did you find out?"

"Nothing except she's expecting you. She was at her OB appointment, so she couldn't talk." Fin kept her voice casual. "Are you free for dinner?"

"If your sister is cooking, I'm definitely free."

"You're so predictable." Fin laughed.

If only she could say as much for herself. Ever since they'd left the hospital she'd been seized with the feeling that her life was about to take an unpredictable turn.

Chapter Five

"We should go inside."

Despite Jeremy's urging, Fin's feet remained rooted to the sidewalk leading up to her sister Ami's home. While outwardly she remained composed, her heartbeat pounded in her ears. Something in Ami's tone this afternoon had put her on alert. She'd yet to figure out the reason for the dinner invitation.

If it was something to do with the baby . . .

No. She would not let her mind go there. If it was a baby issue, Ami wouldn't have insisted she bring Jeremy with her. "I can't figure out why she wanted you here."

"Maybe she knows I don't get nearly enough home-cooked meals?"

"If that was the case, she'd be inviting every single man in Good Hope."

"Okay." Jeremy rubbed his chin. "How about I'm a charming dinner companion?"

Fin rolled her eyes. "I guess the invitation will just have to remain a mystery."

Jeremy took her arm as they climbed the stairs. "I never asked. Had you told any of your family about your engagement to Xander?"

"No."

"Scared?"

Her head whipped around, her gaze pinning him. "I'm not scared."

The amusement in those brilliant blue eyes told her he'd known exactly what he was doing. Getting her riled so she'd pull herself together.

Fin had already made inroads toward accomplishing that task. After dropping Jeremy off at the courthouse, she'd phoned Xander. More often than not he didn't take her calls, preferring to call back on his own timetable. This time he'd answered immediately. No doubt hoping she'd thought up even more ways to put the screws to Jeremy.

"I don't like you pressuring Jeremy when his grandmother's life is at stake." Fin's voice sounded hard, even to her own ears. But darn it, Xander knew better.

"Well, hello to you, too." The amusement in his voice only fueled her anger.

"In case you can't tell, I'm pissed. Seriously pissed. Jeremy is going through a lot right now. He doesn't need you on his back. Trust me, such pressure will only backfire on you."

There was a long pause.

"Apologies. You know me, Fin. When I want something, I want it now. But you're right, it was a wrong move. The mayor won't get any more pressure from me."

Though she couldn't see his eyes, he sounded sincere. And Fin couldn't recall the last time he'd apologized for anything.

"Am I forgiven?"

The hint of boyish contrition mixed with the warmth in his tone melted the last of her resistance. She sighed. "You're forgiven."

They didn't chat long. She'd caught him in a meeting. As a busy professional herself, Fin understood the stresses he was under. Xander simply needed to remember that friendship and loyalty trumped business any day.

"C'mon." Jeremy cupped her elbow in his hand and pushed open the gate. "We don't want the potatoes to get cold."

Fin found herself propelled up the last few steps. While not large by Hollywood mansion standards, Ami and Beck's home was one of the largest on the peninsula. Also, in her opinion, one of the most beautiful. Stained glass topped each window. A black iron fence enclosed a yard that spanned two lots. Leafy trees shaded a spread of sprawling green accented with clusters of colorful flowers.

Fin paused when they reached the porch. Since she'd last walked up these steps, her sister had added another urn of impatiens. The fancier New Guinea variety in salmon and white, their mother's favorite, spilled over the sides of the pot. The white-lacquered porch swing was new as well.

"So much wonderful space." She thought of her postage-stamp-size LA apartment and sighed. "Perfect for a growing family."

Jeremy cast a glance in her direction. "I bet Ami is hoping you're still here when she has the baby."

Fin felt a surge of excitement. "That would be wonderful."

"Before we go in, I want to say again how much I appreciate what you're doing to help Ruby." Jeremy's voice deepened with emotion. "I called her on my way to pick you up, and she's in high spirits. When I told her you and I were having dinner with your family, she said to drink a glass of champagne for her."

"Champagne." Then it hit her. "She thinks we're announcing our engagement to my family tonight."

"Now you'll be telling them about your engagement to Xander with your ex-boyfriend at your side." Jeremy's tone was light but his eyes held shadows.

Impulsively, Fin slipped her arm through his and gave it a squeeze. "I'm glad you're here with me."

The door flew open and Fin didn't have a chance to say anything more.

Ami raced to her, wrapping her arms around Fin and pulling her close. Or at least as close as her sister's big belly would allow.

As Fin hugged her sister, her new niece or nephew—no one knew, since Beck and Ami wanted to be surprised—kicked Fin in the ribs. Hard.

"Wow." Fin cleared her throat as a storm of emotion pummeled her. "You and Beck have got yourself a soccer star."

But Ami had already turned her attention to Jeremy, a warm smile lifting her lips. "It's good to see you, Jeremy."

"I appreciate the invitation."

"Come inside." Beck held the door wide, then stepped aside to let them pass. "Can I get either of you a beer or a glass of wine?"

Beck's chocolate-colored hair and dark eyes provided a startling contrast to Jeremy's blond good looks.

Jeremy smiled. "I wouldn't say no to a beer."

"I'll grab one." Beck glanced at her. "Fin?"

"A glass of red would be great. Thanks."

"Everyone is in the parlor," Ami told her.

"I'll help Beck get the drinks." Jeremy shot Fin a reassuring smile, then strolled down the hallway toward the kitchen.

Fin sniffed the air. The savory scent of pot roast, garlic-roasted potatoes, and fresh bread teased her nostrils. "It smells amazing. I'm sure it will taste even better."

"I invited everyone for dinner." Ami looped an arm companionably through hers.

Fin glanced down at Ami's belly, took in the dark shadows beneath her eyes, and felt a pang. "I wish you hadn't gone to so much trouble."

"I love to cook." Ami gave her arm a squeeze. "Especially for my family."

"I don't understand why we're all here." They were almost to the parlor when Fin stopped short. "Is something wrong?"

"The news is out." A brilliant smile lit Ami's face. "It was quite a surprise, but we're all thrilled and the Bloom family is ready to celebrate. I admit I wished you'd told me yourself, rather than Beck hearing it from Dakota."

Fin cocked her head. "What are you talking about?"

Before Ami could answer, Jeremy and Beck appeared in the hall.

"Is there some reason we're standing out here instead of going in there?" Beck handed Fin her glass of wine, then gestured with his head toward the entrance to the parlor.

Jeremy shot her a questioning glance.

"Ami mentioned Dakota shared some news?" Fin turned to Beck. "What was it?"

"What do you think?" Ami reached down, just as Ruby had done earlier in the day, and lifted Fin's hand. The diamond sparkled in the overhead light. "When were you going to tell us?"

Fin ignored the question. "How did Dakota find out?"

"Her friend Liliana works in dietary at the hospital in Sturgeon," Beck answered. "Ruby told her the news when Lily brought in her lunch tray. Lily also saw you and Jeremy embracing in the hall."

"She told you Jeremy and I are engaged."

Beck nodded.

Fin's heart slammed against her rib cage. "Who else knows?"

"Everyone who was in Muddy Boots heard the story." Beck glanced at Ami. "I forgot to mention Katie Ruth was there and said something about putting the news in the *Open Door*."

Fin closed her eyes. Small-town living at its best.

When she opened her eyes, Jeremy had moved beside her. "Don't worry. We'll get this figured out."

"Figure what out?" Ami's brows slammed together. "First we have to find out you're engaged from someone at the café. Now you're acting like it's some big secret. What's going on, Fin?"

"A big misunderstanding." Fin slung an arm around her sister's shoulders. "I'll tell you and the rest of the family all about it."

Ami's voice lowered as they turned toward the parlor entrance. "Is this something bad?"

As Fin wasn't quite certain what Ami would consider bad, she hesitated, then cursed herself when worry flooded Ami's face.

"No." Fin forced as much reassurance into the word as possible. "Not bad. Just an unusual set of circumstances."

"You're engaged?" Ami spoke tentatively, as if feeling her way through a minefield.

"Yes, but not to Jeremy."

"Who else is there?"

"Xander."

"Well, then." Though she smiled, Ami didn't appear relieved. And her smile didn't reach her eyes. "You're right. This is different."

The second Fin stepped into the parlor, her two younger sisters pounced. Her father stood back, smiling at his girls. Then he moved to her. When his strong arms wrapped around her, Fin's unsteady world righted itself. For the briefest of seconds she closed her eyes and hugged him back.

A lesson she'd learned as a child—that it's better to rip off a Band-Aid than peel it off—had her dispensing with formalities and blurting, "I'm afraid there's been a big misunderstanding."

The laughter and congratulations abruptly ceased. Her sisters stepped back and exchanged glances. Once again, Jeremy moved to her side, a strong, supportive presence. Though Fin knew he'd willingly step in if she needed him, this was her family.

"Despite that huge rock on your finger, something tells me we're not going to be toasting your engagement. Not yet, anyway." Marigold's light tone didn't match her watchful gaze.

"Let's sit." Their father, Steve, swept an arm wide, gesturing to the assortment of chairs, settees, and the new chaise with its ornately carved legs. "You and Jeremy sit there."

Steve pointed to a couple of high-backed chairs that someone had brought in from the dining room.

Hot seats, Fin thought, and had to stop herself from reaching for Jeremy's hand. Instead she cleared her throat and smiled. "That will work."

As the silence was making her nervous, she turned to Max. "Where are the twins?"

Connor and Callum, two redheaded charmers with loads of spirit, had been six when Prim had married Max. They were such a happy family it was easy to forget he wasn't the boys' biological father.

"The twins already had a playdate scheduled with Chris White. When, ah, Jackie and Cory heard we were coming to Ami's to, ah, celebrate, she offered to have them stay for dinner." Prim's cheeks were now as red as her hair.

"A nice pinot. Perfect for any occasion." Beck returned to the room with a bottle in each hand and a liter of ginger ale tucked under one arm.

Beck had proven to be a good brother-in-law and a considerate husband, always thinking of his wife and her happiness.

Will Xander be like that with me? Fin wondered.

Although the movie director had run somewhat hot and cold in the past six months, Fin told herself she and Xander were a good fit. Every relationship had its ups and downs. On the whole, things were good between them. She didn't need hearts and flowers like some women.

There had been no point in waiting for some all-consuming passion that would likely burn out before the ink on a marriage certificate dried.

Besides, she'd eventually like to have a child or two, and she wasn't getting any younger.

Beck made quick work of filling the glasses and dispensing them. Fin idly noticed Prim went with ginger ale. Likely so Ami didn't feel left out. Her accountant sister was considerate like that. Fin, well, right now she wouldn't mind a shot of whiskey. She'd make do with the wine.

Marigold heaved a heavy sigh. "I wish we had chocolate."

The fact that Fin's baby sister was there without her husband meant Sheriff Cade Rallis was on duty this afternoon. Fin never thought she'd see the day when Marigold, hairstylist to the cream of Chicago society, would return to Good Hope to stay.

At one time, not so long ago, Ami had been the only one of the sisters in Good Hope. Now Fin was the only bird who hadn't flown back to the nest.

She'd always been a big-city girl, Fin reminded herself. Always searching for . . . more.

"Delphinium, I believe it's time you explained about your engagement." Steve's eyes might hold worry, but his smile told Fin he was on her side, no matter what kind of news she shared. His gaze shifted to Jeremy. "I thought you'd have come to me, asked my permission. I realize that's a bit old-fashioned, but my girls mean a lot to me, and I'm a traditional man."

When Jeremy opened his mouth to respond, Fin squeezed his hand. "The situation is, shall we say, complicated."

"Are you pregnant?" Marigold blurted out.

Fin blinked. Her heart fluttered. "No. Why would you think that?"

"The sudden engagement. All the secrecy." Marigold gave a shrug. "It's the only thing that seemed to make sense."

Pregnant. Fin forced herself to breathe as the image of herself big with Jeremy's child took shape. The longing that assailed her was sharp enough to bring a stab of pain to her heart and tears to the backs of her lids. But Marigold had sharp eyes. Somehow, Fin maintained her composure and even managed a light tone. "I've only been back in town a week."

"You were back for Marigold's wedding," Prim said pointedly. "And Jeremy took a vacation last month."

"To Naples to visit my parents," Jeremy explained.

Marigold shot him a saucy smile. "So you said."

"Fin isn't engaged to Jeremy." Ami practically sighed the words. "She's engaged to Xander."

"Xander?" Prim and Marigold said in unison.

Fin nodded. "He proposed yesterday."

"Oh." Prim exchanged a look with her husband.

"I thought you were going to break up with—" Marigold stopped when Ami slanted her a warning look.

"It was a wonderful surprise." Fin gazed at her sisters, one at a time, daring them to say different.

Their confusion was totally on her. The last couple of times she'd been in Good Hope, Fin had complained about Xander to any sister who would listen. In February, when she'd made an unexpected trip home, she'd been down on him for canceling their plans to go to St. John. Then, when he'd backed out of his promise to come home with her for Marigold's wedding, she'd been livid.

If Fin were the blushing type, she'd be blushing now as she recalled all the not-so-complimentary things she'd said about her fiancé during the sisterly get-together before the wedding. Marigold was correct. She *had* said she was going to break it off with him.

Fin expected Marigold, the most straightforward of the Bloom sisters, to take the lead. The littlest Bloom didn't disappoint.

"If you're engaged to Xander, why does Ruby Rakes think you're engaged to her grandson? And why is Jeremy with you now?" Marigold sipped her wine and studied her older sister through lowered lashes.

"Funny you should ask." Fin glanced at Jeremy, who offered an encouraging smile. Taking a deep breath, Fin laid it out for her family.

She didn't omit anything except Xander's comments to Jeremy.

"Xander is okay with you pretending to be engaged to another man?" Steve asked.

"It was supposed to be only for a couple of days, a week at the longest, until Ruby had her operation and was stable." Fin glanced at Jeremy.

"My grandmother is scheduled for bypass surgery tomorrow afternoon in Milwaukee." Jeremy expelled a long breath. "We had it all planned out. Fin wouldn't wear her ring while in Good Hope, only at the hospital. We were going to inform all of you, then tell Ruby once she was through the surgery and stabilized. Several days, a week at the most. We never thought anyone in Good Hope would hear the news and run with it."

"We don't like lying to her," Fin acknowledged, "but her life is at stake. She saw the ring and immediately said she'd have the surgery. I was the one who suggested to Jeremy that we play along."

"I agreed." Jeremy reached over and gave Fin's hand a squeeze.

Steve took in the gesture, his gaze thoughtful. "I knew about the heart attack but didn't realize she was still at risk."

Jeremy cleared his throat. "If she doesn't get the operation, she'll die."

Ami's hand rose to her throat. "Ohmigoodness."

"I'll call Katie Ruth." Jeremy pulled out his phone. "Explain the situation and ask her to leave the announcement out of the newsletter."

"Too late." Marigold held her own phone high. "It's already gone out. Do you want me to read it to you?"

Expelling a resigned breath, Fin nodded.

"Congratulations to Mayor Jeremy Rakes and Delphinium Bloom on their engagement. While this news may come as a surprise to some Good Hope residents, it doesn't surprise your editor, a former classmate. Even back in high school, it was apparent these two were meant to be together. Best wishes, Fin and Jeremy!"

"That's sweet." Prim's lips lifted in a soft smile.

"Except it isn't true," Marigold, always the practical one, pointed out.

Ami rested her hands on her big belly. "What are you going to do?"

"I don't know that we have much choice but to continue the charade." Fin rubbed the bridge of her nose, where a headache was attempting to form.

Steve's gaze settled on Jeremy. "You realize the position you've put my daughter in. When she goes back to LA and announces her engagement to another man, it will reflect poorly on her."

"What about Xander?" Marigold sipped her wine. "He can't be okay with this arrangement."

"He understands how ill Ruby is and how much she needs this procedure. He has grandparents. He sympathizes. At the time we spoke, we all thought this engagement would be short-lived. Now it appears we'll have to string it out a little longer to avoid a real mess." Fin slanted a glance at Jeremy. "If that's okay with you."

His eyes never left hers. "Whatever you want to do."

"How are you going to do it?" Prim asked.

"Do what?"

"Pretend to be in love with one man when you're in love with another." Prim glanced at her husband. "I couldn't pull it off."

"I'll think of it as simply playing a part." Fin slanted a sideways glance. "Jeremy and I acted opposite each other in a lot of high school productions, so I know we can do it."

"For how long?"

Was it Ami or Prim who'd shot out the question? Did it even matter?

"I suppose until I'm ready to go back to LA."

Marigold's eyes narrowed. "I thought you were leaving soon."

"The town board will reconsider Xander's proposition at its September meeting." What had initially seemed so simple had sprouted wings. "Xander has gotten my boss to agree to let me stay here until the vote. I'm going to see if I can present arguments to Eliza and Lynn to sway their vote."

"I don't like it." Ami set down her glass of ginger ale, her eyes troubled. "Though if I'm being totally honest, I love the idea of you being here for the next month. You'll get to be here when our baby is born."

Beck, who'd remained standing behind his wife's chair, rested his hands lightly on her shoulders, massaging lightly.

Ami glanced around the circle. "It's been my dearest wish to have all of my sisters with me for this joyous occasion. If you go through with this playacting, you'll be here."

Fin met her sister's gaze. "There's no *if* about it."

"You're a forthright person." Ami's eyes softened. "You and Jeremy both have that reputation. Your word has always meant something. Once everyone finds out—"

"No one will ever know." A muscle in Jeremy's jaw jumped. "When this is over and Ruby is fully recovered, Fin will break up with me and return to Los Angeles. It will be up to her when to tell everyone about her engagement to Xander. If she wants, she can assert this time with me made her realize how much she loved him."

Beck gazed thoughtfully at the couple. "That might work."

"It will work." Jeremy's expression remained placid and under tight control, but Fin recognized the determined gleam in his eyes.

"You'll look like a schmuck." Marigold lifted her glass. "Just sayin'."

"Marigold," Ami shot out.

The youngest Bloom lifted a shoulder, let it fall. "It's true."

"It is true." Jeremy's lips lifted in a humorless smile. "But I'll do anything to save my grandmother. Being thought a schmuck is a small price to pay for her life."

Fin touched his arm. "I'm not going to let you do it. If anyone is going to look like a schmuck, it'll be me. Your life is here, mine isn't, not anymore. We'll have a public blowup where I'll look like the spoiled, self-centered woman most consider me to be. When I toss the ring at you and head back to Los Angeles, all will be right in your world."

Jeremy shook his head, the muscle in his jaw jumping. "Not gonna happen that way."

Fin lifted the wineglass to her lips, her gaze steady on his. "We'll see about that."

Tension simmered in the air as her and Jeremy's gazes locked.

"Since you're going to be doing all this pretending, how about we start by pretending you're engaged to Jeremy?"

Marigold's odd question had Fin breaking the stare-down with Jeremy and turning toward her sister. "What are you talking about?"

"I brought over several bottles of this really good champagne. Ami baked your favorite coconut cake." Marigold sighed hugely. "We don't know Xander very well, but we love Jeremy. So let's kick off your fake engagement by eating a great meal, toasting you two with champagne, and topping it all off with cake."

Before Fin could respond, Ami rose. "I think that's a fine idea."

"I like it, too," Steve said.

Fin glanced at Jeremy.

He smiled. "I love coconut cake."

The tension that had gripped Fin since she'd stepped out of the car slid from her shoulders to pool at her feet. "Well then, bring out the champagne, and let's get this party started."

Chapter Six

Jeremy pulled into the parking lot of the Sweet Dreams Motel just east of the business district, taking the spot next to Fin's vehicle. He'd barely stepped from the car when he saw Mavis Rosekrans, the proprietress, hauling a box almost as large as she was.

"Be right back," he called out to Fin as he sprinted to Mavis's side.

She was a portly woman, almost as wide as she was tall, with tightly curled gray hair and a ready smile. "Oh, Mr. Mayor, you don't need—"

The box was already in Jeremy's hands. Considering its size, it was surprisingly light. He jiggled it. "What's in here, anyway?"

"Christmas lights."

"Hello, Mrs. Rosekrans."

"Delphinium." The woman's smile widened farther. "I read the good news just an hour ago. Congratulations."

"Why, thank you, Mrs. Rosekrans. I'm pretty excited." Fin held out her ring for the woman's inspection.

Jeremy was impressed. Fin was an excellent actress.

He gave the box a little jiggle. "Where do you want this?"

"In the office. If it's not too much trouble."

"No trouble at all."

"What are you doing with Christmas lights at this time of year?" Fin walked beside Jeremy and eyed the box.

Mavis laughed. "First, I'm going to make sure all the bulbs work. I plan to put them up next month and leave them up until after the first of the year."

"Why so early?" Fin called over her shoulder as she hurried to open the door. She let the two step inside the office before following them.

"You've been gone too long, Delphinium." Mavis pointed to a spot on a card table set up behind the counter. "The weather here isn't like California. It's unpredictable. We could have a long fall or it could jump into winter at the end of September. With Ervin gone, I have to put them up myself. I don't like climbing a ladder when it's twenty degrees and the snow is blowing."

"You shouldn't have to climb a ladder. Call me when you're ready." Jeremy offered a warm smile. "Either I'll come out or one of the other rotarians, depending when you want it done, and put those up for you."

Mavis stiffened. "I take care of my own. I don't need charity."

"Mrs. Rosekrans, you've lived in Good Hope all your life." Jeremy placed a hand on her shoulder, let his gaze lock with hers. "Neighbors helping neighbors is the Good Hope way."

The woman's gaze softened, but he could see she wasn't fully convinced.

He tried another route. "Consider it a personal thank-you for making my fiancée so at home here."

The older woman glanced at Fin. "I appreciate you staying in Good Hope when those two with you didn't find it fancy enough."

A startled look crossed Fin's face. "I don't think they thought—"

"I know one of them was your boss and you feel you have to defend him." Mavis's jaw jutted out. "And, granted, where they stayed in Egg Harbor is very nice. But it meant a lot to me to have you choose my motel. Your mother and I were good friends."

Tears filled the older woman's eyes. "I'll do whatever I can to make you comfortable while you're here. Not only because that's the way I run my business, but because of Sarah."

Fin reached out, clasped the woman's hands. "Thank you."

Mavis gave Fin's hand a squeeze, then stepped back, her gaze returning to the box. "Your mother loved Christmas almost as much as I do. That last Christmas she had, well, it seemed extra special. I was glad of it, and glad all you girls could be with her and your dad that year."

Jeremy thought back. "Was that the year we brought in actual reindeer to pull Santa's sleigh in the parade?"

"Yes, and it was a huge hit." Mavis beamed. "That was also when we used the old A&W tracks for the Christmas Polar Express."

"I remember that . . ." Fin's green eyes were dark with memories. "I was older then, but it seemed a big hit for the kids. I know Prim's boys would get a kick out of riding it if they had it now."

"Maybe we can look at bringing it back." Jeremy paused at the look Fin shot him, then turned to Mavis. "I don't know if you heard, but the town board is going to revisit accepting the offer to have that company film here in December. I don't recall you voicing your opinion and wondered what you thought of the idea."

A look of startled surprise flashed across the woman's lined face. "That got voted down. You broke the tie and stood up for Christmas."

"It's not really standing up—"

Jeremy gave his head a barely perceptible shake, stopping Fin's protest. He wanted to hear honest opinions from his constituency. "A lot of the merchants have come to me and said they didn't believe they'd been given a chance to voice their opinions. That's what will happen at the mid-September meeting."

"Why are you against the proposition?" This time Fin's tone was matter-of-fact and free of judgment, something Jeremy very much appreciated.

"I have people who've been staying here every Christmas for as far back as I can remember. They reserve the same unit and know their neighbors in the adjacent units. We're their family, and this community gives them something they can't get where they live during the rest of the year . . . a sense of home and belonging." Mavis fixed her gaze on Fin. "Being here nourishes their soul. I know it probably sounds corny to a big-city girl—"

Fin grasped the woman's hand. "It doesn't sound corny at all."

"I appreciate you sharing your opinion," Jeremy told her. "Thank you."

"Thank you for listening." Then Mavis smiled and a twinkle filled her eyes. She made a shooing motion with her hands. "Now, you two go and do whatever newly engaged couples do with their time, and leave me to my bulbs."

Jeremy slung an arm around Fin's shoulders as they left the office. He told himself it was because Mrs. Rosekrans was watching. The truth was, he wanted the connection. The decision on the film proposition hadn't been easy the first time. It wasn't going to be any easier the second time around.

"Until she'd mentioned it, I'd forgotten she and my mother were friends." Fin's voice was oddly subdued.

"That's not surprising." Jeremy smiled. "Your mother had so many friends."

He stopped when they reached the blue door of her unit. "I thought you'd stay with family while in Good Hope."

"Ami and Beck have less than a month before Baby Cross arrives." Fin's expression softened. "She wanted me to stay, but this time needs to be about them."

How much easier it would be for Fin to simply call one of the many empty bedrooms in the recently remodeled Victorian home. Instead she'd put her sister's needs first.

As if anticipating his next question, Fin continued without taking a breath. "Now that school is in session, my dad goes to bed at nine and is up by six. Not exactly the hours I like to keep."

"It's too bad the apartment over the bakery isn't available." Jeremy thought of the one-bedroom unit over Blooms Bake Shop, where both Ami and Marigold had lived for a period of time. "Ami would never have rented it to Hadley if she'd known you'd be back."

"I'm not back," Fin clarified. "Not permanently, anyway. Just for a month."

Jeremy's gaze returned to her unit's bright blue door. While Sweet Dreams was a nice, comfortable motel, he couldn't imagine Fin lasting a month in such close quarters. But what was the alternative?

A solution came to mind, but Jeremy swiped it away like a troublesome mosquito. Still, the idea continued to buzz. "Your sister is quite a cook."

"After the rocky start to the evening, I thought dinner might be awkward." Gazing up at the moon hanging heavy in the sky, Fin was in no apparent hurry to go inside. "But I enjoyed the food and the conversation. Everyone seemed much more relaxed by the time we left."

"Your dad still isn't sold on the fake engagement idea."

"He's old-fashioned," Fin acknowledged. "He worries about me."

"I worry about you, too." Jeremy had worried about Fin's safety in Los Angeles. Now, knowing she was engaged to the Pompous Ass, he worried for her happiness.

Not that where she lived or who she married was his business. But they'd once been as close as two people could be, and just because she was no longer a part of his life didn't mean he couldn't care.

"I'll wait out here while you pack your bag." He took a deep breath, then let it out slowly. "Thanks for not making a big deal out of spending tonight at the farm. I have lots of empty bedrooms, and this way we can leave first thing in the morning, pick Ruby up in Sturgeon Bay, then head to Milwaukee."

He turned to go, but Fin's hand on his arm stopped him.

"One more thing." She stared intently in his eyes. "Promise me Ruby isn't going to die."

Jeremy started to say there was no way to know for sure, but he stopped himself, seeing she needed reassurance, not worst-case scenario. "She won't have any problems, and she'll be back home, feisty as ever, in no time. Froedtert is one of the top-ranked hospitals for heart bypass surgeries. Her surgeon does dozens of these operations a year. And we'll be there to make sure she has the care that she needs."

It still pained him that his parents hadn't volunteered to forgo their European vacation plans. Still, his grandmother had him and Fin, and the promise of a wedding in the spring.

What had she told him right before they'd left the hospital? Ah, yes, *she couldn't ask for anything more.*

When Jeremy spotted the car parked in the drive, he nearly groaned aloud. He didn't want to talk with anyone right now, not even the woman who'd been his friend since childhood. While many in Good Hope considered Eliza prickly and difficult to deal with, she had a good heart.

Fin slanted a glance at him. "Is that Eliza's Subaru?"

"Yes, it is."

After parking the car in the carriage house, instead of going in through the back door, he rounded the house to the front, Fin still holding the bag she'd refused to let him carry.

Eliza sat on the porch swing but rose when he and Fin climbed the steps. As usual, she was dressed mostly in black, the fitted top accentuated by a leopard-print vest.

He saw Eliza glance briefly at the suitcase in Fin's hand.

"I heard about the engagement." Color rode high in Eliza's cheeks as her gaze remained fixed on Jeremy. "And about your grandmother's upcoming surgery. I came to offer congratulations and to see if there was anything I could do for Ruby, or for you."

"That's very kind of you." Fin spoke before he could, surprising him once again.

Jeremy unlocked the door, pushed it open. "Please, come in. We can talk inside."

They ended up in the kitchen, with Jeremy pouring them each a glass of wine.

"Read any good books lately?" Jeremy knew he was stalling and only prolonging the inevitable, but the thought of ending the friendship he'd enjoyed since childhood pained him.

"I just finished a nonfiction book on organizational management." Eliza took a sip of wine and studied him over the rim. "Later tonight, I'm treating myself with a murder mystery by a favorite author."

Jeremy thought of the book on his bedside stand. "I'm into a thriller that has more than its share of dead bodies."

As if sensing he still wasn't ready to share his news, Eliza obligingly filled the silence with book talk while Fin listened without speaking.

It didn't take long before the book conversation ran its course. Eliza cocked her head and fixed those steely gray eyes on him. "I thought Ruby refused to have the surgery. What changed?"

Jeremy took a deep breath. "She was excited when she found out Fin and I were going to get married. She—"

"Stop." The word burst like a bullet from Fin's mouth, startling him. "Eliza is a close friend of yours." Fin's unblinking green eyes met his. "She deserves the truth."

"We agreed." Jeremy spoke in a low tone, barely above a whisper. "Not—"

"We agreed to tell only a small inner circle the truth." Fin gestured with her head toward Eliza, whose gaze was now sharp and assessing. "Eliza is part of your inner circle."

"What's going on here?" Eliza set down her glass, her focus shifting from Jeremy to Fin, then back to Jeremy.

"Tell her," Fin urged, her voice unnaturally soft.

As Jeremy knew there was no love lost between Fin and Eliza, he was surprised by the encouragement. Yet she was right. He and Eliza had been friends since childhood. Jeremy didn't want to deceive her. Heck, he didn't want to deceive anyone. He prided himself on being a straight shooter.

There was a long pause as he searched for the right words. Then he took a breath and laid it out, topping off their wineglasses halfway through the telling.

Eliza cast an incredulous look in Fin's direction. "You're engaged to Xander Tillman, yet it was *your* idea to go along with the misunderstanding?"

"I couldn't let Ruby die. She's like my own grandmother. I won't lose another person I love." When Fin's eyes took on a distant glow, Jeremy knew she was thinking about her mother.

Jeremy continued, then ended with the surgery scheduled for tomorrow.

Absolute silence filled the air with a kind of watchful waiting.

"Does this have anything to do with Tillman's proposition being back on the agenda?" Instead of the anger and sharp bite so often heard in Eliza's voice, there was only weariness.

"No. That was already decided." Fin glanced at Jeremy, then back at Eliza. "Although while I'm in Good Hope, I will try to get you and Lynn to change your votes."

"What about Jeremy? Do you expect him to break a tie in your favor?"

Fin's smile disappeared under Eliza's assessing gaze.

"That's an insult to him. You know Jeremy as well as I do." Fin's steady gaze never left Eliza's face. "He's an honorable man. If it becomes necessary for him to break another tie, he'll do what he thinks is in the best interest of Good Hope."

Eliza slowly nodded her agreement.

Jeremy couldn't believe that after all these years of sniping at each other, the two women were having a rational conversation. He sat back, took another sip of wine.

"What happens when you go back to Los Angeles?" There was puzzlement in Eliza's voice mixed with a liberal dose of concern. "How are you going to explain the breakup?"

Before Fin could respond, Eliza's focus shifted to him. "Your reputation will be in tatters."

"If that's the price I have to pay for my grandmother's health, I'm okay with it." Jeremy kept his voice casual and offhand, as if losing a reputation that he'd spent his life building was no big deal. "I'll say that I couldn't make Fin happy. That I tried but—"

"Not happening." Fin paused, then continued, softening her tone. "I made it clear to Jeremy that I'm taking the blame. I'm not sure how quite yet, but I'll find a way."

Eliza inclined her head. "I believe you will."

"Not in this lifetime." Jeremy would have said more, but his phone rang, a jarring sound that had them all jumping.

"Is something wrong?" Eliza's voice, often so brusque, filled with concern. "Is it your grandmother?"

Fin's eyes were wide. "Is it the hospital?"

Glancing at the readout, Jeremy breathed a sigh of relief. "It's Kyle Kendrick. I forgot I promised to get back to him about the courthouse renovation project."

"Don't tell me he's staying around longer?" Eliza's gray eyes flashed.

Fin cocked her head. "You don't like him?"

"He's arrogant." Eliza sniffed. "I've no use for arrogant men."

Jeremy smiled and finally answered his ringing phone. He considered leaving the room but was comfortable where he was, so he remained seated.

"Kyle. I'm sorry I didn't get back to you."

Jeremy listened, conscious of both women's eyes on him. "I verified the contract will be ready for you to sign on Monday morning."

They talked for a few minutes longer before Jeremy clicked off. "He seems like a nice enough guy."

Eliza dismissed Kyle with a flick of her wrist. "Listen, I know you've had a busy day, and tomorrow will likely be worse, but before I leave, I'd like to discuss some business with you."

Fin pushed back her chair and stood. "I'll go up—"

"You don't have to leave," Eliza told her. "You might even have some thoughts on this."

Clearly intrigued, Fin sat down.

"In three weeks, Rakes Farm is set to host a Your Wish Fulfilled Christmas event for Mindy Vaughn, a seven-year-old suffering from a brain tumor." Eliza's voice remained even, but Jeremy saw her fingers tighten around the wineglass.

"Is that Owen Vaughn's daughter?" Fin slanted a look at Jeremy. He'd played football with Owen in high school.

"Yes. She's a real spitfire. She reminds me of Grandma Ruby." The smile that had lifted his lips faded as he recalled the last year of treatments she'd undergone.

"Anyway," Eliza continued, "Mindy loves Christmas, and she wants the holiday to come early."

The child had wished for Christmas. Fin found herself idly wondering what she'd wish for, but it had been a long time since she'd allowed herself to wish for anything. Wishing led to disappointment.

"Since she might not make it to December . . ." Eliza paused to clear her throat. When she spoke, her voice was even and under control. "Your Wish Fulfilled, with help from the rotary and the Cherries, will do a Twelve Days of Christmas. It will begin with events at Mindy's home, culminating on day twelve with a big party in the barn and sledding down—"

"Sledding?" Fin interrupted. "It's summer."

"Snow machine," Jeremy tossed in. "The white stuff won't last long, but it'll be here."

"The Cherries will assist with the sledding, the caroling, and the rest of the barn events, but I got to thinking . . ." Eliza paused for a moment, as if gathering her thoughts. "What if we helped take it bigger? Got the whole town involved? The businesses could put up their lights and we could toss in a few of the Twelve Nights events. I know it'd be extra work, but . . ."

"I think it's a fabulous idea." Fin glanced at Jeremy.

Jeremy understood immediately why Eliza was concerned. "You're worried all this Christmas hoopla might look odd now that the proposition is back on the agenda, like we're trying to show the town what they'd miss if we skipped the Christmas festivities this year?"

Eliza nodded. "Conversely, it might also appear as if we're doing it so we can assure people they've already had their taste of Christmas this year."

Fin gave a snort of disgust. "Who cares how it looks or appears?"

"Said the woman who's engaged to one man while pretending to be engaged to another."

When Fin shot her a sharp look, Eliza only grinned.

"I'm just saying." Fin smiled sweetly. "If you go ahead with the plan, I'll be happy to do whatever I can while I'm here at the farm."

"You're living here?" Eliza raised a brow.

"Since when?" Jeremy asked.

"Once Ruby is released, I plan to stay here to help with her care until she's stronger." Fin smiled at Jeremy. "We hadn't talked about this yet, but it makes sense."

"You're going to have your hands full with this one," Eliza told Jeremy, then turned back to Fin. "I accept your offer. Katie Ruth is the Your Wish Fulfilled rep for this area. You can help her coordinate events at the farm. I'll handle the downtown decorating."

"Sounds like you two have it all planned out." Jeremy pushed back his chair and rose.

"It's a good start. And it's time for me to go." Eliza moved to Jeremy, then gave him a swift, hard hug. "Thanks for trusting me with the truth."

Jeremy glanced at Fin for a second, then let his gaze linger on Eliza. "How could I not? You're my inner circle."

"I'll walk you to the door." Fin waited until she and Eliza were out of earshot before she stopped, gripping Eliza's arm. "You have my word I won't hurt him. Not again."

Eliza studied her for a long moment. "I think you believe that. No, I know you believe it. And I hope to God you don't hurt him. But I learned a long time ago that sometimes a person can be hurt despite the best of intentions."

Chapter Seven

Jeremy watched Fin key something into her phone, then hit Send. It wasn't that he was nosy; staring at her simply beat pacing or casting another look at the surgical waiting room clock. The hands of which had moved at a snail's pace all afternoon.

Fin looked up, caught him staring, and smiled sheepishly.

"The way you were concentrating, it looked as if you were transmitting the nuclear codes."

"Hardly that." Fin waved a dismissive hand. "I was just texting Xander my daily update."

Since the update undoubtedly involved him, Jeremy was blunt. "What did you tell him?"

"I told him I checked the city website and confirmed his proposition is on the September fifteenth agenda. I also mentioned that you are actively soliciting opinions of business owners." She paused, as if

Cindy Kirk

seeing the question in his eyes. "I saw no reason to relay last night's conversation with Mavis and her strong feelings against the measure."

"Probably for the best." Not able to sit another second, Jeremy pulled to his feet and began to pace. "Why can't someone stop in and tell us how she's doing? I don't think wanting regular updates is asking too much."

"I wish they could." Fin chewed on her bottom lip. "But I bet everyone in the operating room is pretty busy."

Jeremy paused near the window and tried to ignore the frisson of fear snaking up his spine. "The doctor said it could take three to six hours. It's been nearly three."

"No news is good news." Fin studied him, her eyes dark as jade. Though she appeared calm, the way she was shredding the tissue in her hand told Jeremy he wasn't the only one on edge. "I hate hospitals."

"I never did before," Jeremy muttered. "But I do now."

"We could play cards?" Fin suggested. "It might make the time go faster. God knows it can't go any slower."

Jeremy glanced around. Several families were gathered on the other side of the spacious room, visiting in hushed tones. The solemn atmosphere reminded him of a funeral. He swallowed against the baseball that had become lodged in his throat.

As Fin gazed expectantly at him, he cleared his throat, then did it once again before speaking. "One problem. No cards."

"I have that covered." Fin opened her bag. "Marigold dropped a deck into my purse at Ami's the other night. She said something about hoping I'd find a use for them."

"That seems odd."

"I thought so, too."

If playing cards would take his mind off Ruby and how pale and scared she'd looked when they'd wheeled her off to surgery, Jeremy was all for it.

76

When Fin sauntered to a table near a sunny window, he followed and dropped into a chair opposite her.

Jeremy leaned back in the plastic chair. "What do you want to play?"

"Gin rummy?"

"Works for me."

Fin fumbled around in her purse, then pulled out the deck. Her triumphant smile quickly morphed into a frown. "What the—"

Jeremy leaned close. "What's the matter?"

"These aren't playing cards." She puffed out her cheeks, flipped through several more cards. "They all have questions. Relationship-type questions."

"Why would Marigold give them to you?"

"As a joke." Fin's eyes narrowed. "It's probably a dare. She's probably going to ask me if I played."

"Easy solution. When you speak with Xander tonight, ask him a couple of them. Then you can honestly tell Marigold you and your fiancé played the game."

She gave her head a little shake. "Xander won't take time for such silliness."

The slight catch in her voice tugged at his heart.

Pompous Ass, he thought. "Lay one on me."

Her eyes lit up. "You'll play?"

"I'm willing to answer a question or two, so long as you reciprocate."

Her sudden grin had Jeremy's heart skipping a beat. For a second he forgot all about his grandmother.

She shifted her attention to the cards. "I'll find—"

"No cherry-picking." Jeremy lifted them from her hands. He shuffled, then set the deck on the table and fanned out the cards. "Pick one."

"I want an easy one."

"Don't we all."

Staring at the cards as if she could see right through them, she closed her eyes and pulled one from the middle of the deck. She handed it to Jeremy with a flourish. "You read it."

"If you could write a note to your younger self, what would you say in only three words?"

Fin groaned. "Next card."

"No do-overs." Jeremy wiggled the card. "Do I need to start the timer?"

"What timer?" Fin paused. "Oh, you were kidding. Well, just remember, smart guy, that you have to answer the question, too."

"First I get to hear yours." Jeremy leaned back in the chair and studied her. Had he ever known a more beautiful, more intelligent woman?

"Three words." Fin chewed on her lower lip, her gaze unsettled. "Don't be afraid."

"What?"

"My three words are *don't be afraid*. Now, it's your turn."

"What do they mean?"

"I don't think that's part of the game."

"Of course it is. The point of any of these types of questions is to get better acquainted. Just tossing out *don't be afraid* doesn't serve the spirit of the game."

Fin rolled her eyes.

He linked his fingers together and waited, curious to discover what she meant. The Fin Bloom he remembered was fearless, strong, and courageous. What could she possibly have had to fear?

"When I was younger, I worried that I wasn't enough. Not pretty enough. Not smart enough. I worried I'd disappoint my parents, that I would do something and they would be ashamed and disappointed." Her eyes settled on him. "When we dated, I worried I couldn't be what you wanted me to be."

When he opened his mouth, she lifted a hand, stopping him. "Not that I knew what you wanted, but, anyway, there it is." A look of melancholy settled over her face. "If I could write that note, I'd tell myself to not be afraid, to trust in myself and in the love of family and friends."

Jeremy leaned across the table, said nothing, only gave her hand a squeeze. It felt as if she'd shared something private and intimate with him.

"Your turn." Her lips curved in a slight smile. "If you could write a note, what would you say to your younger self? Remember, use only three words."

The question was, he realized, more difficult when you were the one forced to answer it. But he hadn't let Fin beg off, so he wouldn't ask for clemency. "Go for it."

"Go for what?"

"Go for what I wanted. Pursue fearlessly." Oddly embarrassed, Jeremy shrugged. "I knew by the time I was sixteen that there were two things I wanted in this world. Making my home in Good Hope was one of them."

"And you made that happen. You came back after college, took over the family's business interests, and now you're the mayor." Fin studied his face. "What was the second?"

"That isn't important."

"C'mon, go for it." She grinned. "What else?"

"You." An ache looped around his heart, squeezed. "I let you go. More accurately, I pushed you away. That's my biggest regret."

Her smiled faded. "Everything works out for the best."

He cocked his head. "Does it?"

She flushed, gave a little laugh, and pushed the cards to him.

When she started to reach for a card, he placed a restraining hand on her arm. "My turn to pick."

He pulled a card from the top and handed it to her.

"Name something you've done that you should have apologized to your partner for," she read.

"We should have done one and called it good."

"I read it." Her hands twisted together. "You answer first."

A familiar heaviness centered around Jeremy's heart. He didn't want to answer the stupid question. Didn't want to think about the past. While the cards might fill up the time, they'd also brought the past he and Fin had once shared—along with mistakes he'd made—front and center.

Could this be a blessing in disguise? Maybe this conversation was what he needed for closure.

Jeremy kept his gaze focused on her face. "I never apologized for how I acted right before I left for college. I promised I'd never leave you, then I did. I'm sorry."

She reached over and lightly touched his hand. "I never held that against you. Our families were both in upheaval. My mom was sick and your parents were experiencing . . . challenges. You were afraid they might split."

Though the fears had been real, he waved the excuse aside. "I wasn't there for you, not like I should have been."

When a sadness filled her eyes, Jeremy didn't stop to think. He rose, rounded the table, and pulled her into his arms. Though she stiffened at first, it took only a second for her to relax against him. As they had all those years ago, they melded perfectly. It was as if ten years apart had never happened. He tightened his hold and accepted the comfort she offered.

"She's in recovery."

The unexpected voice had them springing apart and jumping to their feet.

Dr. Lyons, the cardiovascular surgeon who'd performed the surgery, swept off his surgical cap with a weary gesture. "Mrs. Rakes came through the surgery in good shape. She's lucky she didn't wait any longer to have the procedure. With the vessels so blocked, she could have had a massive MI at any moment."

"But she's okay?" Jeremy asked the doctor and felt Fin take his hand.

"Yes." The doctor gestured to the chairs they'd just vacated. "Let's sit down."

Jeremy wanted to see his grandmother, see for himself that she was okay. But he sat.

For a few minutes the doctor talked about the surgery itself before moving on to what they could expect now. "She'll be in ICU the next couple of days. Right now, I'm keeping the tube down her throat. It shouldn't be in long, but if we need an open airway, we have one. Though I anticipate an uneventful recovery, because of her age, I plan to keep her in the hospital another three to five days after she's transferred out of ICU."

"Dr. Passmore told her to expect to be in the hospital a week." Fin's fingers stole over to clasp Jeremy's hand. "That seems to be what you're saying, too."

"If she's doing really well, I may send her home in five days." The doctor turned to Jeremy. "I understand she'll be coming to your house."

"It's actually her home, but yes, she'll be staying with me."

"You can expect her to have some side effects from the procedure." Dr. Lyons leaned forward. "She'll have pain from the incision, and you may notice some short-term memory loss."

Jeremy exchanged a glance with Fin.

"As well as confusion and trouble with time," Dr. Lyons continued. "Those are reactions to the anesthesia and will go away as she recovers. For safety, someone needs to be in the house with her at all times. If that's a problem, I can have our discharge planning staff look at skilled nursing facility placement. There are a number of fine—"

"That won't be necessary." Jeremy cut him off. "If I can't be there, I'll hire someone to help."

"I'll be there, too." Fin's quiet voice was a balm to his raw nerves. "Between us, we'll see she gets the care she needs."

"Okay then, we'll plan on her going home once she's discharged." The doctor's gaze shifted between him and Fin, then he stood and smiled. "Congratulations on your engagement. When I checked on her in recovery she was telling the nurses she decided to have the surgery so she could dance at your wedding. Regardless of the reason, she did the right thing in having the surgery."

Only when Lyons had left the room did Jeremy slide his arms around Fin and pull her close, resting his forehead against hers. "Thank you."

"I didn't do anything." Though she gave a little laugh, he felt her tremble.

"You saved my grandmother's life." He lifted his head, and emotion surged as he gazed into those sea-green eyes.

"Are you certain Xander will be comfortable with you living at the farm?" The eyes that met hers were clear and very blue. "I don't want to cause trouble."

"Xander trusts me." Fin spoke with great conviction even as she wondered if that was true. Or was it that he simply didn't care? Or that he wanted to secure the location site so much that anything went? She shoved the ridiculous doubts aside. "He probably thinks that if you're around me twenty-four/seven, you'll agree to anything just to get me out of your hair, or rather out of your house."

Jeremy looked puzzled by the comment, and Fin decided it would be best if she just kept her mouth shut from now on. She was painting an unflattering picture of both her and Xander.

"Well," he said after a long moment. "I won't forget your generosity."

———

"Jeremy is at the hospital with his grandmother now." While Fin spoke with Xander, she tidied up the hotel suite she and Jeremy had called home for the past five nights. "He's hoping to be there when the doctor does his rounds and find out when she'll be released."

She hadn't expected Xander to inquire about Ruby's health, and he didn't disappoint.

"You've had lots of uninterrupted time with the mayor," Xander's voice probed, soft and smooth as glass. "Do you sense any change in his position on my proposition?"

Fin knew Xander wouldn't believe her if she told him the truth, that she'd barely seen Jeremy since they'd checked into the hotel. The fact was, from day one they'd been taking shifts at the hospital. When Fin was there, he was back in the room, in bed, sleeping. Which was where she needed to be after spending the night in Ruby's room.

"Fin?"

She realized with a start that Xander had asked a question and her foggy brain had yet to formulate a response. What had he asked? Oh, yes.

"I don't sense a change yet, but the Your Wish Fulfilled Christmas event may change some minds."

"When does that start?"

"I think it's already started." *At least at the child's home,* Fin thought. Or maybe it was about to start. Since Ruby's surgery the days had blurred together.

"Good. Keep me updated on how things are going." Xander paused. "You sound tired."

"I'm exhausted." Though he hadn't wanted to FaceTime, she offered a wan smile.

"I appreciate all you're doing for me, Fin. I'll make sure you're handsomely rewarded if you pull this off."

"Good, well, I'm going to bed now."

As Fin was drifting off to sleep, one thought circled in her head. She'd be handsomely rewarded if she pulled this off. What would happen if she didn't?

She woke to find Jeremy leaning over her. He smelled of soap and a familiar warm, male scent that made something tighten in her abdomen. Still half-asleep, she stretched and wound her arms around his neck. "Good morning."

A slow smile turned up the corners of his lips. "It's afternoon, but I've got some good news. They're releasing Grandma Ruby."

"When?" She laughed, for no reason other than the news.

"Now." He laughed, too, his eyes dropping down to her mouth. "Or as soon as we can get the car packed and pick her up."

"That's not good news. That's fabulous news." Giving a little squeal, Fin pulled Jeremy down on top of her.

Even before his lips brushed hers, she knew the feel of his mouth, the softness, the warmth, the gentleness. Her sleepy blood hummed in pleasure as he kissed her with a slow thoroughness that left her weak, trembling, and longing for more.

Somewhere in her passion-filled brain, the thought struck her that Xander was her fiancé, not Jeremy.

When she opened her mouth to inform Jeremy of that fact, he changed the angle of the kiss, deepening it. A smoldering fire burned in her, a sensation she didn't bother to fight. Matching heat, as strong as her own, radiated from him, urgent now and hungry. His hand slid under her top, flat against her hot skin.

Fin squirmed with need as those fingertips inched slowly higher.

When his telephone rang, a harsh, jarring sound resembling a fire alarm, she ignored it and planted a kiss against the base of his throat, reveling in the salty taste.

The phone continued to play the Black Eyed Peas' "I Gotta Feeling" until Fin was ready to snatch the darn thing from his pocket and fling it across the room.

His fingers had almost reached her breasts, and the tips tingled with anticipation.

Still, the song played on.

With a muttered oath, Jeremy jerked his hand back and sat up, pulling out the phone. "Rakes."

He closed his eyes for a second, then chuckled. "It sounds like her. We'll be there within the hour."

Fin propped herself up on one elbow. "What happened? Is Ruby okay?"

"She wanted the nurse to call and say that even though she is eager to go home, we didn't need to rush. She, ah, wanted us to take time to enjoy the room one last time."

Even as Fin's breasts yearned for his touch and her lips longed to meet his just one more time, she knew they'd narrowly escaped disaster. "I'd say that phone rang at just the right time. Or you and I would have been enjoying this room a little too much."

Jeremy's sigh was heavy with resignation. "I'm guessing that means it's time to pack up and head out."

Fin couldn't help it. She leaned over and gave him one last kiss. "You always were a smart guy."

Chapter Eight

Two days after Ruby returned home, Fin moved into Jeremy's house. As Ruby needed someone around and she and Jeremy were splitting caregiver duty, it didn't make sense for her to drive back into Good Hope when her shift was up.

Xander had been ecstatic when she told him the news, telling her he couldn't buy this kind of access to the mayor. She wondered if he'd feel the same if she told him about the kiss she and Jeremy had shared the day his grandmother had been released from the hospital. She planned to tell him; the guilt she felt each time she thought about how she'd responded wouldn't let her keep something so important from him.

What she'd said about window shopping might be true, but that didn't extend to kissing a man, or thinking about doing more with that man . . .

Tonight. She'd tell Xander tonight. For now, she would enjoy the warm sunshine and lunch with Ruby and Jeremy on the terrace.

"Having you join us for lunch is a nice surprise." Fin took the last bite of the goat-cheese-and-olive-stuffed chicken breast, letting the delicious flavor linger in her mouth. She set down her fork with a sigh.

Jeremy's best move since his grandmother had come home from the hospital had been to convince Dinah Pratt, who'd cooked for Ruby before, to come out of retirement to prepare heart-healthy meals for the three of them for the next month or so. Fin had argued she was up to the task, but Jeremy insisted she had enough to do with keeping Ruby occupied and happy.

Having eaten Dinah's meals for the past three days, Fin was glad he'd prevailed.

"This sure beats a cold roast beef sandwich." Jeremy stabbed a piece of perfectly steamed broccoli and popped it into his mouth.

Ruby sat back in her chair and smiled at them. There was healthy color in her face, and every day she grew stronger. She'd been confused a few times, and Fin and Jeremy had both noticed Ruby had difficulty keeping time straight, but the doctor had assured them these symptoms were transitory.

"Mrs. Rakes." Dinah appeared in the doorway. "You have a visitor. He said he has an appointment."

"Bring him out here, please." Ruby straightened in her seat, her hands smoothing her hair. "And if you could bring us another pot of decaf, that'd be splendid."

"Yes, ma'am." Dinah was nearly as old as Ruby, and the two had been acquainted since girlhood. Yet when she was on the job, she refused to call Ruby anything but *Mrs. Rakes* or *ma'am.*

It was puzzling, to say the least, Fin thought.

"Who did you invite?" Jeremy lifted his glass of iced tea. Not a fan of decaffeinated coffee, yesterday he'd asked Dinah to brew some sun tea.

Ruby gave a little laugh, color high in her cheeks. "I don't remember."

Jeremy cocked his head. "You don't remember?"

"I like surprises." Fin gave Ruby's hand a squeeze.

The grateful look Ruby shot her had Fin's heart twisting. She knew these bouts of forgetfulness were hard on the older woman. When they occurred, Fin did her best to make them seem like no big deal.

Still, she was as curious as Jeremy and looked up when the French doors opened.

Pastor Dan Marshall, the senior minister at First Christian, stepped out onto the terrace. He was shorter than Jeremy, with a messy cap of brown hair, hazel eyes, and a ready smile. He looked, Fin thought, very un-pastor-like in khakis and a navy polo.

Smiling broadly, Jeremy stood and stepped forward. "I'm glad you could make it this morning. Dinah is bringing out a fresh pot of decaf. We also have iced tea."

The minister glanced at the patio table, still holding the remnants of their meal. "I interrupted your lunch."

When Fin saw a look of distress cross Ruby's features, she stood and began to gather the dishes. "Actually, you have perfect timing. We just finished."

Relief skittered across the young minister's face. "Good."

Dan stepped to Ruby's side, crouched down, and clasped her hand in his. "How are you feeling this morning?"

"Very well, Pastor." Ruby's smile lit her entire face. She made a sweeping gesture with one hand. "I'm surrounded by love."

The minister's gaze slid around the table. At Fin, with a stack of dishes in her arms, and at Jeremy, who'd risen to help and now had his arms full, too.

"Since I'm here to speak about love, it does appear the timing couldn't be better."

"Be right back," Fin called over her shoulder.

Once they were inside and Dinah had confiscated the dishes, Fin pulled Jeremy into the parlor. Conscious of the woman in the kitchen, she kept her voice low. "What's he doing here?"

Jeremy shrugged. "I assume visiting members of his congregation who have recently had surgery is one of his duties."

Some of the tension in Fin's shoulders eased. "You're probably right. Pastor Schmidt stopped by often when my mother was ill. There was just something about the way he looked at me . . ."

Jeremy's gaze sharpened. "As if he's got the hots for you?"

"No, not like that." Fin chuckled. "Though it might be interesting. I've never been hit on by a minister before."

"You're engaged." Jeremy lifted her hand.

Fin gazed down at the diamond. Yes, she was engaged, and she needed to remember that fact. "We better get out there. Hopefully he'll want to talk to Ruby about church things and we can make a quick exit."

"Your mouth, God's ear."

She gave him a quick jab to the gut with her elbow.

"Oof." He pretended to double over.

"Wuss."

They were both laughing when they stepped back on the terrace, where the table had been cleaned and only a carafe of coffee and Jeremy's iced tea glass remained.

Ruby and Dan glanced up when they stepped out.

"I know you three have a lot to discuss." Ruby slowly rose to her feet. "I'm going to my room so you'll have some privacy."

Fin's heart skipped a beat. "What do we need privacy for?"

"Usually premarital counseling is done with just the minister and the engaged couple." Dan smiled warmly at Ruby. "When she called yesterday, Mrs. Rakes told me that you two were eager to get started on these sessions."

Fin froze.

Jeremy stiffened beside her.

Ruby's smile faltered. "Oh dear, did I get that wrong?"

"No." Fin shot her a reassuring smile. "You were right. Jeremy and I are eager to get started."

"It's just that we know how busy Dan is at this time of year." Jeremy spoke slowly, as if feeling his way through a dark room. "We certainly don't want to take time—"

"No worries." Dan shot Ruby a wink. "Your grandmother made that clear. But today works for me, if it still works for you."

Though Ruby's expression gave nothing away, Fin noticed the older woman's tongue moistening her lips. Since the surgery, she'd seen Ruby doing that whenever she was anxious.

"Perfect time." Fin reached over and squeezed Jeremy's forearm. "Right?"

"Absolutely."

Fin hoped Xander appreciated all she was doing to help him. Last night he'd reminded her that he was a results guy. He didn't care how it was done, he just wanted the approval.

The conversation had left her feeling uneasy.

Jeremy's hand slid down her arm to take her fingers in his warm, firm grasp. It was as if he'd told her, "I'm here. No worries."

She looked up and fell headfirst into the liquid blue depths of his eyes.

This can't be worse than the relationship cards, she told herself, then hoped that was true.

Once they were seated, Dan took several minutes to explain the purpose of premarriage counseling. This was an opportunity for the three of them to become better acquainted, to see where they were on their spiritual journey, and to discover if there were any problem areas in their relationship that needed addressing.

Fin listened to the minister's words and felt dread wrap around her like a straitjacket. This was definitely not what she'd signed up for. But other than hopping up and running into the house—or feigning a panic attack—she saw no other option than to soldier on.

The minister reached down to pull a portfolio out of his messenger bag, and Jeremy's thumb stroked Fin's palm in a gesture meant to soothe.

Dan's gaze dropped to their clenched hands and nodded approvingly. He put the papers on the table in front of him, then leaned forward. "Who wants to tell me how you met?"

"That's easy." Fin glanced at Jeremy, then proceeded forward. "We've always known each other."

Jeremy picked up the conversational ball. "Fin's sister Ami and I were in kindergarten together. Their mother, Sarah, was one of the room moms. She brought Fin with her to one of the class parties. I don't know where the other two girls were . . ."

He glanced at Fin, and she gave a little shrug. She had no memory of the party.

"I thought she was Ami's twin." Jeremy chuckled. "I asked the teacher why she wasn't in school with her sister."

Dan leaned back, his eyes sharp and assessing. "You two go way back."

Fin nodded and began to relax. If all the questions were this easy, she'd been worried for nothing.

Dan cocked his head. "When did you begin dating?"

"My freshman year in high school." Fin glanced at Jeremy, and his fingers tightened around hers. "He asked me to a school dance."

"We were together until I left for college." Jeremy shrugged. "Fin still had a year of high school left."

If the breakup had to be discussed, Jeremy had done a nice job of making it sound as if his leaving for college had precipitated them going their separate ways.

"Is that why you broke up?" Dan asked.

Suddenly grateful for the coffee, even if it was decaf, Fin took a long sip.

"I'm sure it was part of it." Jeremy grabbed his tea and took a gulp.

"What else?" Dan set down his pencil, completely focused.

Coffee cup still in hand, Fin managed to feign boredom at the line of questioning. "It was such a long time ago. It scarcely matters now."

Dan's pleasant expression didn't waver. "It may or it may not matter. Sometimes patterns of behavior that were developed early follow us into adulthood."

Fin took another sip of coffee.

When neither of them spoke, Dan smiled. "Humor me. What caused you to go your separate ways all those years ago?"

Guilt.

One word said it all. But it was the word she wasn't about to say aloud. Instead she fell back on the story she'd been telling for so many years she almost believed it herself.

"My mother had been diagnosed with leukemia that spring." Even after all these years, simply thinking about the day they'd gotten the diagnosis brought a lump to Fin's throat. "Though she ended up living many more years, her initial prognosis was dire. She was given only weeks to live. It was a very stressful time for our family."

Dan's hazel eyes softened with sympathy. "It was a very stressful time for you."

She knew what he was doing, pulling the conversation back to her, making it personal.

Fin thought of the tension in her home, thought of what had happened in Milwaukee, thought of how she'd had no one to turn to for answers, for support. She exhaled a ragged breath. "Yes."

Dan glanced from her to Jeremy. "Instead of this incident drawing you closer, it pulled you apart."

Fin didn't like the way the minister was regarding Jeremy. Didn't like it one bit. "Jeremy was good to me."

"I was getting ready to leave for college. My parents were having marital difficulties." A shadow passed over his expression, and Jeremy's voice rang heavy with regret. "They resolved their issues, but I wasn't there for Fin, not like I should have been."

When the minister began to nod, Fin saw red. It wasn't fair for Jeremy to take the fall. Not when she knew who was really to blame.

"It wasn't your fault." Fin turned in her seat to face Jeremy. "It was mine. I pushed you away. Because I—"

She reined herself in just in time. When she realized not only Jeremy, but the minister was waiting for her to continue, she took another sip of coffee. "I'm not sure why."

Okay, she was probably going to hell for lying to a minister, but she was not going to talk about this, not now, not ever.

"I have an assignment for you." Dan sat back in his chair, his eyes grave. "Before we meet again—"

"Meet again?" Fin strove to keep the panic from her voice and thought she did a pretty good job. "I assumed this was a one-shot thing."

Dan arched a brow as if that surprised him, then offered an easy smile. "It's more of an eight-week thing."

Fin's own smile froze on her lips. "Good to know."

Good to know because she would be busy anytime the minister, and his emissary, Ruby, tried to schedule another one of these sessions.

Something in the way the pastor gazed at her made her wonder if mind reading was also one of his skills.

"Before we meet again," Dan began again, "I want the two of you to sit down and discuss that time in your lives. I want you to talk about why you reacted the way you did, and how you would handle the same situation now."

Fin felt perspiration pool at the base of her spine. "What's the point? It's the past."

She glanced at Jeremy, hoping for a little support.

"That was over ten years ago, Dan." Jeremy rubbed his chin. "Instead of focusing on the past, I'd think we'd be looking ahead to the future. Or at least the here and now."

Dan's lips lifted in a half smile. "I'm sure you've both heard the saying 'The past does not determine the future.'"

Fin nodded at the same time as Jeremy.

"The saying has a lot of merit. It tells us that just because we reacted—or acted—one way in the past doesn't mean that's how it has to be in the future." Dan folded his hands in front of him. "It can also mean the sins of the past don't have to color our future."

Sin.

A chill traveled along her spine.

Keeping her face expressionless, Fin nodded as if she saw his point and agreed. She'd briefly considered pushing Jeremy's point about looking ahead but sensed Dan had a stubborn streak. He obviously wanted to give them homework, and that's what he was going to do.

"What happened all those years ago is still between you." Dan glanced from her to Jeremy. "You need to discuss it, bring it out into the light of day. Only then will you be able to heal that part of your past, a part I sense still stands between you."

"Understood. Our first assignment is to discuss that time and figure out where we went wrong."

The minister narrowed his eyes at her flippant tone, then his expression softened. "Your assignment is to be completely honest with each other about what you did or didn't do during that time, about what you said or wished you'd said. This is a chance to grow closer. Good communication is at the heart of any successful union."

Fin carefully placed the empty china cup on the table and stood, signaling the session was over. If the two men wanted to stay and talk, that was fine, but she'd had enough prying into her past.

This was why she rarely went to church. She could only imagine how Dan would look at her if he knew everything. Worse, she could imagine how Jeremy would look at her.

The men stood. Dan followed her and Jeremy through the house.

She was almost home free. They'd reached the porch when Dan clapped a hand on her shoulder, his voice low and reassuring. "Never forget there is no sin too big to be forgiven."

Jeremy left to head back to work right after the minister left. Ruby was still resting in her room when Fin sat on the porch swing and pulled out her phone.

"Xander, hi," she said when he answered.

"How's it going at the farm?" His tone, almost jovial, had her smiling.

"The minister stopped over."

"Sounds as if it's a laugh a minute in Good Hope." Xander's voice deepened. "But it's a beautiful place to film. Are you making progress?"

"These things take time." When Fin found herself moistening her tongue, she thought of Ruby and stopped. "There's something I wanted to tell you."

"This sounds serious," he teased. "Should I make sure I'm sitting down?"

The fact that he was being so kind made the telling even more difficult.

Just spit it out, Fin told herself. *Tear the Band-Aid off.*

"I kissed Jeremy Rakes. When we were in Milwaukee. I don't quite know how it happened, but I swear it will never happen—"

"Delphinium, it's okay. I don't want to say I don't care, but it really isn't major. I've kissed other women since we've been dating plenty of times." He paused. "Did Rakes kiss you back?"

Shame flooded Fin. "He did."

"Even better."

"I don't understand."

"The mayor obviously still has a thing for you. We can play on that to get what we want."

Fin was far from naive. The sole reason Xander had left her behind in Good Hope was due to her connections in the community. Because she believed strongly in a well-informed vote, she'd been happy to take on the task of ensuring that not only Jeremy, but those town board members who'd voted against the proposition, were aware of the value the filming would bring to the community.

But to use Jeremy's feelings for her to influence his vote . . . well, that smacked of pandering. Still, she might be reading too much into Xander's simple comment. "You want me to use Jeremy's possible feelings for me to influence his vote?"

"Whatever it takes." Xander's voice turned persuasive. "You're doing a good job for us, I know that. Just don't let some Midwest moral high ground stop you from going all out in pursuit of the goal."

"Are you saying that—"

"Sweetheart, it was good to hear from you, but Harvey just walked in." Xander lowered his voice. "It looks like the joint project we've been discussing is a go. I'll tell you all about it when I have the time. Ciao."

He clicked off.

Fin pushed with her feet and sent the swing moving back and forth. Instead of feeling as if she'd cleared the air between them, she was more confused than ever.

And what the heck did Xander mean he'd kissed plenty of women since they'd been dating?

Chapter Nine

After a morning spent baking—and decorating—sugar cookies in Jeremy's amazing kitchen, Fin and her sisters decided to take a short break.

"I felt as if I was being interrogated by a CIA operative," Fin told her sisters when Ami brought up the topic of last week's counseling session with Dan. "Worse, I think Jeremy is on board with completing the homework assignment."

"Max and I were married by Pastor Schmidt." Prim's hazel eyes grew thoughtful. "We had several sessions with him, but he focused more on our spiritual journey than past stuff."

Instead of sitting at the table, Fin stood by the stove, carefully adding sugar to a pot of water.

Ami lifted her hands. "We had Schmidt, too. Our experience was pretty much the same as Prim and Max's."

"I could ask Marigold. Dan married her and Cade. Then again, what does it matter?" Fin would be returning to LA in a few weeks. Despite what Dan believed, there was no point in dredging up the past.

"I don't understand why you participated." Ami's steady gaze remained focused on Fin.

"I wondered that, too." Prim inclined her head. "Why didn't you simply put him off?"

"Ruby." As far as Fin was concerned, the one word said it all.

"It's not like you to be so . . . agreeable." Prim spoke hesitantly.

"I know." Fin gave a half laugh. "Believe me—I've wondered more than once why I keep falling into step."

"Why do you?" Ami appeared genuinely puzzled.

"I guess because I know how difficult it's going to be for Jeremy and Ruby after I split." Fin's heart swelled. "It won't be easy for you, either. Or for Dad."

Ami's eyes softened. "It's going to be difficult for you, as well."

Through the kitchen window, Fin spotted a ruby-throated hummingbird hovering above a hanging pot of impatiens. "Don't worry about me. I'll be fine." She kept her tone light. "I'll be back with my fiancé."

Fin saw no reason to mention Xander hadn't returned her most recent call or text. Another woman might be worried, may have even called friends to make sure he was okay. Fin had no such concerns. This behavior was standard operating procedure for him.

When he was ready to talk, he'd call. Or more likely, text.

At least when they were married, she'd see him when they both got home at night. But she had difficulty picturing the scene.

She couldn't imagine Xander sitting on a sofa, feet up on an ottoman, sharing a bowl of popcorn with her. Relaxation wasn't in Xander's nature. He loved to work, and he played just as hard.

Fin glanced at Ami's pregnant belly and wondered what Xander thought about kids. Not that she wanted a baby right away, but she wasn't getting any younger. Did Xander even want children? Though she didn't appreciate the minister's prying questions, Dan had made Fin realize she and Xander had a few things to discuss before walking down the aisle.

Prim reached for a cookie. "This feels good, all of us here together."

"Except for Marigold," Fin pointed out.

"Her salon has really taken off." Ami spoke with the voice of a proud mother. "I don't believe I've ever seen her happier."

"It was a blessing she and Jason broke up." Prim rose and moved to the large coffeemaker. "It was clear they'd never be happy together."

Jason had been her baby sister's boyfriend in Chicago. They'd broken up when she discovered his career mattered more to him than her happiness.

But wasn't Xander the same way? Everything came second to his career.

The knowledge chafed, like a too-tight shirt collar. Fin shoved the uncomfortable question aside and deliberately shifted the conversation's direction. "Do you two have something fun planned for tonight?"

"Dinner, showers, read a few books, then bedtime." Prim gave a little laugh. "That's how we roll in the Brody household."

But the shine in Prim's eyes said she wouldn't have it any other way.

"Beck and I plan to go for a long walk after dinner." Ami's hand lowered to her belly. "The doctor said the baby is ready and can come any time. My doula said sometimes walking, especially curb walking, can speed things along."

Fin cocked her head. "Curb walking?"

"Once I reached thirty-eight weeks, I tried it a couple of times." Prim shrugged.

Since that didn't really answer her question, Fin tried again, feeling every bit the odd one out. "What is it?"

"You walk with one foot on the curb and the other on the street, then you switch and go the other way," Ami explained.

"It supposedly opens up the pelvis and helps the baby to drop." Prim chuckled. "It looks really odd."

"I tried eating spicy foods and drinking red-raspberry-leaf tea." Ami shook her head. "Not even a Braxton Hicks."

A tiny smile tugged at the corners of Prim's lips. "There was only one thing I found that worked."

When Prim didn't continue, Ami circled one hand. "Don't bail on me now, Primrose. I need your expertise."

"Sex." Prim blushed. "My doula said it worked the best for stimulating labor."

Ami glanced down at her huge belly. "Because of that early bout of preterm labor I experienced last month, we'd curtailed our lovemaking and—"

"TMI," Fin interrupted, drawing a smile from her sisters. "Is there some science behind all this?"

"There's science behind it." Prim cast a mischievous glance in Fin's direction, as if aware of her discomfort. "I'll keep this general. I wouldn't want to offend your delicate sensibilities."

Ami chuckled. "Yeah, like she and Jeremy have never done the deed."

Fin laughed along with them. She wished she could say any intimacy with Jeremy was so far in the past she barely remembered. But that would be a lie. It only took one look from those gorgeous blue eyes to have her remembering.

Each touch.

Every caress.

Somehow, when she was in his arms, everything seemed right with the world . . .

Fin jerked. Blinked. "Did I just hear the words prostaglandins, semen, and orgasm come out of Prim's mouth?"

Ami and Prim exchanged glances and laughed.

"Okay, I'd say that's our cue to get back to work."

"You're probably right to crack the whip, Fin." Ami sighed and pushed up from the chair. "Eliza and our fellow Cherries will descend on Rakes Farm in less than an hour." Ami returned to the spacious counter in Jeremy's kitchen and began arranging decorated Christmas cookies on several large platters. "Now that we've lured Fin over to the dark side, all we need is for Marigold to become a Cherrie."

Prim looked up from where she was measuring scoops of ground coffee into a large silver coffeepot. "I predict within a year our baby sister will join us."

Turning from the stove, Fin lifted the stirring spoon from the pan where she was dissolving sugar into water for homemade lemonade. "You two seem to be forgetting something. I'm not a Cherrie."

"You seem to be forgetting that you're about to attend a Cherries meeting at the special invitation of the executive director." Ami gestured with one hand, then glanced at the cookie in her hand and smiled. "These are very pretty, if I do say so myself."

"I enjoyed our baking marathon this morning." Ruby stepped into the kitchen, her warm gaze lingering on the three sisters. "Thank you for letting me be a part of it."

"We enjoyed having you join us." Ami moved to Ruby's side and gave her a hug. "Since we're going to be discussing Mindy's Wish Fulfilled, Christmas cookies seemed appropriate."

Fin waited for Ruby to sit down, then breathed a sigh of relief when she did. Though Ruby had sat while decorating the sugar cookies, Fin worried the excitement of the morning might prove too much for the older woman.

Thankfully, instead of being fatigued, Ruby appeared energized by the conversation and laughter that always accompanied a Bloom baking marathon.

"Decorating cookies, being part of a family, makes me realize all over again how much I love Christmas." Ruby accepted with a smile the cup of herbal tea Prim hurried to set before her. "I can't wait for

December. Even though Fin and Jeremy won't be married yet, you girls are already part of my family, and I love you all."

"We love you, too." Prim brushed a kiss across Ruby's cheek before returning to the coffeepot.

Behind Ruby, Ami shot Fin a pointed glance.

Fin didn't know what her sister expected her to say. Tell Ruby that, while she might be eagerly anticipating Christmas, Fin was doing her best to see it got postponed for a year?

"I think we may have gone overboard with the Christmas cookies." Fin kept her tone light.

Three sets of eyes shifted to her.

"I mean, we're going to get plenty of Christmas cookies at Mindy's Wish Fulfilled event in a couple of weeks." Fin patted her flat stomach. "I don't need to start eating them now."

"Already thinking of the wedding." Ruby chuckled. "No need to worry. You'll be a beautiful bride no matter how many cookies you eat."

"On that most special of days your groom will look at you as if you're the only person in the world who matters." Ami's face grew dreamy. "I remember standing at the end of the aisle and Beck seeing me for the first time in my dress. I'll never forget that moment. It was . . . magical."

Prim sighed. "It was the same with me and Max."

Fin tried to imagine Xander looking at her in a magical way but couldn't quite pull the image into focus. She *could* imagine Xander looking around to see who was in the audience, or rather, the church. She could see him assessing her dress and hair, wanting to assure himself his bride-to-be was presentable.

"Jeremy will look at Delphinium that same way." Ruby expelled a happy sigh. "My heart will burst with happiness. Once the wedding is over, they can move on to the next step."

Prim turned on the coffeemaker, then inclined her head. "What step would that be?"

"Children." Ruby clasped her hands together. "I cannot wait for them to have a baby."

The spoon in Fin's hand stilled. "A baby?"

"Oh, not right away." Ruby laughed. "But I know you and Jeremy. You won't wait long. You'll want your children growing up with their cousins."

The picture Ruby painted was so vivid and so close to an old dream that the impact carried an extra punch. Fin knew she should respond, but she didn't trust her voice.

As if sensing her sister's discomfort, Ami filled the void by steering the conversation down a side path. "I recall this one time when Beck and I were dating—we weren't even engaged—and he asked me if a husband and children had a place in my dreams of the future."

This was the first Fin had heard of this conversation. The way Prim was looking at her eldest sister indicated this was news to her, too.

Ruby inclined her head. "What did you tell Beckett?"

A faraway look filled Ami's eyes. "We were at our house—his house then—and I looked down the hall. That's when I saw them."

"Them?" Though Fin had found her voice, it held a raspy quality. She cleared her throat. "Who did you see?"

"I saw a small, dark-haired girl in footie pajamas running toward me with outstretched arms. Beck stood beside me. He had a baby in a blue blanket cradled in his arms. A toddler, also in blue, gripped his legs." Ami blinked at the tears filling her eyes. "It was all so real. At that moment, my heart swelled with a longing so intense it was a wonder it didn't burst."

"If your vision holds true, your firstborn will be a girl with Beck's dark hair." Prim touched her own hair. "Not brown like you or strawberry blonde like me."

"I like your color, and the twins couldn't be cuter with their red hair," Ami insisted.

"They are cute," Prim agreed. "As they get older, I see Rory more and more in their features."

"Your first husband was a handsome man." Ruby offered a sympathetic smile. "It's a shame he died so young."

Fin barely listened to the conversation, her thoughts drifting to the baby who'd have been *her* firstborn. She didn't know if it had been a boy or a girl. Would it have looked like her as it grew? Or like Jeremy?

What did it even matter? With lips pursed, she stirred the sugar, wondering how much longer the blasted substance would take to dissolve.

Finally the sugar dissolved. Lemons were squeezed and the juice added, along with more water. Focusing on the task allowed Fin to ignore most of the conversation between her sisters and Ruby.

She commented just often enough to show she was listening. But Ami's statement about a longing so intense it brought tears to her eyes kept circling in Fin's head. She understood what it was like to feel such raw emotion, how strong it could be, how it could touch one's very soul.

Fin understood because that's how she felt about a baby she hadn't known she wanted, a baby she'd never had a chance to know, the child she'd lost that would always be her and Jeremy's firstborn.

Eliza ran the Cherries meeting with an iron hand.

Watching the executive director keep the thirty women who'd shown up on task was a monumental accomplishment. Fin silently applauded her. She had the feeling that, left on their own, a scheduled two-hour session could have easily turned into an all-afternoon event.

Fin had been in her share of meetings where reports on various projects were given. Never had she been in one where there were so many projects going on at the same time.

Since Lynn Chapin was out of town, Katie Ruth Crewes gave the committee report on the All About Kids project. The focus was on increasing child care options for everyone from high school students who found themselves pregnant to families with limited income who didn't qualify for Medicaid.

Lindsay Lohmeier, whose mother had once dated Fin's father, updated everyone on the plans for the upcoming Septemberfest celebration. Fin discovered the farm would be hosting a gathering prior to the Taste of Good Hope. As he'd apparently done for the previous two years, Jeremy had scheduled a mini event for participating merchants to be held in the big red barn.

As the barn would be used if the Taste of Good Hope got rained out, the mini event served as a trial run to ensure each merchant knew where their table would be located so they could get set up quickly and efficiently.

Fin was wondering how Jeremy kept track of all the events held here when she heard her name.

"Fin Bloom has agreed to coordinate the Wish Fulfilled activity that will be held at Rakes Farm. This doesn't mean she'll be the only one responsible. There's a sign-up sheet on the back table. I'd like at least five volunteers to assist her." Eliza paused when a hand shot up from the back row. "Yes?"

Fin nearly grimaced when her gaze landed on her dad's former girlfriend. Though Anita had to be one of her least-favorite people on the peninsula, Fin had to admit the woman was attractive. Her dark hair was cut in a style that flattered her angular face and large hazel eyes. Though she was only in her fifties, the slight relaxing of her skin Fin had noticed on recent trips back to Good Hope was nowhere in evidence.

Someone had had a little Botox . . .

Anita caught her staring and lifted her chin. "I'm shocked and dismayed that you appointed a person who is not a Cherrie to coordinate the event."

The only sign that being questioned irritated Eliza was a slight tightening of her red lips. Her gaze remained cool and her face expressionless. "If you'd been at our last meeting, Anita, you'd know that Your Wish Fulfilled is not solely a Cherrie project. As previously explained, the Your Wish Fulfilled organization relies on local groups to help with the granting of wishes to terminally ill children. In Mindy Vaughn's case, both the rotary and the Cherries are lending their assistance."

The executive director's delivery of the facts would have made most quiver. But Anita was like a banty rooster, clawing the dirt and ready to scrap.

"As far as I'm aware, Fin Bloom is not a member of the rotary, either." Anita's jaw jutted out.

Yep, Fin thought. The woman was definitely in a scrapping mood.

Eliza merely lifted a brow. "Since you're so well informed, you should also be aware that Delphinium is engaged to our mayor, Jeremy Rakes, the owner of the property where part of the wish will be fulfilled."

"Anita." Ruby's normally cheery voice held a hint of frost. "Let it go. You won't win this one."

"I was just asking." Two bright spots of color dotted the woman's cheeks.

"Now that we have that settled." Eliza smoothly transitioned into talk of Christmas planning.

Fin sat back and sipped her iced tea, amazed—and a bit dismayed—by how much planning had already been completed on this year's upcoming Twelve Nights celebrations. She was glad there would be a definitive vote by mid-September, before planning went any further.

As she listened to all the reports, Fin realized this was no sewing circle. These women were focused and dedicated. They cared about Good Hope and worked to make it even better. For the briefest of moments, Fin let herself imagine what it would be like if she'd returned home after college and married Jeremy. Would she be one of these women? Very likely. But without the experience and life lessons she'd learned in Los Angeles.

"We're at the new business portion of our meeting. As I don't see that anyone submitted an item for—"

"I have some new business." Gladys, who'd been sitting next to Ruby, not-so-quietly chatting with her old friend through the entire meeting, surged to her feet.

A pained look crossed Eliza's face, but with the sweep of a hand, she yielded the floor.

A wise move, Fin thought, because if Eliza hadn't yielded to Gladys, the older woman would have seized it anyway.

"Some of you may have heard that I have announced my retirement from acting once *Annie* ends its run at the community theater." Gladys waited, taking time to soak in the dismayed gasps and accept the groundswell of sadness expressed. "I started in the theater working on sets, then I handled the lighting before finally being given a chance to be onstage. There is only one aspect of the theatrical process I have yet to experience. I've never directed a play or a musical."

When Gladys's gaze lingered on hers, Fin couldn't help but smile. She could only hope when she was in her midnineties, she'd also be looking for the next great adventure.

Smiling back at Fin, Gladys continued. "I've been offered the opportunity to try out my directing skills by showcasing a small portion of the wonderful musical *Holiday Inn*. I've chosen the scene where Bing Crosby and Martha Mears sing 'White Christmas.' If it goes well, I'll be the director of the full production set to run during January at the playhouse."

"That's crazy. Why not in December? Wouldn't that be more appropriate?" Andrea Dunlevey, who lived just down the street from Ami, spoke without raising her hand.

Eliza cast her a censuring glance but remained silent, letting Gladys respond.

"There are two reasons. Since you and Scott usually spend the winter months in the land of the cacti, you've likely forgotten that *A Christmas Carol* runs in November and December." Gladys continued without waiting. "Second, as *Holiday Inn* is the story of a farmhouse turned inn that offers performances to celebrate holidays throughout the year, it's appropriate for any month."

Fin felt a surge of excitement. If Xander's measure passed, this theater run would give the Good Hope community something holidayish to enjoy in January.

"That's super exciting," Katie Ruth piped up. "Do you already have the couple in mind you'll use for the showcase?"

"I do." Gladys gave a dramatic exhale. "This couple epitomizes not only the best of Good Hope, but what true love is all about."

"Don't keep us in suspense." Ami leaned forward in her seat, her green eyes sparkling. "Who will it be?"

When Gladys's gaze slid to her, despite the warmth of the woman's smile, Fin felt a chill all the way to her toes.

"Why, your sister, Fin. And the love of her life and our beloved mayor, Jeremy Rakes."

Chapter Ten

"Seriously? She said I was the love of your life?" Jeremy grinned. "I always liked Gladys."

"Be serious." Fin had waited until they were alone in the car to bring up the subject. Jeremy had sprung the rotary event on her at the last minute, giving her the option of going as his date or staying home.

As Ruby was having friends over for dinner, Fin chose to tag along. Dinah had promised to stay with Ruby until she and Jeremy returned home.

Fin crossed her arms over her chest. "Though you haven't asked, I'm not doing it."

"What does she want us to do?"

"Basically, she wants us to re-create the piano scene in front of a fire."

Jeremy's brows pulled together as he turned the car toward town. "It's been so long since I've seen the movie, I'm not sure I remember that particular scene."

"Bing Crosby plays the piano, and he and Martha Mears do a duet of 'White Christmas.'" Fin had always loved the vintage movie—and she loved Gladys—but a woman had to draw the line somewhere.

"That song is a favorite." Jeremy's hands relaxed on the steering wheel. "We definitely have to watch the movie."

"Sure, we'll watch the movie. But tomorrow I'll call Gladys and politely decline." Fin relaxed against the seat. "I'll say we're just too busy and while we—"

"It doesn't sound as if it'd be much work." Jeremy slanted a glance in her direction. "I'd have to brush up on my piano skills, but 'White Christmas' isn't difficult to play."

Fin turned in her seat to stare at him. "Are you saying you want to do it?"

"Gladys is one of my grandmother's oldest friends." His expression turned serious. "If I can help her out, I will."

"I won't do it."

Jeremy exhaled a breath but said nothing for a long moment. "I'd much rather do it with you, but I'm sure Eliza would step up. Her voice isn't nearly as good as yours, but it isn't as if either of us are signing up to perform onstage. The way you've described it, this would be a onetime thing."

"Well, I'm glad we got that settled." But Fin didn't feel glad, she felt uneasy, as if she was about to let something precious slip from her grasp.

During the rest of the drive, Fin kept the conversation light. When she told him about the meeting and Anita's battle of wills with Eliza, he smiled.

"She should know better than to take on Eliza."

"If Gladys gets to direct *Holiday Inn* in January, it could help Xander's cause."

Jeremy shot her a glance, clearly startled by the abrupt change in topic. Well, he wasn't the only one.

"You're probably right," Jeremy agreed. "But that isn't a reason to get behind her on this venture. We have her back because she's our friend and we want her to succeed."

Fin nodded. She'd learned that lesson on her father's knee. Somewhere along the way, she wasn't sure exactly when it had occurred, she'd begun to embrace the "you scratch my back, I'll scratch yours" mentality.

"You realize I haven't sang in years." She spoke into the silence, not glancing in Jeremy's direction.

Keeping his gaze straight ahead, he reached over and took her hand, bringing it to his lips. "Sometimes, change starts with a single step."

After a restless night, Fin rose early. She found more than coffee when she reached the kitchen. Dressed for the day, Jeremy turned from the coffeepot and offered a smile. "Good morning, sunshine."

"Good morning back." Good Hope might not be LA, but seeing Jeremy's suit and tie made Fin glad she hadn't followed her first inclination and bopped down the stairs in casual attire. Though she'd always taken pride in her appearance, during her year with Xander she'd learned the importance of always being camera ready.

She may have dressed down her mint-green cotton sheath with wedge sandals instead of heels, but she hadn't skimped on her makeup.

"Lookin' good, Finley." Jeremy twisted the top onto the to-go cup he'd been filling even as his gaze lingered. "What's on your agenda today?"

Fin flushed with pleasure at the appreciative look in his eye. "Dinah is going with Ruby to cardiac rehab at the Y, then a group of women are coming over in the afternoon to play mah-jongg. That's a long way of saying I have the day free, I thought I'd track down Lynn and find out why she voted against the proposal."

Jeremy rested his back against the counter and continued to study her. He sipped his coffee. "I realize you're eager to get started, but I suggest you wait a couple days."

While the thought of taking a few more days to relax and enjoy some time with her family was appealing, Fin thought of Xander. Easing into anything wasn't an option. She lifted the cup from Jeremy's hands, took a drink, then handed it back to him. "Why would I wait?"

"With our engagement being the talk of Good Hope, likely the only thing Lynn will want to discuss is the wedding. You'll be spinning your wheels."

As Fin considered the point, she glanced longingly at his cup.

He handed it to her without comment. "You grew up in Good Hope. You know how it is here."

Fin sighed and shoved the cup back into his hand.

With her optimistic mood in danger of crumbling, Fin strode across the room and grabbed a cup from the cupboard and gestured to the stainless-steel percolator. "Mind if I help myself?"

"No need to ask. For the next month, consider this your home." Jeremy rested his back against the counter, no longer appearing in a hurry to leave.

Fin poured, then lifted the red mug to her lips, taking a moment to inhale the rich aroma before fortifying herself with a big gulp. "I enjoyed the rotary dinner last night."

"You sound surprised."

Finding comfort in the easy conversation, Fin sipped her coffee. "A dinner honoring high school athletes sounded boring. But it was fun. Took me back."

Although Fin and her sisters hadn't been any star athletes, they'd participated in most sports.

"I was thankful Dinah stayed with Ruby. That way we could enjoy the evening without worrying."

"Your grandmother is doing remarkably well."

"She's a remarkable woman." The admiration in his voice matched the look in his eyes.

What would it be like, Fin wondered, to have someone look at her that way? She glanced away for a second, then forced a casual tone. "What time will you be home?"

"Since I've been out of the office so much, I still have some catching up to do." Jeremy reached for his briefcase. "I'll try to be home by six."

Fin set down her mug and closed the distance between them. With a wifely gesture, she adjusted his tie. "Have a good day."

For a second she thought he might kiss her, but that was absurd.

Since Dinah would be around all day, after Jeremy left, Fin called Blooms Bake Shop and confirmed Ami was working. Though her sister warned the morning rush might make taking a break impossible, Fin decided to swing by anyway.

Before leaving the house, she phoned Xander. Once again, the call went straight to voice mail. Fin pasted a smile on her face so her tone wouldn't reveal her irritation.

"Hey, Xan, quick update. Speaking with Lynn Chapin, one of the two board members who voted against the proposal, may have to wait a few days." Fin saw no reason to say Lynn would be too excited about her pretend engagement to Jeremy to want to talk business.

With the phone still pressed to her ear, Fin opened the French doors and took her coffee out to the back terrace. "There's also the possibility of the community theater performing *Holiday Inn* during January. I'll tell you more about that when we talk. I'm seeing that as a positive for our side."

Is there an "our" side? Fin wondered. Shouldn't the decision come down to not only what was best for Xander's film, but what was best for Good Hope?

"Hope all is well. Talk soon." She hesitated for a long moment. "I—I love you."

Fin wasn't sure why she found it so difficult to say the words. Probably because they were new. New for him, too. Until he proposed, Xander had never even hinted he loved her.

Before that day at the Pfister Hotel, his hot-and-cold act had her wondering exactly how he did feel about her. Yet Fin couldn't imagine him giving her such a large diamond unless he really did love her.

Fin held the ring up to the morning sun, admiring how the stone caught the light. She and Xander were perfect for each other. They both enjoyed fine dining and travel. Their sense of humor was in sync, although Xander's could be caustic at times. But he did his best to not go too far when joking.

The chink was that he wasn't particularly family-oriented. Xander found the closeness she shared with her sisters and father difficult to understand.

An only child, he'd been estranged from his parents for as long as she'd known him. Celebrating holidays and special occasions with family was a foreign concept. Which, she assumed, was why he'd never accepted any of her invitations to come to Good Hope, preferring to spend holidays in exotic locations or with film-industry friends.

While she didn't kid herself that he'd embrace family togetherness as her sisters' husbands had, Fin hoped when he spent time in Good Hope for the filming, he'd get to know her family and eventually grow to like them.

There were some hopes she knew would never be realized. Fin tried to picture Xander playing pond hockey with his brothers-in-law or relaxing with a beer on her father's back patio while Prim's twins pelted each other with water balloons.

The thought of his horrified expression had Fin smiling all the way to the bakery. It faded when she drew close and saw the crush of people inside. There was no way she and Ami would be able to share even one second of conversation.

"I just got back in town last night. I hear congratulations are in order."

Fin whirled. Lynn Chapin, head of the Chapin banking empire and current president of the Cherries, offered a bright smile. "Your father told me the wonderful news. I'm thrilled for you and Jeremy."

Fin smiled.

And the charade begins.

For many reasons, including Lynn's seat on the town board, Fin was glad to see the woman. She'd always liked the pretty blonde, admired her coolness under pressure, whether business or personal. She totally approved of her father dating Lynn.

"Thanks." As Fin took note of her trim summer suit in ice blue, for the second time that morning she was glad she'd chosen to look her best. "Jeremy is a great guy."

When Fin offered up the sentiment, it sounded completely sincere. Probably because it was sincere.

Lynn's gaze returned to the packed bakery. "I haven't yet had my caffeine boost. Do you have time to grab a cup of coffee at Muddy Boots?"

This was life in Good Hope. A day could be as fluid as you allowed it to be. "I'd like that."

As they walked past the bakery window, Ami glanced out. When their gazes met, Fin mouthed *I'll call you*, and Ami responded with a thumbs-up.

In minutes Fin sat across from Lynn in a booth with a steaming mug of freshly brewed coffee in her hand.

"Your ring is lovely." Lynn's gaze lingered on Fin's left hand.

"It came as such a surprise." The words were out of Fin's mouth before she could pull them back. Actually, Xander's out-of-the-blue proposal had been more shock than surprise.

"Oh, I imagine not so much of one." Lynn smiled around her cup and took a sip. "I daresay there are any number of people in Good Hope who always believed the two of you would end up together."

"Grandma Ruby never lost hope." The thought of how Jeremy's grandmother would feel once Fin returned to LA brought a ping to Fin's heart.

The greater good, Fin reminded herself. That's what this charade was about. She'd done this for Ruby.

And, also, she reluctantly admitted, for herself.

She had a lot riding on the outcome of a repeat vote. Both personal and professional.

"Was it difficult to leave your job in LA?" Lynn forked off a bite of coffee cake.

"I haven't left." Fin took a drink of coffee. "I'm on temporary leave."

"Really?" Lynn's perfectly tweezed brows drew together.

The suspicion that filled her eyes had Fin carefully choosing her next words.

"I can't quit right now. I'm in the middle of a big project. Jeremy and I agree it wouldn't be fair to leave the company in the lurch." Bring her fake fiancé in, Fin told herself, say his name to make it seem more personal. "Jeremy is very understanding. And I'll be back in Good Hope before I'm even missed."

Again, true. Yes, she would stick as much to the truth as possible. She *would* be back, for holidays and baptisms and all sorts of family events. But when she returned, Xander would be on her arm, not Jeremy.

"When will you need to go back?" Lynn gazed at her over the top of her mug.

"Mid-September." Again, true.

"A woman can get a lot of wedding planning done in a month." Lynn's expression turned soft, almost dreamy. "I love everything about weddings. Unfortunately, it will be years before Greer walks down the aisle. The girl doesn't even have a steady boyfriend."

Lynn's daughter and Marigold had been friends in high school. "How is Greer?"

"Doing well. Back in Good Hope. Learning more about the local banking industry every day." Lynn's smile held a touch of pride. "When I'm ready to step down—which won't be anytime soon—the family's banking enterprises will be in good hands."

Keep her talking, Fin thought. She offered an encouraging smile. If Lynn was busy updating Fin on her children, she wouldn't be able to pump her for information about wedding plans.

Jeremy had warned her. The questions Lynn was asking were the same ones she'd be asked a thousand times in the next month. She and Jeremy should have done more to prepare. Fin idly wondered if he was fielding similar questions.

"Anyway, enough about me and my family." Lynn leaned forward, her blue eyes fixed on Fin. "Have you chosen a venue for the wedding?"

Sometimes, Fin decided, a woman must make an executive decision. As both Fin's family and the Rakes family always attended services at First Christian, that made it the logical venue for the ceremony. She'd once hoped, if Xander did propose, that she could convince him to be married in Good Hope.

Being married in her hometown was no longer an option. She knew how the citizens felt about Jeremy. No matter what the spin, after the breakup, Fin Bloom would be persona non grata in Good Hope.

Her heart rose to her throat, and for a second—a very brief second—she found herself fighting back tears.

"Perhaps you're considering having it outdoors, like your sister?" Lynn asked when Fin didn't immediately respond.

"Marigold's wedding was lovely." Fin summoned a smile, recalling how breathtakingly beautiful her little sister had looked under an arbor of flowers on a stage specifically built for the ceremony. The property

Cade had purchased prior to their marriage overlooked Green Bay, so the view had been breathtaking. "Being married on the same land that will eventually be the site of their home made the ceremony incredibly special."

"Each couple brings their own personality and flavor to a wedding."

Fin could see where this conversation was headed. She recalled a tidbit of information that might get this conversation off her and Jeremy. "Someone mentioned at the reception that your son David and his wife's home is just down the road from Cade and Marigold's property."

"That's correct." Lynn set down her mug, her expression inscrutable. "David designed the house. It's very special to him."

Okay, so it appeared Lynn didn't want to discuss her eldest son and daughter-in-law. Fin wondered if the rumors of trouble in their marriage were true.

Lynn leaned forward, resting her forearms on the table. "So, yes or no to the outdoor wedding?"

"No. I'd like to be married at First Christian. It might sound crazy, but . . ." Fin hesitated, then plunged ahead, "whenever I'm in the sanctuary, I feel my mother's presence. If I got married there, perhaps she could be part of my special day."

The sweet, heavy mass that filled her chest took Fin by surprise. She didn't consider herself to be an overly sentimental person. Which meant she must be more tired than she realized. She cleared her throat to dislodge the lump that settled there.

Lynn reached across the table and covered Fin's hand with hers. "Sarah wouldn't miss your wedding. She was so proud of you."

Would her mother be proud of her now? Fin wondered. Would she understand that Fin had agreed to this charade out of love for Ruby?

Fin's head began to ache. She was about to motion to the waitress for another cup of coffee when she stilled. Her heart gave a little leap.

Jeremy stood inside the doorway of the café. His eyes lit up when he saw her.

Fin lifted her hand in welcome, the headache disappearing in a rush of pleasure.

He immediately began weaving his way through the tables to the booth, followed by another man who Fin barely noticed.

Lynn swiveled in her seat, intent on seeing who'd caught Fin's eye. Her lips curved. "Well, this is perfect timing."

"Isn't that your fiancée by the window?" Dan asked Jeremy when the two men stepped inside Muddy Boots.

Jeremy had run into the young minister on the sidewalk, and they'd decided to grab a cup of coffee together.

Following the direction of Dan's gaze, Jeremy spotted Fin in the booth by the window. He was embarrassed to admit his day got just a little brighter. "She's with Lynn Chapin."

That fact didn't surprise Jeremy. Even though he'd suggested she give Lynn time to adjust to news of their engagement, Fin did as she wanted.

Dan shot Jeremy a questioning look. "Shall we see if we can join them?"

"I'm sure Fin won't mind." Jeremy reached the table a half second before the minister. Going with instinct, he leaned over and touched his mouth to Fin's. "This is a nice surprise."

Her lips curved in a slow smile. "Hello."

Jeremy fully understood Fin was playing this part for two reasons: to help out her real fiancé and out of love for his grandmother. But when she gazed up at him and her eyes locked on his like they did now, he felt the connection.

She was simply playing a part, he reminded himself. She'd always been a stellar actress.

"You remember Pastor Dan." Jeremy gestured with his hand to the broad-shouldered man at his side.

Fin's smile was warm and friendly. "Will you join us?"

Fin's years in advertising and now as a development executive showed. But when her green eyes lingered a few seconds longer than necessary on the minister, Jeremy was seized with the insane urge to tell Fin that Dan was dating Lindsay Lohmeier.

Instead he kept his lips shut and shifted his attention to Lynn. As president of the local bank as well as of the Women's Events League, commonly referred to as the Cherries, Lynn was a force to be reckoned with in Good Hope.

Jeremy both liked and respected her. "I hope we're not interrupting."

"You're not." Lynn made room in the booth, and Dan slid in beside her, while Jeremy took a seat on the bench next to Fin. "I can stay for a few minutes longer before the business world beckons."

"I was about to update Jeremy on the All About Kids project." Dan spoke directly to Lynn, his hazel eyes intense. "As co-chair, you'll likely have information to add."

Practically vibrating with excitement, Lynn turned to Fin. "I know you'll be busy with wedding preparations, but this project is dear to my heart. I'd love it if you could find time to help me with it."

Jeremy slanted a glance at Fin. The opportunity to spend time with Lynn was being served up to her on a silver platter.

"I'll make the time," Fin told Lynn. "All I ask is you give me some assistance on the Wish Fulfilled event at Rakes Farm."

Lynn held out her slender hand. "While I'm not sure what that will involve, it's a deal."

As Dan and Lynn took a moment to catch up, Jeremy turned to Fin. "How's it going?"

"It's looking up." Fin's voice lowered, and she slanted a glance at Lynn, who appeared deeply engrossed in her conversation with the minister. "She asked about wedding arrangements. I told her First Christian."

He nodded, appreciating the heads-up. If they *were* engaged, where the ceremony would be held was one of those early decisions.

Jeremy took her hand, threading his fingers through hers. "Will you have time to help with Lynn's project?"

"Don't you dare try to dissuade her, Jeremy Rakes." Lynn's voice broke through, and he realized the intense conversation that she and the minister had been having had concluded. "I need her expertise."

Fin gave a little laugh. "That's nice to hear, but I'm not sure what this project entails."

"You heard the gist from Lindsay at the Cherries meeting yesterday." Lynn exchanged a smile with the minister. "Dan is on our board and has been involved with the project since the beginning."

"I mean, I'm not sure what you want me to do." Fin's tone remained light, and her sea-green eyes were firmly focused on Lynn.

"Clay and I were talking, and several things he said got me to thinking about the needs of those who become parents in high school." Lynn's expression turned serious. "As a high school principal, my youngest son is committed to seeing all students graduate. Every year there are a handful who get pregnant and drop out because they can't manage both school and caring for a baby."

Jeremy felt Fin stiffen beside him. Automatically he reached under the table to take the hand he'd released only seconds before.

"I don't understand where I come in," Fin said again.

To Jeremy's surprise, she made no move to pull her hand away.

"You're young with a quick mind. You've also been away from Good Hope for a number of years." Lynn took a sip of coffee. "You have a worldly view that I believe will come in handy as we consider options. As with the issue of closing down the town in December, what I'm proposing may be controversial. I'd like you to offer a young person's perspective as we formulate the talking points to help gain community acceptance."

"You mentioned students getting pregnant and dropping out." Fin's laugh sounded slightly strained. "I have no experience in that area. Neither does anyone in my family."

"I realize that." Lynn's tone remained matter-of-fact. "But I'm confident you have the capacity to put yourself in that student's place as well as look at it from the perspective of an adult. That ability, as well as your advertising background, should help us personalize the talking points."

"The number of high school students giving birth in any given year is small, but we'd like to offer them a way to continue their education." Dan's eyes glowed with passion. "This project will also benefit parents in our community who need quality child care at a reasonable cost. We're toying with the idea of using the setting for classes in early childhood education."

"Which will also encourage buy-in from the community," Jeremy commented.

"As you can see, we have lots of ideas." Lynn's gaze returned to Fin. "Can I count on you?"

Fin hesitated. Though she hid her reluctance well from the others, Jeremy could tell she had no interest in the project. Yet she was smart enough to realize that with Lynn so busy, this might be the only access to the woman.

Fin flashed a bright smile. "Absolutely."

"Wonderful." Lynn leaned back in her seat. "Now, let's talk weddings."

Chapter Eleven

That evening, Fin drove up the winding driveway with Jeremy's vehicle right behind her. The only car still parked in the back was Dinah's Buick, which told her the mah-jongg crowd had already departed. She and Jeremy walked together to the house. As the day remained warm and sunny, they didn't rush.

While they strolled side by side, he asked about her day, then filled her in on his. Fin enjoyed hearing him talk about everything from parking issues to water quality concerns. Clearly, the man had a passion for governance. Under his leadership, Good Hope was thriving.

Dinah met them at the front door. "I'm sorry to rush, but my granddaughter is stopping over tonight and I need to pick up the house."

"How's Ruby?" Fin asked, feeling Jeremy's hand settle against the small of her back.

Was it an unconscious gesture or a deliberate one to show they were a couple?

"Your grandmother is in high spirits. She won the last game."

"She's a lucky one," Jeremy said.

Dinah nodded vigorously, sending her tight gray curls bobbing. "She's very lucky and she's getting stronger every day. I can see it."

"I really appreciate all your help, Dinah." Jeremy's amazing blue eyes settled on the older woman. "You've gone out of your way for Ruby and for me. I won't forget it. If there's anything I can ever do for your—"

"It's my pleasure." Dinah blushed. "And you know as well as I do that neighbors helping neighbors is the Good Hope way."

"See you tomorrow." Fin waved as Dinah hurried off.

"I'm in the parlor," Ruby called out as soon as they stepped inside.

Fin and Jeremy exchanged a smile, then strolled into the parlor.

When she took a seat on the sofa and Jeremy dropped beside her, she caught Ruby's nod of approval.

"How was your day?" Ruby asked, her eyes bright with interest.

Fin glanced at the man at her side. "Jeremy and I ran into Pastor Dan this morning."

"Ohh. I can't tell you how happy I am that he'll be the one performing the ceremony." A smile blossomed across the older woman's face. "Pastor Schmidt was nice but could be a grouch at times."

"Schmidt could be intense." Fin vividly recalled the time the silver-haired minister had called her out for talking in catechism class. Still, there'd been a forthrightness about the man that she'd admired. She'd been sad when she'd heard he'd retired. "Dan walked into Muddy Boots with Jeremy when I was having coffee with Lynn Chapin."

"You're eager to get the church booked. I don't blame you. Can't let this one get away a second time." Ruby didn't appear to notice Jeremy's startled look as she'd already returned her focus to Fin. "Tell me about your conversation. Don't spare the details."

Ruby's request reminded Fin of her sisters. Whenever the Bloom women gathered and one of them had something to share, three things were mandatory: Wine. Chocolate. Spare no detail.

"What would you like to know?"

"For starters, will you be getting married in the church? Or will Pastor Dan officiate at another location?"

"At First Christian."

Ruby's smile dimmed slightly. "I have to admit I hoped you'd get married at the farm."

The easiest thing to do would be to agree to the change. What did it matter? The wedding plans were merely a sham anyway.

Yet Fin couldn't seem to bring herself to tell one more unnecessary lie.

"I don't know if I even told this to Jeremy." For effect, Fin slanted a glance at her fiancé and received an encouraging smile. "Whenever I'm in the sanctuary, I feel my mother's presence. I'd like her at my wedding. I know that may seem silly, but—"

Ruby leaned over and touched Fin's arm with fingers as light as butterfly wings, her expression soft with understanding and love. "I feel that way when I'm in the flower garden at the farm. It's as if Eddie is there, watching me with that little smirk on his lips."

"Now you know why we chose the church." Jeremy took Fin's hand, brought it to his mouth, and kissed her knuckles.

Ruby's gaze shifted from Jeremy to Fin. "Remember all of us who love you also loved Sarah. We want her with you on your special day."

Tears stung the backs of Fin's eyes. She blinked rapidly to keep them from spilling down her cheeks. Why hadn't she simply told one more lie?

Jeremy's arm stole around her shoulders. As Fin rested her head against his chest, drawing comfort from the closeness, she told herself it was simply because the gesture was something Ruby would expect.

But when Jeremy brushed a kiss against her hair and her heart swelled once again, Fin admitted that was simply another lie.

Conversation flowed easily through dinner with Ruby making no attempt to bring up the wedding.

His grandmother had obviously noticed the emotion storming in Fin's eyes when she'd spoken of her mother. Jeremy had seen it too and had wanted nothing more than to pull Fin into his arms and kiss away the pain. How easy it was to forget she wasn't his.

"I believe I'm going to retire to my room and do some knitting," Ruby announced, pushing back from the table and standing.

"Are you feeling okay?" Fin glanced at the clock sitting on the fireplace mantel. "It's not even seven."

"I didn't get my nap in today." Only then did Jeremy see the weariness in her eyes. "Playing mah-jongg and seeing my friends was quite lovely, but I'm rather fatigued now."

"Where are you going?" Jeremy called out when Ruby angled toward the stairs.

"It was nice of you to let me use your suite while I was recuperating, but I'm feeling stronger. I'm moving into the green room. It's the one I've always used when visiting."

"Should you be climbing those stairs?" Fin rose, a worried frown creasing her brow.

"I'm not an invalid." Ruby softened the words with a smile even as she waved a dismissive hand. "Jeremy belongs back in the master suite. Besides, I've always loved the way the light streams in through the windows of the green room in the morning."

Fin shot a pointed look in Jeremy's direction.

"Ah, right now Fin's bags are in there. But we can move them across the hall." Jeremy caught Fin's slight nod of agreement. "I'll take care of that right now."

"You most certainly will not." Jeremy had no doubt if Ruby had a cane in her hand she'd have given the floor a solid thump. "I know exactly the game you've been playing. I'm telling you it's quite unnecessary."

Jeremy stilled. "Game?"

"Pretending you're sleeping in one room while your fiancée stays in another." Ruby cackled. "If that's how you want to play it with Pastor Dan, I won't give you away. But we're all adults here."

Her gaze shifted to Fin, then back to her grandson. "Oh, cut the shocked look, Jeremy. Eddie and I were aware the two of you were canoodling back in high school. I hardly think you're settling for a handshake at the end of the day now."

Fin's green eyes closed for a moment. Jeremy saw her chest rise and fall as she took a breath.

A bit resentful that she had the luxury of punting while he was forced to stay in the game, Jeremy took a step forward. "Grandma—"

"Save your breath. I won't believe you anyway." Ruby smiled. "Move Delphinium's things back into your room where they belong. Then you two will be able to enjoy the rest of your evening as much as I'm about to enjoy mine."

Jeremy returned fifteen minutes later and dropped down on the sofa in the parlor. "She's all settled."

While he'd been upstairs, Fin had cleared the table and loaded the dishwasher. Then, as she subscribed to the notion you could never have too much wine, she'd pulled out a bottle of Shiraz and filled two glasses.

"I thought you might need this." She handed him one. "After your grandmother's comments, I may need several glasses."

He grinned. "I put your bags in my room."

"Sacrifices must be made."

"She wouldn't have it any other way. Nothing I said could dissuade her." Though Ruby appeared to be safely tucked upstairs, Jeremy kept his voice low, as if fearing they might be overheard. "If I'd refused or insisted you move to another room upstairs, she'd have become suspicious."

"You're right." Fin dropped into an overstuffed chair that practically begged to be sat in and gestured with one hand to the nearby sofa. "And regardless of how good she looks, she's still healing."

She kept her voice equally soft. While Ruby might not mean to eavesdrop . . . Fin stopped the thought and grinned suddenly.

Jeremy took a seat, inclined his head. "What's so funny?"

"I was thinking Ruby wouldn't deliberately listen in on our conversation." Fin paused to take a sip of wine. "Then I realized, yes, she would."

"Absolutely she would." For several heart-tugging seconds, they shared a smile. Fin supposed she should bring up the sleeping arrangements, but they could deal with that when it was time for bed.

Bed.

Fin felt a stirring in her lower belly but immediately dismissed it. She would text Xander before the night ended. See if he was free to talk. There was a lot she could tell him about her day.

"I couldn't believe my luck in running into Lynn Chapin this morning." Fin deliberately steered the conversation back toward business.

Jeremy took a drink of wine. "I never asked how that came about."

"I went to the bakery hoping to grab a latte and a few moments with Ami, but they were slammed. Standing room only."

"I stopped there, too." Jeremy shook his head. "Couldn't even get inside the place."

Another sip of wine had the troubles of the day easing from Fin's shoulders. "Lynn happened by. We got to talking and decided to slip over to Muddy Boots for coffee."

Jeremy studied her with unreadable blue eyes. "Smart move cozying up to her."

"Thanks," Fin said, though she wasn't sure he'd meant the comment as a compliment. "I didn't even bring up the project."

"Another smart move." Jeremy lifted his glass in a mock salute. "Best not to be too obvious."

"I've always liked Lynn." Fin couldn't understand why she sounded defensive.

"Good thing, since she's dating your father."

"Yes." Fin relaxed against the leather. "A vast improvement over I-Need-a-Man."

Anita Fishback was the kind of woman who struck fear in the hearts of any young woman with a widowed father. Anita was sweet as pie when she was with Steve but had a tongue that rivaled a snake if you caught her alone.

Jeremy spoke conversationally. "She's dating again."

"Who does the piranha have in her sights this time?" Fin really didn't care who Anita dated, as long as it wasn't her father, but she was curious.

"Adam Vogele."

Fin, who'd been in the process of removing her shoes, paused. "The Adam that Vanessa Eden brought to Marigold's wedding?"

At her sister's reception, Fin had assumed the guy dancing with Max's mother had been a friend of her son. Until Prim told her the thirty-some-year-old and the just-turned-fifty Vanessa had been dating for nearly a year.

"The same."

Sitting forward in the chair, Fin circled both hands in a hurry-up gesture. "Don't stop there."

"What more is there to say?"

She might have been fooled by Jeremy's innocent expression if she hadn't seen the twinkle in his eyes.

"Let me see if I've got this straight Vanessa and Adam broke up and now Anita has latched on to the hunky organic farmer?"

"That would be correct."

Fin wondered what her dad thought of his former flame dating a man twenty years younger than she was. Then hoped Steve Bloom never gave Anita a second thought.

"If you'd kept your subscription to the *Open Door*, you'd be up on the local gossip."

Fin lifted a brow. "How do you know I don't read it religiously?"

His gaze pinned her. "Do you?"

"No," she admitted, taking another sip of wine. "I unsubscribed a couple of years back."

When she'd first moved to LA, Fin had found comfort in keeping up with Good Hope events. But reading the newsletter had begun to feel uncomfortable, like she was trying to wear a too-tight shoe that no longer fit.

It would be easy to say that was because the lifestyles of those she loved had begun to seem pedestrian compared to the fast and exciting world of the rich and famous in LA. Fin knew it went deeper than that. It hurt to realize she was no longer part of Good Hope except in only the most superficial of ways.

"Is there any other Good Hope news that I can catch you up on?"

"Let me think." Fin tapped a finger against her lips and was pleased when his attention riveted to her mouth. "Tell me what you know about Lynn's project."

Jeremy could put off going to bed no longer. "I'm calling it a night."

Ignoring his outstretched hand, Fin rose with a languid grace he'd always admired. They'd spent the last half hour talking about the child care needs in Good Hope. Jeremy had no doubt the Pompous Ass, er, Xander, would have been glancing at his Rolex in under three minutes.

Like Fin, Jeremy still wasn't sure exactly what role Lynn wanted her to play. Whatever it was, Fin would go along. Being able to spend time with Lynn under the guise of volunteerism was a perfect way to stay close to the town board member.

Fin's willingness to do whatever it took—within reason, of course—was something Jeremy needed to keep in mind when old feelings for her threatened.

He told himself being this close was a good thing. Several times Eliza had accused him of never getting over Fin. Though he denied the accusations, deep down he wondered if there might be some truth to the words.

The time he and Fin would spend together would be his opportunity to get her out of his system for good. It was obvious by her engagement she'd moved on. It was past time he did the same.

He realized with a start she was staring at him, those brilliant green eyes sharp and assessing.

"How are we going to handle this?" she asked.

"Based on the fact that you're asking, I'm guessing you don't trust yourself to sleep in the same bed with me." His lips twitched. "Totally understandable. You're obviously afraid you won't be able to resist this magnificent bod."

"Don't flatter yourself, Rakes." Fin rolled her eyes. "It's just that I've experienced those roving hands."

He'd loved to touch her and still recalled each place that could make her moan. Jeremy shoved those memories aside. "Sleeping in the same bed with me is a problem for you?"

There was a blatant challenge in his tone that even he could hear.

Fin had never been able to resist a dare. Despite knowing that, he'd still thrown down the gauntlet.

He could take the words back. All he needed to do was laugh, pretend it had all been a joke, and tell her he'd sleep on the pull-out sofa in the sitting room.

Fin surveyed him from under lowered lashes.

Jeremy knew how her mind worked—or, rather, how it had once worked. By the smug look in her eyes, she'd decided how far she was willing to go to call his bluff.

"I'll be sleeping on the sofa."

Jeremy fought a surge of disappointment, then chastised himself, knowing she was the only one in the room displaying even a modicum of common sense.

"And there'll be no sleeping au naturel," she added.

"I haven't worn pajamas in years."

"Then it's time to pull them out of the drawer." The teasing look on her face turned serious. "I'm engaged, Jeremy."

"If you're so concerned about that, why are you sharing my suite?"

She looked at him, raised a brow.

Ruby.

He let the subject drop.

Fin finished off the wine she still held in her hand and set down the glass. "We're both adults, and all we'll be doing is sleeping. But you need to remember that not only am I in love with another man, I made him a promise."

Fin's promises were golden, Jeremy thought. In all the time they'd been together, despite her popularity with other boys, he'd never worried about her cheating on him.

The only promise she'd broken had been the one they'd exchanged at fourteen, and that had been a promise between children.

She was a woman now, and he was a guy who knew the score.

"All right." Jeremy exhaled a melodramatic breath. "I'll dig out the pajama bottoms."

"And the top," Fin added.

"You drive a hard bargain, Ms. Bloom."

Fin smiled. "You ain't seen nothin' yet."

Jeremy ended up taking the sofa bed. His even breathing told Fin he was asleep.

She had a good view of the sofa from the huge four-poster. Sharing a room for a few hours of sleep every night should be easy. She'd crashed in college with several guy friends and even a couple of times in LA when she'd first moved there and needed a place to stay for a couple of days.

There had been no sex involved, not even a thought of sex. Of course, those boys—men—had been friends. There'd been no past intimacy to rear its head and remind her how good it had once felt to hold him close, to feel his hands on her . . .

Stop.

She would not let her thoughts go in that direction. Xander was the man for her. He was her fiancé. He was the one she would spend the rest of her life with, have children with . . .

A knife lanced her heart, so sharp Fin was surprised when she lifted one hand to the source of the pain to find her nightshirt dry instead of wet with blood.

Her breath now came in fast little puffs and sleep had never been further away. Silently, she eased off her side of the bed, her bare feet making no sound on the hardwood. She glanced at the clock. One thirty. Still early in LA.

She'd meant to phone Xander, truly she had, but the change in sleeping arrangements had done a number on her head. She'd forgotten all about her fiancé.

After removing her phone from the charger, Fin crept out of the room and silently down the hall. The moon shone through the large windows at the back of the home, so there was no need to turn on the lights.

Fin considered the best place to have a private conversation with Xander. With Ruby in the house, it needed to be somewhere she could be assured of not being overheard.

Outside.

Either the front porch or back patio.

The front porch with its swing won. Once she was comfortably settled, she called Xander. To her surprise, he answered on the second ring, sounds of clinking glasses and laughter in the background.

"Fin, this is a nice surprise." The pleasure in his voice warmed her as much as the summer air. "I won't be long."

"Are you at a party?"

"Oh, Chad invited a couple of people over." Xander tossed the name out there as if of no consequence.

Fin knew differently. Uberwealthy and a patron of the arts, Chad Kingston was the money behind many top independent films. And Xander, well, he had an indie he was dying to direct . . . as soon as the funding was secured.

"Did you speak with him about backing the film?" She settled back against the swing and realized just how much she'd needed to touch base with Xander.

"Not yet." The sounds of crystal and conversation muted, and she assumed her fiancé had moved to somewhere more private to talk. Still, his voice continued low and for her ears only. "I just arrived."

Doubtless anyone in Good Hope would find it odd not only to have a party on a Tuesday night, but for a guest to show up shortly before midnight. She'd once found that behavior strange, too.

"I miss you." She whispered the sentiment into the phone while holding up her hand to stare at the diamond.

"Miss you too, babe," he said, then called out, "I'm talking business. I'll be out in a minute."

"Talking business?" she teased.

"No other reason will do." His tone was as light as hers. "How's it going there?"

She wanted to tell him about dinner with her sisters and about Jeremy's grandmother, but even with two thousand miles separating them, Fin sensed his impatience.

"I met today with one of the town board members who voted against the proposal." Fin kept her words short and to the point as she went on to explain she'd agreed to help Lynn with a project.

"Smart move." Approval rang in Xander's voice, though he'd started to sound distracted again. "I've used that tactic myself. Ingratiate yourself by doing a favor, then let them do a solid for you."

"It's not really—"

"I'll be right there." Charm returned to his rich baritone.

Fin could almost see the flash of his perfect white teeth.

"Time for me to get back to the party. Sounds as if you're making progress. Keep up the good work."

The connection broke, and Fin stared at the phone in her hand. *He didn't even say goodbye.* Or that he loved her.

A welling of some emotion she couldn't quite identify rose inside her. Then she told herself she was being too sensitive. Xander was at a party hosted by a potential investor. Of course he couldn't hang out on the phone chatting with her all night.

"Can't sleep?"

Even as her heart flip-flopped, Fin's head jerked toward the doorway. Jeremy's lean figure stood swathed in shadows.

"Just enjoying the evening air." Fin set down her phone, then gestured with one hand toward the sky. "And loving the full moon. What about you?"

Jeremy ambled across the porch. "I'm a light sleeper."

So he'd heard her get up and had come to check on her. She wondered how much of her conversation with Xander he'd overheard.

"How's Xander?" The swing creaked as he sat beside her.

"He's doing well." Fin wished she had a drink, more for something to do with her hands than because she was thirsty.

By the way Jeremy shifted in place, she knew he was probably wishing for a prop, too. "I imagine parties are essential for someone in his position."

"They are." Fin was grateful he understood. The last thing she needed was someone making a remark about her fiancé attending a party without her.

"I know being here, without him, is difficult." Jeremy cleared his throat. "I appreciate the sacrifice."

"You could ease my pain by saying you'll vote yes this time."

"Good try." He grinned and she felt warm all over.

"I suppose I should attempt to get some sleep." Fin pretended to yawn, fighting a sudden urge to close the distance between them. "Tomorrow will be another busy day."

Despite the words, Fin made no move to walk to the door, not even when Jeremy stood and crossed to the rail. When he inclined his head back to look up at the sky and moonlight bathed his face, Fin's heart gave a lurch.

"I understand him." Jeremy's voice was a low rumble.

Curious, Fin rose and slipped to the rail. "Xander?"

Jeremy turned his head slightly and nodded before returning his gaze to the moon. The golden orb sat large and heavy in the dark sky, surrounded by a million sparkling stars.

"How could he not love it here?" Jeremy's gaze met hers. "Who knows? Eventually you and the director may end up settling in Good Hope."

Though Xander had grown up rural, he'd made it clear he was big city to the core. She understood. Like her, he'd built a life in California. "I don't think—"

"Door County is a boomerang."

Fin was familiar with the saying. People might leave to pursue their education or a job opportunity, but they always returned. There was something special about Good Hope that made it like no other place on earth.

"For most, yes," Fin acknowledged. "Not for all."

"You don't think you'll ever be back to stay."

It was a statement, not a question, but one Fin felt compelled to answer.

Before she did, Fin breathed in the scent of evergreen. The air was so clean here, so fresh. Once she "jilted" Jeremy and married Xander, she would have effectively closed the door on ever returning to Good Hope to live.

"No." Fin lifted her gaze to the sky and pushed aside the regret. "That's why I plan to enjoy every second."

Chapter Twelve

By the time Fin woke the next morning, Jeremy was gone. His pillow and blanket were off the sofa and back on the bed, likely in case his grandmother glanced in the room to check.

Ruby.

It wasn't the older woman who should be checking in on her, it was she who should be checking on Ruby. Fin glanced at the clock and realized Jeremy had likely been gone for hours. She hoped he'd made sure all was well with his grandmother before leaving.

Fin pulled on the pair of jeans and tee she'd borrowed from Ami. She didn't wait to put on her shoes. She took the steps two at a time but found Ruby's room empty.

After checking the other rooms on the second level, she headed back downstairs. When she called out and didn't receive a reply, her heart began to race.

Fin pulled out the phone she'd stuffed in her pocket. She wished she'd thought to put Jeremy's number on speed dial. As she scrolled through her contacts, she called out again, this time raising her voice several decibels. "Ruby."

"We're out here."

Relief surged. Fin let out the breath she didn't realize she'd been holding. Only then did the words fully register.

We're? Fin pulled her brows together. Had Jeremy decided to stay home and tend to his grandmother? It would be like him, she thought with a rush of warmth. She scurried toward the back of the house in the direction of Ruby's voice.

She found Jeremy's grandmother on a back terrace that overlooked a sprawling expanse of green. A plate of pastries and a carafe sat beside a vase of daisies on the glass-topped table. Two sets of eyes turned in her direction when she stepped out.

"Ami and I were beginning to wonder if you'd ever wake up." Ruby gestured to a chair, looking regal in a blue silk caftan. "Sit. Your sister brought the most wonderful pastries for us to sample."

"This is a nice surprise." Fin glanced at Ami, who thankfully was also dressed casually in jeans and a green gingham shirt. The only difference was her sister wore shoes.

Fin curled her toes into the flagstone, hoping if she didn't look down, no one else would either. "I thought you'd be at the bakery."

"Already there and done." Ami covered a yawn with her fingers, the huge diamond on her left hand sparkling in the morning light.

"You need to take care of yourself." Fin dropped into the chair next to her sister. Worry surged at the sight of the dark shadows beneath Ami's eyes. "Your baby could come anytime. You shouldn't be pushing yourself so hard."

"I told her the same." Ruby gave a decisive nod. "Ami's priority needs to be her child."

Bad things happened in a pregnancy when you didn't take care of yourself, when you pushed too hard.

Panic had Fin's throat in a choke hold. Some of what she felt must have showed on her face, because Ami reached over and gave her hand a reassuring squeeze before smiling at Ruby.

"You two can relax. I've already had that lecture from my husband." Ami's gaze dropped to her swollen belly, and a little smile lifted her lips. "This was my last morning. I won't be working at the bakery until after the baby is born. Hadley is now in charge and assures me she'll keep everything under control."

Fin had met Hadley, Ami's second-in-command, numerous times. Though the woman had shown up in Good Hope with no references and a sketchy backstory, Ami had hired her on her baking skills alone.

While Ami held Hadley in high regard, Fin had always thought there was something secretive about the woman. She wondered if Hadley thought the same about her.

Fin shoved the thought aside as of no consequence and refocused on her sister. "I'm glad you're taking these last few weeks to rest."

"That's what makes your return to Good Hope so perfect, Delphinium. You and your sister are now free to spend time together. That wouldn't be possible if you were in LA." Ruby warmed her own coffee, then glanced at Fin. "May I pour you a cup?"

Fin stared at the carafe, then at Ruby. "Should you be drinking coffee?"

Dear God, I sound just like my mother.

From the twitch in Ami's lips, she agreed.

"It's decaf." The older woman leaned forward as if imparting a secret. "But you'd never know it. It's full flavored and robust."

"I brought some with me for Ruby to try. It's Café Du Monde's chicory decaf." A soft smile lit Ami's face. "Beck found it for me on Amazon."

Fin hadn't been convinced any man would be worthy of her sister. Beckett Cross had proved her wrong. "Your husband is a sweetie."

The comment widened the smile on Ami's lips.

Beck was a lot like Jeremy, Fin mused. Both men liked to do nice things for those they loved. Fin had no doubt the pretty flowers on the table were from Jeremy to brighten his grandmother's day.

"I love gerbera daisies. I'm especially fond of the yellow ones." Fin touched a petal the color of lemons with one finger.

Ami lifted the dainty china cup to her lips. "They've always been your favorite."

"I believe that's why my grandson chose them for you."

Ruby's comment had Fin shaking her head. "They're yours, I'm sure of it."

"Not according to this card." Ami pushed a small manila envelope across the tabletop. "The delivery boy and I hit the porch at the same moment."

Fin eyed her name neatly printed on the front of the card. She cocked her head. "What does it say?"

Ami chuckled. "I may have brought in the flowers and Ruby may have carried them outside, but we stopped at reading the card."

"Your sister can be very strict," Ruby informed Fin, her blue eyes twinkling. "Open the card."

Fin hesitated, deciding she'd paraphrase if there was something a little too personal in the note. Then she nearly laughed aloud. How personal could it be?

She slipped the tiny card from the envelope.

Having you back in my life makes every day brighter.

Assuring herself, despite the sudden tightness in her throat, that the message wasn't intimate, she read it aloud. When the women sighed, Fin resisted the urge to sigh right along with them. While the sentiment might not be in-your-face intimate, it spoke volumes . . . and had red flags popping up.

"My grandson has his soul mate back."

More red flags.

"I'm ready for coffee." Fin refocused. She had to admit the aroma was heavenly. But decaf? And chicory? She almost shuddered.

Steeling herself, Fin took a sip. Then another. "This is really good."

"Told you," Ami and Ruby said in unison, then both women laughed.

A light breeze ruffled Fin's hair and a bird cawed in the distance. Any worries she'd had slipped from her shoulders to pool at her feet. She glanced at the pastry plate. "Are those bite-size kouign amann?"

"They're part of our new party platter line." Ami relaxed against the back of the comfortable patio chair. "Perfect for office parties or for individuals or families who like variety."

"Spoken like a businesswoman." Ruby nodded approval, her bony fingers wrapped around a dainty china cup.

Fin placed a tiny kouign amann on a floral plate. She took a bite, then closed her eyes as sugar, butter, and caramelized goodness came together in a delicious explosion of flavor.

"This is amazing," Fin told her sister. "You can pop over anytime."

"Actually, she came because I called." Ruby smiled brightly.

Ami patted the woman's hand. "I'm so glad you did."

Fin cocked her head. She'd thought her sister had simply stopped over to see her, or maybe to visit Ruby. It appeared there was more to the unexpected visit than she first thought.

"If we're going to pull off a March wedding, we need to start planning now." Ruby bit into a tiny cherry Danish and munched happily.

Fin's second bite of pastry stuck in her throat. To get it moving, she gulped coffee. "I don't recall saying anything about March."

"I spoke with Dan. Not only is the man gorgeous, on the phone his voice is like cream over whiskey." Ruby's eyes sparkled with mischief. "If he was fifty years older, I'd jump him. He could even quote Bible verses while we did the deed."

"He, ah, he seems very nice," Fin managed to utter, wondering if she was still in her bed and this was simply a nightmare. "What does Dan have to do with a March wedding?"

"All the Saturdays in May and June were already taken," Ami informed her.

There was a definite smile lurking in Ami's green depths.

Fin hated to ask the obvious, but it appeared necessary when neither woman elaborated. "Why does that matter?"

"I know my grandson. He's waited ten long years for you, Delphinium. Jeremy won't want to wait any longer than absolutely necessary to make you his wife. Plus, we needed to secure the church before moving ahead with other wedding plans."

"What other wedding plans?" Fin wondered if ten a.m. was too early for a shot of whiskey. Forget the cream.

"The cake, photographer, musicians." Excitement bubbled in her voice, and Ruby's cheeks were now a healthy shade of pink.

Fin, who'd been about to shut down the discussion, swallowed. The last thing she wanted was Ruby depressed because her future granddaughter-in-law refused her wedding help. "You seem to have a good handle on all this."

"What can I say?" The older woman gave a little laugh. "I haven't been this excited since Sly and the Family Stone took the stage at Woodstock."

That left only one question. Fin cocked her head. "You were at Woodstock?"

Fin changed into a white sundress with bold red poppies and heels of the same color, then arranged to meet Jeremy for a late lunch at Muddy Boots. The wedding plans discussed this morning reminded her of a large boulder perched at the edge of a precipice.

One little push would have it careening out of control. Still, she didn't want Jeremy to upset his grandmother by refusing to play along.

She could see him doing it, not understanding the entire picture. Fin felt she had a good grasp on what was going on and how to best deal with the situation.

Though she knew Jeremy had to be busy, when she called he didn't make her feel as if she was bothering him. He answered immediately, informed her he was in a meeting and would call her in ten minutes. Her phone rang in eight.

Despite being a Wednesday and past the lunch hour, the small café on Main Street buzzed with activity. Several tables held groups playing cards while a rectangular table near the back wall had been claimed by a Bible study group.

Fin chose a table without any neighbors, hoping for some privacy. Or at least as much privacy as one could hope for in a small town. While she waited, she picked up the menu and studied the selections.

"Hey, beautiful." Jeremy brushed a kiss across her cheek and took the chair next to her. "I hope I didn't keep you waiting."

"I just got here myself." She placed the menu on the table. "Thanks for coming. And thank you for the flowers. They're lovely. Gerbera daisies are my favorite."

"I remember." An emotion she couldn't quite identify filled Jeremy's blue eyes, then he blinked and it was gone. "You said there was something we needed to discuss. It sounded urgent."

Fin was considering how best to explain what his grandmother had planned when the bell over the front door jingled, drawing her attention.

Eliza stepped inside and glanced around, looking stylish as always in a lace overlay dress, which Fin recognized as a Marc Jacobs. The color of lemon chiffon, it was the perfect foil for her dark hair, and the simple cut flattered her lithe figure.

When their eyes met, Fin smiled and lifted a hand in greeting.

Fin was glad she looked Eliza-ready. Jeans and a tee might be okay for Ruby and Ami, but meeting up with your fiancé's former flame looking as if you just finished working in the garden would be a major faux pas.

"Is my grandmother okay? When you said—" Jeremy stopped when Eliza strode up. He started to rise, but she motioned him down.

"Eliza. What a pleasant surprise." The smile he offered Eliza seemed especially warm. "Can you join us?"

"I stopped to pick up a to-go order, but I'm five minutes early." Her gaze flicked to Fin.

"Please, sit." Fin's encouragement earned her a smile from Jeremy.

Eliza took a seat with an innate gracefulness Fin envied. "I'm happy I ran into both of you. I'd like to come out on Sunday. Getting the barn Christmas-ready for Mindy is going to take time. We need to get started."

Fin shot Jeremy a questioning look. "I don't think we have anything planned for that day?"

She cursed her insensitivity when the smile froze on Eliza's face. Though the woman was a master at hiding her emotions, for an instant Fin saw pain spark in the smoky depths.

Darn it, Fin thought as sympathy surged. The *we* made it sound as if she and Jeremy were a real couple.

Jeremy didn't appear to notice the faux pas. "I'm completely open. How 'bout I see if I can round up some additional help?"

"That'd be wonderful." Eliza smiled, and her eyes locked with his.

Fin fought back a surge of jealousy, reminding herself that his friendship with Eliza wasn't her business.

After arranging to meet at noon on Sunday, the three of them chatted easily for several minutes before Eliza rose to get her order.

Jeremy's gaze followed his old friend out the door.

"Do you love her?" Fin forced out the words, grateful the delivery was casual, even nonchalant. Perhaps she was a better actress than she thought.

When he hesitated, breathing became difficult. Before Jeremy could respond, a middle-aged woman Fin didn't recognize came to take their order.

When the waitress left, Fin wasn't sure what she'd even ordered. She waited until the woman returned with their drinks to press for an answer. "Do you love her?"

"As a friend." Jeremy lifted the plastic tumbler and guzzled the tea as if he'd been working in the hot sun all day. "Our friendship goes way back."

"Your mother always hoped you'd end up together." Fin liked Cheryl Rakes well enough, but even back in high school had sensed a Bloom sister wouldn't be his mother's first choice for a daughter-in-law.

Fin paused when Jeremy only continued to stare at the doorway where Eliza had recently stood, then continued, "She had a rough time in middle school. Between braces and being super skinny . . ."

"Those were difficult years for her." Jeremy's fingers curved around the tumbler, but he didn't lift the glass.

"It could have been so much worse. Everyone knew she was your friend." And from kindergarten to graduation, Jeremy had been one of the cool kids. "That helped."

"She's a beauty, now."

Fin ignored the stab of jealousy the words provoked. "By the time the ugly duckling morphed into a beautiful swan, you and I were together."

"As I've said before, Eliza and I were never more than friends." His fingers drummed against the table.

"I don't sleep with my friends." Fin gave him a thin smile. "I guess that's the difference between you and me."

He shot her a steely glance.

"Do you think you'd have ever proposed marriage to Eliza?" Fin took a sip of tea, resisting the urge to guzzle.

"No," he said after an interminable silence. "The affection I feel for her isn't romantic."

"Yet you slept with her."

"It was a mistake." His blue eyes were thoughtful. "Or perhaps it wasn't."

Fin covered her sharp intake of breath with a cough.

"Sleeping with her made me aware I didn't care for her in the same way she cared for me." He twisted a spoon between his thumb and forefinger. Back and forth. Back and forth. "She told me it didn't matter if her feelings were reciprocated, that sex for sex's sake was okay. Afterwards, I realized she was lying. To herself. To me. If we continued being intimate, I would hurt her. I'd already hurt her."

"You probably did her a favor."

He cocked his head. "What do you mean?"

The hope-filled look he shot her tugged at her. Jeremy had always had a kind heart. He'd always been a nice guy. Too nice. Fin would have kicked Eliza to the curb years ago after some of the stunts she'd pulled.

"It isn't fair to lead someone on." She held up a hand when he opened his mouth and she saw the protest forming on his lips. "I'm sure you didn't intentionally do it, but you admitted she's always hoped for more with you than just friendship."

After a long moment, he gave a reluctant nod.

"Despite making it clear that you thought of her only as a friend, I'm sure she kept hoping."

"You're saying now she'll quit hoping."

"She'll move on and hopefully find her prince." Fin nearly groaned aloud when the word slipped past her lips.

A slow smile lifted Jeremy's lips. "Prince?"

If Fin had been looking for a way to lift his spirits, she'd obviously scored with the ridiculous remark.

Fin waved a dismissive hand. "Just something my mother used to say."

"Tell me more."

Fin knew he would press and cajole until she did. "It's not all that interesting. My mother used to say that when she met my dad, she found her prince. She wanted each of us girls to find our princes, too; the man who we would love and who would love us for eternity."

Jeremy waited, as if sensing there was more.

"All my sisters have declared they've found their princes and will live happily ever after." Fin chuckled. "Cue the violins and cherubs."

She sighed.

Jeremy's gaze searched hers. "Do you think their marriages won't last?"

"It's not that." Fin's tone turned pensive.

"Then why the sigh?"

"It's just that not all marriages are hearts and flowers." She gave a little laugh. "From what I've observed, it certainly isn't that way in Tinseltown."

"You found your prince."

"Our relationship is only temporary," she pointed out.

"I wasn't talking about us." Jeremy's eyes never left hers. "I was referring to you and Xander."

Before Fin could come up with a proper response, the waitress appeared and set a salad with shrimp in front of her and a hamburger steak with green beans and french fries before Jeremy.

The waitress cast Jeremy an inquiring look. "Ketchup?"

"Absolutely, and also some A-1 if you have it, Helen."

"Coming right up, Mr. Mayor." The woman shifted her gaze to Fin. "Anything I can get you, ma'am?"

Ma'am.

Though Fin inwardly cringed, she smiled. "I'm fine. Thanks."

"Red meat isn't good for you." She found herself parroting what Xander had said to her the few times she'd ordered a burger.

Jeremy smiled as Helen returned with his ketchup and steak sauce.

"Everything in moderation." Jeremy picked up a fry. "Now, tell me why you felt we needed to meet. Other than, of course, you missed me terribly and couldn't wait to see me again."

There was something about that slightly lopsided smile he gave her that made her feel all flustered and high schoolish. She didn't much like the feeling. Xander never made her feel that way. "That will be the day."

She watched his smile fade, saw his eyes turn cool as a stiff winter breeze over Green Bay. He picked up his phone, glanced at the time. "Tell me why you called."

It was smart to keep distance between them, Fin told herself. Especially with them sleeping in the same room. Otherwise things might become . . . difficult.

"I want," she lifted the glass of tea and took a leisurely sip, "to know if you're okay with a March wedding. Your grandmother already booked the church."

Jeremy held up a hand and visibly swallowed the chunk of meat he'd just popped into his mouth. "Back up the train and start at the beginning."

"Your grandmother decided that we—meaning she, you, and I— couldn't move forward with wedding plans without a date."

Jeremy drowned a french fry in ketchup, said nothing.

Fin snatched a fry from his plate. *Everything in moderation.* "Ruby was distressed to learn the church had various events booked for every Saturday this spring. That's when she decided March would be perfect."

"March?" Jeremy's blue eyes took on a slightly glazed appearance. "We usually still have snow on the ground."

Fin lifted a shoulder, let it drop.

His eyes turned sharp and assessing. "You went along with this?"

"I didn't know what to say."

"Since when?" He must have seen her stiffen, because he waved a hand before she could reply. "Why not a later date?"

Fin glanced at her salad but didn't pick up her fork, feeling strangely embarrassed to say the words. "Ruby insisted you wouldn't want to wait that long to make me your wife."

Instead of saying something sweet, which she absolutely didn't expect, Jeremy dragged a hand through his hair.

"This is just great," he muttered. "Once you return to LA, these plans will have to be undone. It would have been much simpler if you'd told her you wanted a big wedding. From what I hear those often take years to plan."

"I'll slow down the planning." Fin leaned forward, lowered her voice. "What does it matter if the church is confirmed? It isn't as if there are dozens of brides-to-be hoping for that Saturday in March."

"Good point."

"I could have given your grandmother a date far into the future," she admitted, "and it would have been difficult for her to argue. But you should have seen her face, Jeremy. She was so happy. To have insisted I wanted a wedding a year or two from now, well, it would have been cruel."

Though not entirely accurate, it was the only word that came to mind. She stabbed a shrimp with her fork. "When she started talking about how March is a slow time for Good Hope merchants and our wedding would help them through the after-Christmas slump, what could I do but agree?"

Warmth returned to his blue eyes, and the approval she saw there had her world going steady again. "There wasn't anything else you could do. You're a good person, Fin."

"You didn't think so a few minutes ago."

"You can be prickly."

When she sputtered, he only chuckled.

"Enough about the wedding." Fin set down her fork. "Let's move on to more important matters, like why you vetoed Xander's proposition."

Jeremy didn't appear surprised. It was almost as if he'd expected her to bring up the topic. "First, let me ask you a question. What comes to mind when you think of celebrating Christmas in Good Hope?"

Fin had a good idea where Jeremy was going with this and could easily skew her answer to support Xander's position. She fought back the urge, determined to be honest.

"I'd have to say caroling in the town square on Christmas Eve." Fin didn't have to close her eyes to visualize the scene: the crisp night air, the heavy scent of pine, and fat flakes falling from a star-filled sky. "When Loretta Sharkey steps to the podium to lead us in song and a hush falls over the crowd, well, it just does something to my heart. I love holding the candles when we sing 'Silent Night' and seeing the colorful lights from shop windows reflect off the pristine white snow."

"Beautiful."

When she glanced at him, ready to agree, she found him staring. At her.

Trying not to blush, she stole another french fry from his plate. "What about you?"

"I think of the Twelve Nights celebrations. All those activities are what make Good Hope so special at holiday time."

His light tone didn't fool her. She saw the emotion in his eyes.

The Twelve Nights hadn't changed much since Fin had been a child. For the four weeks leading up to Christmas, activities were scheduled every weekend. These events were kicked off by the lighting of the Christmas tree in the town square.

"Delaying the holiday celebrations until January would be a onetime thing." Instead of going for the hard sell, Fin kept her voice matter-of-fact.

"What about the people who already have plans to come here for Christmas?" Jeremy's tone remained equally conversational. "Those flying in won't be able to change their reservations. Not even if they were given notice now. Yet when they arrive to celebrate Christmas in Good Hope, they won't find any signs of Christmas."

The agreement stipulated that the entire business district of Good Hope would be available for filming purposes during the month of December. As winter, not Christmas, played a part in the story Xander would be shooting, there could be no evidence of the holiday along Main Street.

"That's true." Fin took a sip of tea and felt herself steady. "But this will be a major Hollywood production with A-list actors in town for the shoot. Not only is Xander willing to pay big bucks to the town's coffers, residents and visitors alike will have a chance to apply to be extras. Or simply watch the filming."

"It won't be the same." Jeremy lifted his glass and took a long drink of tea.

"That isn't necessarily bad." Fin kept her tone light despite the sudden ache that had invaded her own heart.

"I don't know." Jeremy wiped the condensation from the side of his glass with one finger, his gaze thoughtful. "What I have to decide is, will accepting this proposition make life better for the community of Good Hope? Not just in December, but during the rest of the year."

"Having the increased revenue will help you get to projects that are currently languishing because of lack of funds."

"True." Yet something in those serious blue eyes told Fin he wasn't convinced. "On the other hand, I believe coming together during the holidays strengthens our sense of community and reminds us once again why we live here. In Good Hope, *neighbors helping neighbors* isn't just something we say but something we believe and practice. When we come together to celebrate and rejoice, we become stronger because of it. I'd hate to lose that over extra road construction money."

Not knowing how to respond to that argument, Fin gestured to Helen for more iced tea and focused on eating the salad she'd barely touched.

Jeremy had pulled out his wallet to pay the bill when Fin stopped him with a hand on his arm.

"Give it up, Finley." His lips curved and he pulled out a couple of bills. "I don't care if you invited me, I'm not letting you pay for lunch."

"That's not it, although I wish you'd at least let me toss in half."

"Not happening." When her hand remained on his arm, he cocked his head. "Something else?"

"There's one more thing to do with your grandmother that I forgot to mention."

"What is it?"

"She's throwing an engagement party for us Saturday night."

Chapter Thirteen

"Too bad I have a prior commitment or I'd come to the party." Amusement laced Xander's tone. "It's not every day a man is invited to celebrate his fiancée's engagement to her ex-boyfriend."

"I'm glad one of us thinks this is funny." Fin's fingers relaxed around the phone. She hadn't been sure how Xander would take the news. But FaceTime allowed her to see that his brown eyes were as warm as his smile. "Ruby is determined to have the party. We argued it was too soon after her surgery, but the plans are now all in place."

"Where will this grand soiree be held?" Although Xander lay on top of his bed, relaxing against a pile of propped-up pillows, he was fully dressed. She wondered if he was planning on going out once he got off the phone.

"At the farm."

He lifted a brow. "Farm?"

Fin gave a little laugh "Sorry, I forgot you said you didn't make it outside the town limits when you were here. Rakes Farm is a huge venue in Door County. Around here most people simply refer to it as the farm."

"Is it?"

"Is it what?"

"A farm?"

"I suppose it qualifies as one, since last I knew it had five hundred acres of tart cherry as well as some apple and pear trees," Fin conceded. "But it's definitely not the kind you're imaging. The house is this amazing old Victorian and the property has a beautiful old barn that has been renovated and is used for a variety of community and private functions."

"A barn."

"Since you're from a rural area, you're undoubtedly familiar with the structure."

His lips twisted in a grimace. "Don't remind me."

Fin was poised to tease, but the edge in his voice stopped her. In the time they'd been together, Fin had learned that Xander preferred to keep his life in rural America firmly in the past.

She'd always found that odd, considering it had been their shared Midwestern roots that had originally drawn her to him. In a city of pretense, he seemed real.

Or he had. Over the past year, as success had come calling, as the movers and shakers in the film industry had accepted him into their inner circle, she'd watched him slowly change.

He was a talented man and Fin had been happy to see his confidence get a much-needed boost, but not all changes had been positive. She liked to think she centered him. That she kept him—and his healthy ego—grounded.

"Even though you won't be attending," Fin kept her tone light, "you'll be pleased to know the party won't be held in the barn. It'll be in the house, and it will indeed be a grand soiree."

"It's being held in Wisconsin. There's no way it'll be a soiree, grand or otherwise." The smug tone pricked her temper. "Good Hope may be the perfect setting for this movie, but it isn't the most cultured of areas."

"You haven't spent enough time here to make that assessment." Fin's tenuous control on her temper now hung on a single thread. "We're not all Cheeseheads and beer drinkers. Not that there's anything wrong with either of those."

Xander's smile thinned. "Just don't change too much while you're there."

"What's that supposed to mean?"

"What is that you're wearing?"

Fin glanced down. Her dad had invited her over to play a fast and furious game of badminton with him and her nephews. She'd almost declined, but Jeremy had encouraged her to go, insisting she enjoy her time in Good Hope fully. "It's a T-shirt."

With the University of Wisconsin's mascot, Bucky, across the front.

Fin lifted her chin. She would not apologize for wearing a shirt appropriate for hitting a birdie over a net. She only regretted that when she'd decided to call Xander, she hadn't given a thought to her appearance.

"Don't forget who you are, Fin." A subtle warning ran through Xander's tone. "The woman I want at my side on the red carpet isn't a small-town girl from Wisconsin."

Don't forget who you are.

Even after Fin ended the call and headed downstairs for something to drink, the words circled like a song on repeat.

She found Jeremy in the kitchen, dressed in cargo shorts, sneakers without laces, and a striped polo shirt. If Xander thought she was too casual, he'd most certainly sneer when he caught sight of Jeremy.

But Fin liked Jeremy with his tousled blond hair and stubble. In fact, she liked him better this way than in a suit and tie.

He looked up from where he was rummaging through the refrigerator. "How'd the call go?"

She'd warned Jeremy she wasn't sure how Xander would take the news of a big engagement party.

"He was amused."

"I bet that was a relief." Though Jeremy smiled, his gaze remained watchful.

"I thought it might bother him." The words slipped past her lips before she could stop them.

"It didn't."

"Like I said, he thought it was funny."

"I realize all this must be difficult." Jeremy shut the refrigerator door, giving her his entire attention. "Celebrating your engagement to me when you should be celebrating yours to him."

"It'll be fine. Your grandmother is—" Fin glanced in the direction of the stairs.

"Asleep," Jeremy answered the unspoken question. "I just checked on her before I came down."

"I feel badly she's going to all this work."

"She's not actually doing the work and she's enjoying every minute of overseeing the action."

"But to do all this only to have it end—"

"Hey." His hand closing over hers had the rest of what she was about to say dying in her throat. "Think about it. When you get right down to it, today is all we're guaranteed. Grandma Ruby has been through a lot in her life. My engagement ending is something she'll be able to handle. Let's let her enjoy the moment."

"You're right." Fin pulled her hand from his and crossed the room, then paced back again. "I don't know what's wrong with me. I feel edgy."

It wasn't stress over the upcoming party that had her in such a state. Not entirely. It was being this close to Jeremy. "I think I'll go for a run."

"It's dark."

She glanced out the window and sighed. "I need to burn off this lu—ah, energy."

Dear God, had she really almost said *lust*?

"I'm having the same problem settling." Jeremy's gaze remained fixed on her face, making breathing difficult.

"Any thoughts what we could do?"

The spark in those blue eyes and the answering tingle deep in her belly told her his mind was traveling the same road as hers.

"Wii bowling."

Fin inhaled sharply. "What?"

"It's set up in the back parlor." Jeremy gestured vaguely in that direction. "Gram loves to play."

"Great."

Fin thought she'd done a good job of hiding her disappointment until his eyes turned dark as the night sky.

"Unless you have something else in mind?" His words were soft as a caress.

Fin licked her lips, saw his eyes grow darker still. But she realized there were lines she couldn't cross, no matter how tempted. She forced a smile. "Wii bowling it is."

"You and Jeremy spent the night bowling." Marigold's husky voice was incredulous. Then her blue eyes narrowed. "Are you making that up?"

When Fin stopped by her youngest sister's salon the next morning, Marigold promptly pulled her into the chair. There weren't many people she could trust with her hair, but Marigold was one of them.

"What was I supposed to do?" She gave a laugh that sounded hollow. "Have wild, hot sex with him?"

"Sounds better than Wii bowling." Marigold gave a little snip. "You *are* engaged."

"Not to him." Fin wasn't sure why Marigold seemed determined to forget that important fact.

The bells over the front door jingled. Marigold spoke without looking up. "I like Jeremy. He's cute, in that scruffy, surfer-dude kind of way."

"Happy I meet with your approval." Humor laced Jeremy's voice.

Marigold turned, batted her long lashes. "Did you miss the scruffy part?"

"I didn't think I'd see you until tonight." Fin struggled to keep her voice steady, even as her heart skipped a beat. It was as if she was sixteen again. "What a nice surprise."

"Ditto." He crossed to her, pleasure filling his blue eyes. "I was walking by and saw you through the window."

"Fin didn't really need a trim." Marigold's gaze turned sharp and assessing. "But you could use one. Why don't you exchange places with her? I won't charge you since you're almost family."

Almost family.

Fin thought about reminding her sister—again—that her engagement to Jeremy was only temporary, but kept her mouth shut. To her way of thinking, the less said about the arrangement the better. Sometimes in Good Hope, it seemed as if the walls had ears.

"Thanks, but not this time." Jeremy gave Marigold a wink. "I promise to make an appointment soon."

Marigold waggled her shears at him. "I better not see you going into Golden Door."

The upscale salon was Marigold's fiercest competitor on the peninsula.

Jeremy swiped his fingers across his heart. "Never. We're family. Almost."

His teasing smile made Marigold grin as she swept off the cape and motioned to Fin to get up. "Go. Keep your fiancé company."

Fin remained seated. "I didn't think you were finished."

Marigold gave a little shrug. "You only needed some fine-tuning."

Rising slowly, Fin gazed at the littlest Bloom. At five foot three, Marigold might be the smallest in stature of the sisters, but she was also the feistiest. "Thanks for the trim."

"Stop by again. Or maybe Cade and I will stop out sometime."

Fin smiled. "I'd like that."

She and Marigold had battled wills many times in the past, most recently when Fin had pushed hard to get Marigold to relocate to LA rather than New York. In the end her youngest sister had fallen in love with Cade Rallis and decided to stay in Good Hope, making the decision moot.

The door pushed open.

"Am I invited to this party?" Other than the weapon at his hip, Cade looked very un-sheriff-like in jeans and a henley.

Marigold beamed and rushed to his side, lifting her face for a kiss. "I believe we can make room for one more."

Cade's mouth closed over hers. The welcome kiss lasted a little longer than Fin anticipated and had her and Jeremy exchanging smiles.

Newlyweds.

Although she didn't know him well, Fin liked Marigold's husband. Physically, he reminded her of Beck with his dark hair and lean frame. But Cade had a few more muscles and just seemed more . . . physical. Like Beck, he clearly adored his wife.

Fin swallowed the envy that rose to her throat.

With his arm slung around Marigold's shoulders, the sheriff turned to her and Jeremy. "I'm sorry I couldn't make the dinner at Ami's house the other night. The stomach flu was making an early appearance in the sheriff's department and there was no one who could take my shift."

"We didn't even miss you."

Jeremy's comment had Fin widening her eyes. Then she heard Cade chuckle and realized these two men were friends.

Cade's gray eyes turned serious. "I'm happy for you both."

Jeremy took the hand he extended. "Appreciate the good wishes."

Fin stilled. Had she slipped into some kind of Twilight Zone? Surely Marigold had told Cade that her and Jeremy's engagement was a farce? She glanced at her sister, but Marigold was looking up at her husband with such love that Fin felt as if she was intruding on a private moment.

"Will you be able to make the engagement party Saturday night?" Jeremy asked Cade.

"Count on it." Cade shifted his gaze to Fin. "You've got yourself a good man here."

What else could Fin do but agree?

"I'd like to see a little more greenery in that bouquet." Fin gestured to a vase of flowers the size of Texas. "I believe it'd give the arrangement more depth."

Lindsay Lohmeier, floral designer at the Enchanted Florist, took a step back and eyed the centerpiece that she'd just placed on a round table in the home's main parlor.

"You're right." The pretty blonde's pursed lips made the scar on her cheek more pronounced. "It definitely could use more cocculus."

"Thanks." Fin exhaled a breath, pleased to find Lindsay so agreeable.

Ruby had made it clear that while she planned to act as hostess tonight, Fin called the shots on everything else.

Lindsay glanced up from the flowers now sporting extra green. "It's nice having you here."

"It's good to be back." Fin studied the arrangement with a critical eye, and this time gave an approving nod.

"I meant having you around to coordinate." Lindsay flashed a smile. "Normally we're on our own."

Fin cocked her head.

"Jeremy throws a lot of parties. He normally tells us what he wants, then trusts us to get it done. He doesn't like being bogged down in details." Lindsay turned from the bouquet, her back resting against the glossy burl table. "The freedom is appreciated, but it's also nice having someone to bounce ideas off and give direction."

A whole truckload of flowers had been delivered that morning. Other than this bouquet, no input had been necessary. "You did an amazing job on the floral arrangements. I can see why he trusts you."

"I want it nice for you and Jeremy." Lindsay met Fin's gaze. "While Eliza and I are close, I consider you a friend, too."

"Thanks, Lin." The last lingering bit of tension fell from Fin's shoulders. "That means a lot."

With all the flowers now in place, Lindsay appeared ready to kick back and chat. "Mom said you'll be going back to LA before the wedding."

Fin lifted her shoulder in a nonchalant gesture. Lindsay likely meant nothing by the inquiry, but she knew Lindsay's mother was always mining for dirt. Dirt she'd gleefully smear on every member of the Bloom family.

Ever since Fin's father had ended his relationship with Anita, the woman's acerbic tongue seemed especially directed toward his daughters.

"Fin *has* to go back to Los Angeles." Prim, who'd been busy adjusting the angle of tables that would soon hold appetizers and desserts, spoke in an authoritative tone. "You know how it is when you relocate. There are always loose ends to tie up. I shudder when I recall how much effort it took to make the move back home."

Back home.

Not back to Good Hope, Fin noted. But *back home.*

Other than Ami, who'd only left to attend college in Madison, that's how her other two siblings always referred to their return . . . coming home. Fin was beginning to understand the sentiment.

This visit marked the longest amount of time she'd spent in Good Hope since leaving for college.

"I sometimes wonder what my life would be like if I'd moved away." Lindsay's tone turned pensive. "Though I admit I never did give it serious thought."

"Your mother probably would have tracked you down and dragged you back." Fin spoke in a matter-of-fact tone. Everyone knew she was Anita's favorite child.

Lindsay's lips quirked. "There's no *probably* about it."

"I hear you and our hunky pastor are an item." Prim's hazel eyes sparkled. "He's a real cutie."

"You're dating Dan Marshall?" Fin couldn't keep the surprise from her voice.

This time it was Lindsay's turn to go for nonchalant. "He asked me to be his date for Marigold's wedding. We've been seeing each other since. Dan is a nice guy. We have a lot in common."

Something in the way Lindsay said the words reminded Fin of how she spoke of Xander. *He's a nice guy,* she'd say, then add, *we have a lot in common.*

There was no reason to expect to see a flush in Lindsay's cheeks or hear an excited tremor in her voice. No reason to expect it at all. After all, practical trumped romantic any day.

Ami waddled, er, sauntered, into the room.

"I feel the need to sit for a few minutes and that lovely swing on the porch is calling my name." Ami glanced at Lindsay. "Would you mind if I borrowed my sisters for a few minutes?"

"Not at all." Lindsay looked up from the bouquet she was still fussing over. "I'm good here."

"I can't sit long." Fin offered Ami an apologetic look when the three Bloom sisters settled themselves on the swing. "It's my party—"

"Which means you can do whatever you want." As Ami adjusted her dress, Fin found her gaze drawn to her sister's belly. She'd never paid much attention to pregnant women. In Hollywood, unless currently en vogue, pregnancy was often regarded as something to get over quickly with the goal of regaining the prebaby figure as soon as possible.

Even in the soft twilight, Ami positively glowed. Her summer dress, the color of freshly mown grass, flattered her very-pregnant figure.

Fin felt an odd tightening in her throat. "You look incredible."

"I feel like a beached whale." Ami's quick smile said she was loving every minute of her whale time.

"I'm happy Ruby was able to get everything arranged so quickly." Ami patted Fin's arm. "My OB says the baby could come any day, and I'd have hated to miss this."

Prim's eyes took on a faraway look. "I remember those last few weeks before the twins were born. Rory and I were so excited and yet scared, too. Everything in our lives was about to change."

"How's Beck holding up?" Fin asked. They were all aware that Beck's first wife had been seven months pregnant when she and their unborn baby had died in a car accident.

"We're both feeling confident." If there was anything worrying Ami, it didn't show. "We've been visualizing an easy delivery and a healthy baby."

Unexpected tears stung the backs of Fin's eyes.

"I could get used to this." Jeremy's voice, filled with good humor, sounded from the steps to the porch. "Coming home to three gorgeous women waiting for me on the porch."

Fin jumped up. "We were taking a break."

Before she could say more, he climbed the steps and crossed to press his mouth to hers in a sweet kiss. "None more gorgeous than you, Finley."

Though she thought Jeremy was laying it on a little thick, Fin couldn't stop the rush of pleasure that swamped her. But was it really necessary to lean into him and rest her head against his shoulder?

Ami rose to her feet with surprising ease. "Prim and I are going to take a short walk, then get back to work."

"Thanks for coming and helping. I—"

"That's what family does," Prim interrupted him. "Marigold would be here, but she already had a full day of appointments."

Fin smiled. "I'm just happy her and Cade are able to come this evening."

"Well," Ami looped her arm through Prim's, "we're off to walk."

"Just don't walk so much the baby decides to make an appearance this afternoon," Fin warned.

Ami only laughed. "Your mouth, God's ear."

Feeling more than a little off balance, Fin stepped inside with Jeremy and made a sweeping gesture with one hand. "What do you think?"

His hand, warm and firm, remained on her shoulder as he surveyed the parlor. "It looks amazing. You always did have a talent for entertaining."

"If you're talking about my father's party a couple years back, my sisters did most of the work."

His eyes never left hers, and Fin found herself lost in the liquid blue depths. It was as if the world had suddenly shrunk in around them.

"Actually." He paused and tucked a strand of hair behind her ear with one finger. "I was referring to the one you threw for your parents when you were seventeen. The one for their anniversary."

"Oh." Recalling that night brought a tightness to Fin's chest.

"I remember that party. It was right before the car accident." Lindsay, who'd been surveying the mantel, crossed over and moved a mason jar an inch to the right. "Your mother was going through chemo. You single-handedly pulled the event together."

"My sisters helped—" Fin began, but Lindsay interrupted.

"*You* did it, Fin. Credit where credit is due." Lindsay's gray-blue eyes turned soft with the memory. "It was wonderful and meant so much to them."

"We all needed a boost." Fin hadn't been certain if a party was the answer to the family turmoil, but she hadn't known how else to help.

For the first time in her life, Steve and Sarah Bloom had been totally absorbed in their own struggles. Understandable, given the circumstances, but they'd always been her anchor. Ironic that she'd been cast adrift just when she'd needed them most.

She hadn't even had her sisters to lean on. Ami, always so solid, had taken their mother's diagnosis extra hard and floundered. Prim and Marigold had been too young. Because of his tenuous home situation, even Jeremy had been distant.

Fin had hoped being busy would keep her mind off what had happened in Milwaukee. That part of the plan had failed miserably.

"Your mother and dad were so happy that night." Lindsay slid the rustic mason jar filled with a formal flower arrangement of coral and white back to its original spot. "It seemed as if everything in the Bloom household was back to normal."

Normal hadn't lasted. There had been Ami's accident a couple of weeks later. Then Fin's breakup with Jeremy . . .

Fin took a breath to steady herself. When she looked up, she found Jeremy's eyes on her.

"You've always been strong."

"Spoken like a man in love." Lindsay spoke before Fin could respond. Her eyes held a hint of envy. "But I agree. Fin handles whatever life tosses her way."

Out of necessity, Fin thought. Who would pick up the pieces, if not her?

Jeremy glanced around the room. "What can I do to help?"

"Everything is under control." Fin was relieved to once again focus on the here and now. "The Muddy Boots catering staff should be showing up with the food any minute. The alcohol has been delivered, and the bartenders and servers should arrive around six."

"Sounds as if everything *is* under control." His gaze searched hers, and what he found there must have reassured him, because he nodded. "I'll go keep Grandma Ruby company."

"She's not here," Fin called to his retreating back.

Jeremy spun around. "Where is she?"

"Gladys took her out for a drive." Fin smiled reassuringly. "She offered to stay and help, but I worried she might be too tired to enjoy the party."

"Ruby listens to Fin," Lindsay told Jeremy. "I swear she already thinks of her as family."

"Yes, well." Fin cleared her throat, made a show of pulling out her phone and checking it, although the grandfather clock less than ten feet away could have given her the time. "I'm going to call Create Events. They're doing the decorations for the party. I expected them thirty minutes ago."

"I'll take care of that task." Jeremy lifted a hand when she opened her mouth to protest. "It's my engagement party, too."

Fin hesitated only a second. "Thank you."

His eyes never left hers. "Anytime."

When he strode out of the room, Lindsay sighed. "He's a great guy."

Yes, Fin concurred. Jeremy *was* wonderful.

And, for the next few weeks, he was all hers.

Chapter Fourteen

"Ed and Cheryl should be here." Ruby's voice held a hint of censure.

Though his grandmother usually refrained from criticizing her son and daughter-in-law, it was obvious she'd expected them to come running when they heard about the engagement party.

"They had the trip to Capri planned for months." Jeremy was secretly relieved his parents hadn't canceled their European vacation.

"You're their only child." Ruby's jaw set in a hard line. "You only get engaged once."

"Engagements are broken every day." Jeremy kept his tone light.

"Not if you've chosen the right person." Ruby's gaze shifted to Fin, who was currently on the dance floor with her father. "Delphinium and you are meant to be together for eternity."

The flowery words might have made Jeremy smile if they didn't so closely match how he felt.

His grandmother placed a hand on his arm. "The way you feel about her shows."

Jeremy stilled, hoping that wasn't true. For now he was keeping his feelings for Fin on a need-to-know basis. And Fin didn't need to know. Not yet. He wouldn't scare her off by pushing too hard or fast.

He gave his grandmother's arm a squeeze. "I'm going to grab another dance with my fiancée before the band takes a break."

The band consisted of four talented musicians and their female lead singer. A popular local group for wedding receptions, they played everything from current hits to the big band sounds of the forties.

Jeremy stepped onto the dance floor that had been set up in the back parlor and tapped Steve on the shoulder.

Fin's father turned and his smile dimmed. Jeremy understood. Steve wanted the best for all his daughters. The high school teacher obviously still worried that when the engagement ended, his daughter's reputation would be sullied.

Jeremy stood by his promise. He would do whatever it took to keep Fin from being hurt. But he knew to a protective father, those were only words.

"May I cut in?" Jeremy held out his hand.

"I believe that can be arranged." Fin's bright smile arrowed straight to his heart. She brushed a kiss against her father's cheek. "Let's do this again very soon."

"Count on it." Steve shifted his gaze to Jeremy. "I'm entrusting my girl to your care."

Fin moved into his arms, her laugh breathless. "Dad can be a bit old-fashioned."

"You're safe with me."

"But are you safe with me?" Fin's eyes glittered like emeralds, and Jeremy wondered how much she'd had to drink. "That's the question."

The band launched into "My Girl" by the Temptations. Instead of moving to the music, Fin stiffened in his arms.

He gently stroked her back. "What's wrong?"

"It's nothing." This time the bright smile she flashed didn't reach her eyes.

"Tell me." Jeremy kept his tone low and soft, encouraging confidences.

"This was my mom and dad's song." She kept her gaze on the band. "I can see them dancing to it."

He tugged her closer. "Sounds like a happy memory."

"A bittersweet one." Fin rested her head against his shirtfront. "All I can think is she should be here now, dancing with Dad, surrounded by her children and friends."

"That would be nice." From the second Sarah Bloom had handed him a cookie when he was five, Jeremy had fallen for her. She'd had Marigold's bright blue eyes and Prim's strawberry blonde hair. Ami had gotten her sweet temperament, while Fin's strong will was classic Sarah.

"You love my daughter." Jeremy recalled how her bony fingers had gripped his hand one day when he'd stopped over. "Promise me you'll take care of Fin. Make sure she's happy."

Guilt, hot and swift, swept through Jeremy. At that time he and Fin hadn't been a couple for years. But he'd made the promise, then forgotten about it. Fin had been in LA and, from all reports, was happy there.

The lyrics of the song washed over Jeremy as they danced. *I don't need no money, fortune or fame . . .*

The songwriter nailed it. Nothing mattered without the one you loved by your side.

Jeremy realized he wouldn't give up. Couldn't give up. He would fight for Fin, for *them*. Not because of a promise made to a dying mother. Or because his grandmother was convinced Rakes married their first loves.

He would fight for Fin because she was the woman he loved. No one, especially not some Pompous Ass Hollywood director, could love her as much as he did.

Fin might not realize she was engaged to the wrong man, but she would soon realize there was only one man for her.

That man was Jeremy Rakes.

"I wasn't sure what to expect." Fin slanted a sideways glance at Jeremy as they walked, fingers entwined, toward the bedroom.

He paused when they reached the door and turned to face her. There had been so many people, so much activity, that it had been difficult to keep track of Fin.

Each time his gaze had searched the room and settled on her, she'd been laughing or talking with someone different. Even though her entire family had been there, she'd seemed determined to make all the guests feel welcome.

Her ability to make a person feel special had always been one of her many strengths.

Without giving himself a chance to reconsider, Jeremy swept her into his arms. He began to dance with her, humming a tune he hadn't been able to get out of his head.

"Hey, what are you doing?" Fin asked, even as she swayed back and forth with him.

Though the hall didn't give them much room to move, it was enough. Especially since he held her extra close. "I would think it'd be obvious. We're dancing."

He dipped her low and she laughed.

"The tune is one we danced to earlier." Jeremy's heart swelled with emotion as he recalled the lyrics.

"I like it." Fin threaded her fingers through his hair. "And I like you, my temporary fiancé."

"Good to know." Somehow he managed to keep his tone light, even as the words "they can't take that away from me" ran through his head.

As Fin continued to thread her fingers through his hair, the words changed to "they can't take *you* away from me."

"The party was a blast. How could it not be?" She leaned back in his arms. "You and I have so many friends in common. It was like one big reunion."

Now that the house was empty save for Ruby, who'd gone up to bed a few minutes ago, Jeremy brought up the name of the man he'd avoided mentioning all evening. "Is it like that with you and Xander?"

Confusion clouded her eyes. "What are you asking?"

How things stood between her and Pompous Ass should be none of his business. "Do you have a lot of mutual friends?"

He half expected her to toss off some answer that said nothing, or maybe make a joke. Instead, her brows drew together as if carefully considering the question. "I'd say most of the people we socialize with are his friends. A few have become mine. I don't have that much in common with them."

Jeremy wasn't certain if she was speaking about the friends or Xander. "What about the film industry? You have that in common."

"In a way." The tiny little pucker remained between her brows. "But the development company I work for is more on the fringes of the industry, while Xan and his friends are in the trenches."

A knot formed in Jeremy's stomach. She had a pet name for the guy. *Xan.*

Jeremy wasn't sure what he planned to say next, because when she stroked his arm, it short-circuited his brain.

Not only did she look terrific, she smelled unbelievable. The pleasant, citrusy scent, either perfume or shampoo, had caught his attention several times tonight when she'd stepped close.

The party had been enjoyable, so much so that as he'd accepted congratulations, it had been easy to forget that their engagement was a sham. Jeremy wondered if it had been the same for Fin. If not, she was one heck of an actress.

He forced his attention back to the conversation, to her remark about Xander and his friends. "What do your friends think about you two getting married?"

"They don't know. It happened so quickly." She waved a vague hand. "I'm sure he's waiting for me to return so we can tell them together."

"Will they be surprised?"

"Some will be." Fin spoke in an offhand tone that he guessed was anything but offhand.

Jeremy suddenly recalled Marigold's remark about Fin planning to break up with him. He was beginning to get a good picture of the state of Fin's relationship with the Pompous Ass. "Answer a question for me."

Fin smiled. "Anything."

"Are we going to stand out in the hall all night?" He reached around her and flung open the door to *their* bedroom. "Or step inside and get comfortable?"

Fin opened the bedroom door. The sight of the vase of daisies on the mantel brought a smile to her lips.

The sitting room off Jeremy's master suite had begun to feel like a sanctuary. It was a place where she could slip off her shoes and prop her feet up on the ottoman. A place where makeup and hair didn't matter. Heck, where even clothes didn't matter.

Not that she would ever run around naked in Jeremy's presence, but the cotton pajamas she'd borrowed from Ami would work just fine. "I'm going to—"

Fin paused at the silver bucket on a table by the mantel. "What's that?"

"I don't know." Jeremy strode past her and pulled out a bottle of Dom Perignon.

"Nice." Fin loved the taste of expensive champagne. "Who's it from?"

"There's a note." Jeremy lifted the card tucked under one of the flutes as Fin crossed to him.

She stared at the elegant script. "That looks like your grandmother's handwriting."

While Jeremy scanned the note, Fin realized it was just like Ruby to go to the extra effort to make an already wonderful evening even more special.

Without saying a word, Jeremy handed the ivory vellum card to her. She'd been wrong. The champagne wasn't from Ruby but from Jeremy's parents. Her throat tightened as she read the words Ruby had written: *Ed and Cheryl couldn't be with you tonight, but they want you to know how pleased they are with the engagement.*

His grandmother's flowery script continued. *To you, Jeremy, they say, "We knew when you were sixteen that Fin was the only woman for you. We view this engagement as love and destiny joining hands and coming together." To you, Delphinium, they say, "As you take this next step on life's journey with our son, remember love is best when shared with a partner who is not only your true love, but your best friend." Love and best wishes to you both as you begin this beautiful journey. Mom and Dad.*

Tears stung the backs of Fin's eyes. She couldn't believe Jeremy's parents had given their blessing.

"Wow." She was the one to finally break the silence. "That was unexpected."

Jeremy moved behind her and began gently kneading her shoulders, his voice even deeper than normal. "Not so unexpected."

"Sure it is. They always hoped you'd end up with Eliza."

"My dad always referred to that as Cheryl and Patricia's plan." His voice held a touch of humor. "They're both smart enough to realize I need to choose my own wife. Marriage can be challenging, even when you marry your best friend."

She wondered if he was thinking about his parents. "Yours went through that rough patch when you were in high school."

"They did." Jeremy's hands stilled on her shoulders. "My dad confided they made it through that time because, when all was said and done, the love he felt for my mother was stronger than what life tossed at them."

Fin thought of Xander. His parents had split when he was ten. During their time together he'd made a couple of remarks about sometimes needing to cut your losses and move on. Of course, they'd been discussing a situation where an actor had been physically abusive to his wife.

She'd agreed, but realized now that they'd never discussed couples staying together when love wasn't fresh and new anymore.

Fin thought of the words Jeremy's parents had written. Was Xander her best friend?

The feel of Jeremy's lips on the back of her neck had Fin inhaling sharply, and thoughts of Xander fled.

If she'd been thinking, Fin might have whirled around and asked what he was doing. But at the moment, her mind was focused on the sweet sensations traveling all the way to the tips of her toes.

"You smell so good." Those treacherous lips were on the move, stopping at the sensitive area behind her ear. "I need to see if you taste as good as you smell."

Fin tilted her head to one side, giving him greater access to that side of her neck. When guilt threatened to rear its ugly head, she reminded herself Xander had said kissing Jeremy was okay with him.

Right now, it was okay with her, too.

With hands on her shoulders, Jeremy spun her around to face him. The eyes that bored into hers were dark and almost feral. For a second Fin thought he was going to say something. Instead his mouth closed over hers.

This kiss bore little resemblance to the ones they'd shared since she'd returned to Good Hope. This was a kiss of possession, one that said more clearly than any words *this woman is mine.*

Fin wound her arms around his neck and let herself sink into the exquisite sensation. After all these years, after everything that had happened between them, how could being in his arms still feel so darn right?

Only when his fingers moved to the zipper at the back of her dress, only when she felt the cool air on her bare skin, did alarm bells sound. It was time—past time, really—to call a stop to this madness.

Yet the feel of his warm palms sliding up her bare skin brought an ache of longing so intense it took all her strength to utter a single word. "Stop."

His hands stilled on her now-burning flesh, and the lips that had been planting kisses along the underside of her jaw froze.

Jeremy raised his head, and his hands dropped to his sides. He didn't say a word, only stared.

Fin felt her face warm. "I-I'm engaged." Then before he could speak, she added so there would be no confusion, "To another man. My word means something."

His mouth tightened and he stepped back. "That's convenient."

The mocking tone had irritation taking the place of the passion that had burned so hot seconds earlier. She pulled her dress up, settling it back into place with quick, jerky movements. "What do you mean by that?"

He whirled, then turned back just as abruptly, a belligerent look in his brilliant blue eyes. "I seem to recall you once promising to love me forever. You didn't have any problem breaking *that* promise."

Beneath the cold expression, the icy tone, Fin saw the hurt. For a second she was tempted to come clean. To break down the wall she'd erected between them for her own self-preservation. To tell him what had happened all those years ago on the show choir trip to Milwaukee.

Would he understand how scared and alone she'd felt? How guilty? She hadn't even confided in her sisters. She'd kept the shame all to herself.

But she feared if she told him, even now, he might blame her as she blamed herself. Plus, he had a lot on his mind right now. She didn't need to add to that overflowing plate something that had happened a lifetime ago.

"I was a child when I made that promise, Jeremy."

He stared at her for a long moment, and she watched the fury fade. "You've always known your own mind, *Finley*."

Relief flooded her at his pet name for her. She exhaled a ragged breath.

"Back then, you may have decided you no longer wanted me. But we both know you wanted me tonight." His gaze dropped to the front of the dress she hugged against her chest. "You made a promise to Xander, but your actions tonight prove you haven't given him your heart. I suggest you think long and hard before you marry a man you don't love."

"Do you think God wants to see you pay for the things you've done?"

The pastor's voice, deep and passionate, filled the nearly full sanctuary.

The last place Fin wanted to be this morning was church. But Ruby had suggested the three of them attend together, and Fin couldn't disappoint her.

So after a night filled with visions from the past, Fin had drenched her eyes with Visine and covered the dark shadows with expertly applied concealer. Thankfully, Jeremy had already left the suite by the time she'd rolled out of bed.

Fin had found him and Ruby in the kitchen, laughing about something over a cup of coffee. For Ruby's sake, she pretended everything was fine between her and Jeremy. By the time they reached the church, Fin felt confident she had her emotions firmly under control.

That is, until Dan had launched into his sermon. For several minutes it felt as if he were speaking directly to her. Which was why she tuned him out.

"Such a wonderful message about forgiveness and grace," Ruby whispered.

The minister was a good orator, Fin would give him that, but she wasn't buying what he was selling. She was still reeling from last night's turmoil.

After their conversation, she and Jeremy had gotten ready for bed in silence. When he called good night to her from the sofa bed—in an obviously conciliatory gesture—she'd wanted to weep.

Actually, at that moment, she'd wanted nothing more than to pack her bags, get in the rental car, and drive back to California. Only the promise she'd made to Xander, and yes, to Jeremy, kept her head on the pillow. Regardless of what Mr. Jeremy Rakes might think of her, she kept her promises. Even one made long ago to a boy under the light of the moon.

Being back in Good Hope was turning out to be more of a challenge than she'd anticipated. But she was strong. She'd get through this just like she'd gotten through all the other difficult times in her life, one step at a time.

"God does not keep a record of your sins."

Fin fought a sudden urge to put her hands over her ears to more fully block Dan's voice. She had enough to handle without letting the past mess with her head.

Finally, *thankfully*, Dan stopped preaching. Soon after, the service ended. As was their habit during nice weather, the parishioners gathered on the front lawn. Jeremy remained by her side, playing the role of the devoted fiancé to perfection.

Ruby took off with several friends for an impromptu brunch celebrating her return to good health while Fin's family left for Muddy Boots. Ever since Beck had taken over the café several years earlier, it had become *the* place to gather on Sunday mornings. Apparently this was especially the case for singles.

How had Marigold referred to it? Ah yes, the postchurch Sunday meat market.

Fin listened as Jeremy got an earful from Floyd Lawson. The portly rotarian with the snow-white beard played Santa Claus every Christmas. Though he appeared currently up in arms about some water pollution issue, Fin found herself wondering what Floyd's stand was on delaying the Christmas celebration until January. She decided it best not to ask Santa.

"Fin." Lynn Chapin strode up, hands outstretched. "Such a lovely party last night."

Fin smiled warmly, grateful for the distraction. "I'm happy you could make it. Is my father with you?"

"I haven't seen him." Though her voice remained casual, two bright spots of pink dotted Lynn's cheeks. "Not since he dropped me off at my house a little after midnight."

"Oh." Fin couldn't hide her surprise. "I assumed the two of you . . ."

Catching sight of the minister out of her peripheral vision, Fin let her voice trail off.

"Your father and I are taking things slow." Lynn's bright smile dimmed slightly. "The breakup with Anita was difficult for him. Though Steve came to realize she wasn't the one for him, he still cares for her."

"It's not easy to let go of the safe and secure." Fin stopped, not sure where her thoughts had been headed. "But I'm glad he did."

"Me too." Lynn flashed a quick smile, then lowered her voice. "I can tell Floyd is winding down, so I wanted to make sure of the time."

"Time?"

"Decorating the barn for Mindy."

Fin nearly groaned. She'd forgotten all about that activity. Good Hope might appear to be a sleepy little community, but Fin swore there was more going on here than in LA. "Eliza said noon, but come whenever works for you."

Floyd, dapper in his three-piece suit, shook Jeremy's hand, nodded to Fin and Lynn before striding off.

Jeremy turned to Fin. "Sorry. Floyd can be a bit long-winded."

"No worries." Fin let her gaze linger on her fake fiancé. During the service her wandering gaze had observed men wearing everything from shorts and flip-flops to suits. Jeremy's khakis and cotton shirt fell somewhere in between.

The thin blue stripes in the shirt made his eyes look extra blue, and the way the fabric stretched across his broad shoulders had her mouth going dry. He looked absolutely yummy. And he smelled just as terrific, like hot buttered rum.

While Jeremy couldn't have gotten much more sleep than she had, he looked surprisingly well rested. He offered Lynn a warm smile. "How are you this morning?"

"I'm doing well." Lynn settled a hand on Fin's arm. "I was just telling your fiancée that Steve and I plan to come out and help decorate the barn."

For the first time that morning, Jeremy gave Fin his entire attention. "Glad to hear it."

Then Jeremy surprised her by slinging a warm arm around her shoulders. If it wasn't an apology, it felt like one. Any remaining tension slid from Fin's body into the soft grass at her feet.

As the three of them chatted, Fin leaned against Jeremy in her own gesture of apology. When she looked up at him and he smiled back, she knew they were back on solid footing.

At least for now.

Chapter Fifteen

"I can't believe it all got done." Fin stood next to Jeremy in front of the barn, now festooned with brightly colored strings of lights and ever-green wreaths with big red velvet bows.

Volunteers had shown up in such numbers it had taken all of Fin's organizational skills to keep everyone productive. Jeremy and a few other men, including her brothers-in-law and father, had taken on the task of putting the lights on the barn. Kyle Kendrick had surprised everyone when he'd shown up, bringing scaffolding and some of his crew to assist in the effort.

Once the men had finished, they'd moved to string miles of pink fairy lights—pink being Mindy's favorite color—inside billowing pale pink glittering tulle from the barn's rafters. Once again, Kyle's equipment had proved invaluable.

A life-size reindeer stood at the entrance to the corn maze. A large wreath had been placed around his neck, and his antlers held candles with tips that lit up at the flick of a switch. He wore a pink tulle skirt and sparkly pink ballet shoes had his hoofs *en pointe*. The plan was for Santa—also known as Floyd Lawson—to be waiting with treat bags and a big ho-ho-ho for the children as they exited the maze.

Izzie Deshler, a local painter whose artistic eye extended to photography, would be there to capture the memories.

Inside the barn, a photo booth had been set up with a variety of props including fluffy Santa beards and oversize red-and-green glasses. Eliza had told Fin that they wanted to make sure that Mindy and her parents had plenty of pictures of this event.

Tables that would be used as cake-decorating stations, then for writing letters to Santa, stood ready.

"If we wouldn't have had all the volunteers, and Kyle's equipment, it would have taken all day instead of a couple of hours." Jeremy's smile widened. "Thanks for helping, Dan."

"It was my pleasure." The minister glanced around. "Mindy is going to love this."

"How's she doing?" Fin thought Your Wish Fulfilled events were only for terminally ill children, but Katie Ruth had clarified it was also for kids with life-threatening illnesses.

"Her last scan showed some tumor shrinkage. Owen is hopeful." Dan lifted a hand when Lindsay stepped from the barn. "Thanks for lending your barn. I know it's much appreciated."

"It's the Good Hope way," Fin found herself saying. "Neighbors helping neighbors."

"Any word from Tessa?" Jeremy asked in a too-casual tone that had Fin's ears pricking up.

Dan's warm smile faded. "Not a word."

Fin frowned. "Who's Tessa?"

"Mindy's mother. She left shortly after Mindy was diagnosed." Dan's voice held no judgment. "She said it was too much for her. She and Owen are divorced."

"Poor, sweet girl." Fin knew what it was like to lose a mother.

"She's a sweetheart," Dan agreed, then glanced around. "Ah, there's Lindsay. If you'll excuse me . . ."

As the minister strolled off, Fin caught Jeremy staring.

Jeremy slung an arm around Fin's shoulder and gave her a one-armed hug. "You've got such a big heart."

Fin brushed aside what sounded like a compliment with the flick of one hand. "I still wish we could have had snow."

"The Your Wish Fulfilled coordinator told Katie Ruth there was some screwup with the scheduling." Jeremy's gaze slid back to the barn. "It looks like Christmas."

"Yes, it does."

All the volunteers appeared in high spirits, including nine high school girls, who composed Good Hope High's Triple Trio. They would be back on the big day to serenade Mindy and her friends.

Without realizing what was happening, Fin found herself harmonizing to a version of "Sleigh Ride." She flushed when she caught Jeremy staring. "What?"

"Nothing." As if to divert her attention, he lifted his hand and motioned to Lynn and her father.

The gesture appeared totally unnecessary, as the two were already headed their way.

"This was so much fun." Lynn's cheeks were flushed and her blue eyes sparkled.

Even dressed casually in jeans and a simple, sleeveless top, Fin thought she looked exceedingly pretty this afternoon. From the way her father was gazing at her, he agreed.

"Having all my girls, including this one"—Steve bumped Lynn's shoulder with his—"here and working together . . ." Her father paused to clear his throat. "Well, I can't imagine a better day."

"I know it's been a busy one." Lynn hesitated. "Steve and I were wondering if you and Jeremy would join us in a round of miniature golf this afternoon. We've been wanting to play but hadn't found a time."

"Since we got through with the decorating so quickly . . ." Steve slanted Fin a hopeful glance.

Fin considered. Hadn't she promised herself she was going to make the most of her time here?

When she glanced in Jeremy's direction and got a nod, Fin smiled. "What time do you want to meet?"

Xander's laughter boomed through the phone. Fin tightened her fingers around it, grateful she'd put him on speaker once she'd stepped outside.

"I don't see what's so amusing." Despite her irritation, Fin kept her tone pleasant as she strolled down the garden path. Still feeling a little guilty over what had almost happened with Jeremy in the bedroom Saturday night, she'd called her fiancé.

To her surprise, Xander answered on the first ring. As this was the first time they'd had a chance to speak in several days, she kept a smile on her lips and in her voice.

"Mini golf, that's what's so funny." The laughter eased a bit, but humor still laced the words. "Does this course have a little windmill thing with paddles?"

To calm her rising temper, Fin focused on the brilliant autumn red of a burning bush as his laughter began again. "You seem in a good mood today."

"My life is finally taking off," Xander continued, bringing up the club he'd been to last night, bragging about who'd been there and the conversations he'd had with movers and shakers in the film industry. "Once you nail down this site for me, it's smooth sailing."

She waited for him to say something about how much he appreciated her efforts. Actually, she hoped he'd say he missed her and couldn't wait until they were together again.

When he only continued to drop names of people and places, she took the offensive. "I bet it felt strange not having me there."

"What?" He paused, and she realized he'd started up again about the party. "Of course. But you'd have been bored silly. Even Jessica was ready to leave early."

Fin's ears pricked up at the name. "You were at the party with Jessica Atherton?"

For a millisecond, silence filled the line.

"Not *with* her." Xander gave a hearty chuckle. "She was there. I was there."

"Did you two leave the party together when she got bored?" She kept her tone steady even as her blood began to boil.

Fin had once suspected Xander had a thing for his young assistant, but he'd assured her the only relationship he was interested in cultivating was with Jessica's director father, Harvey.

"I gave her a lift home after her friend ditched her." Annoyance now filled Xander's voice. "Just because you've got a ring on your finger doesn't mean you get to put me on a leash and bring me to heel."

Fin spoke through gritted teeth. "I asked a simple question."

"Don't play the innocent with me. You're out there snuggled up with your former lover and I'm taking the heat?" Xander's voice turned sharp as a steel-edged blade. "Ever heard of projection? Tell me, what games have you and the good mayor been playing that has you suddenly questioning my behavior?"

Fin spent the last five minutes of the call explaining herself to him. It wasn't until he'd hung up that she realized Xander had once again put her on the defensive.

The man was a master at turning the tables anytime she questioned his behavior. She wondered if he'd done more than take Jessica home. If he had, no one would raise a brow, even if they'd known he was engaged.

"Everything okay?"

Fin closed her eyes at the sound of Jeremy's voice. She took a deep breath and let it out slowly while dropping the phone into her bag. When she turned, a smile was on her lips. "Everything is fine. Just updating Xander."

His gaze searched her face. In the sunlight's glow his eyes were clear and very blue. "I want to speak with you."

"Did you change your mind about golfing?"

A puzzled look stole across his face. "Why would I change my mind?"

"It's a silly game." She couldn't get what Xander had said—especially the sneer in his voice—out of her head. "Who gets excited over hitting a ball into a windmill?"

"Easy for you to say, Miss Mini Golf Champion. I don't recall your ball being smacked back to you by one of those revolving sails."

The teasing comment had Fin's lips curving in a genuine smile. Her prowess on the mini golf course was legendary. From the time she could whack a ball straight into the clown's mouth, her sisters had threatened not to play with her.

Jeremy had always seen the losses as a challenge.

"You're going down." She shot Jeremy a teasing look. "I'll even spot you two strokes. It won't matter. You'll still lose."

"Sassy as ever." The wink he shot her said he approved. "I have a question."

Fin reached over and pulled a couple of cherries from a tree next to the path. Breaking the stem apart, she handed a cherry to Jeremy and kept one for herself. "Ask away."

"When was the last time you played?" His gaze remained on her lips as she popped the bit of fruit into her mouth and chewed.

Under the direct gaze, her lips began to tingle. Likely a reaction to the cherry's tartness.

"High school, probably." Fin's forehead furrowed as she tried to recall if she'd played since. "For sure it hasn't been since they built the new course."

"I played last month. I had the low score of the foursome." Jeremy's boast matched his smug smile.

"Who were you playing with?" Fin immediately regretted asking. If he said Eliza, well, she didn't want that image in her head.

"It was an end-of-the-school-year activity sponsored by the education council."

She narrowed her gaze. "End of school?"

"I golfed with three fifth-grade boys."

A picture came into sharp focus. She rolled her eyes. "Three boys who likely spent their time on the course either swatting one another with the clubs or making farting noises by putting the balls in their armpits."

"How did you know?" Astonishment flickered across Jeremy's face. "You have sisters."

"I have twin nephews. All I have to do is picture Callum and Connor in three years." Fin laughed. "No wonder you won."

"You're altogether too confident." Jeremy studied her through slitted eyes even as a smile tugged at the corners of his lips. "You're the one going down."

"Wanna bet?" she taunted.

"I won't need a two-stroke spot, either."

"Ohhh, big words." It was a ridiculous conversation, but it felt good to be back on solid footing. Felt good to laugh and tease. "Willing to put money on the line?"

"Not money." Jeremy's gaze held a wicked gleam. "We can talk about payment once I win."

"Okay. We'll talk about payment . . . once I win." Fin twirled the empty cherry stem between her thumb and forefinger. There was no reason for further discussion on the payment he planned to exact.

There was no way he was going to win.

Fin had seen no reason to mention to Xander she'd be playing the course with her father and his girlfriend. In his mind that would likely make the Sunday-afternoon adventure sound even more lame. Of course, he may have approved if he'd remembered her dad's girlfriend was Lynn Chapin.

Looking stylish but comfortable in pale blue capris, a white collared shirt, and a pair of Toms, Lynn clearly was comfortable on the course. Fin had no doubt the banker could have achieved a respectable score if she hadn't spent so much time talking.

When Fin found herself on the verge of telling the others to get serious, she realized they were on a miniature golf course, not Pebble Beach. How long had it been since she'd allowed herself to simply relax and have a good time?

Impossible to say.

"Gladys is hysterical on the golf course," Lynn told her and Steve while Jeremy eyed the volcano, which had red lava painted down its sides and boasted a single small hole at its base. "We had two subs round out our foursome at the country club last week. Gladys told the women, when they asked her handicap, that she was a scratch golfer."

"Really?" Fin inclined her head. "She's that good?"

Lynn smiled. "When they looked suitably impressed, she told them if she doesn't like a score, she scratches it out."

Steve chuckled.

"They didn't know what to say." There was fondness in Lynn's smile. "I only hope I'm that sharp at ninety-six."

Fin didn't know what to think when her father slipped an arm around Lynn's shoulders.

"You're a good friend to her." Steve's warm tone matched the look in his eyes.

The obvious affection in the words had Lynn's cheeks turning a becoming shade of pink. "She's a good friend. An amazing woman."

Jeremy looked up in triumph when his ball slid down the ramp and straight into the mouth of the red volcano.

"Not bad, hotshot." Fin exchanged a high five with Jeremy before returning her attention to Lynn. "Did having different opinions on the movie shoot cause any tension in your friendship with Gladys?"

Lynn turned slightly to Fin, obviously content to remain close to Steve. "You're referring to the proposal to delay the Christmas festivities until January?"

Fin nodded and saw her father's smile slip.

"When we were elected to the town board, Gladys and I agreed to disagree. We each take our fiduciary duty seriously and strive to make the best decisions possible."

"You're up, Lynn." Steve's tone seemed overly jovial.

Lynn pursed her lips. "A mighty small little hole in that volcano."

"Piece of cake for a golfer of your caliber." Steve gave Lynn's shoulders a supportive squeeze, then stepped back.

When Lynn moved to the line to study the slope leading up to the hole, her father spoke in a low voice to Fin. "Do you have to discuss business *now*?"

Puzzled by his terse tone, Fin hesitated. "I thought that's why you invited her."

"I invited Lynn because I like her. I want her to get to know all my girls." Steve's whisper held a hint of warning. "I don't want talk of business to ruin the afternoon."

Jeremy moved close. Knowing he'd overheard, Fin tensed and waited for him to side with her father.

"Your daughter is under an extremely tight deadline." Jeremy's tone, while respectful, was firm. "She needs to seize every opportunity."

The look he shot Steve dared him to disagree.

"I suppose." Her father's agreement came haltingly, with obvious reluctance.

"Yes." Lynn's fist shot into the air.

Fin glanced at the green and watched the ball disappear into the tiny hole.

They all cheered. In deference to her father, Fin waited until they stopped for ice cream to revisit the topic.

"I'm fascinated by city government." Fin paused to lick the dribble of key lime ice cream snaking down the side of her cone. "Can you tell me anything about the discussion surrounding the decision to turn down the Christmas proposal?"

Her father bit off the top of his chocolate cone.

"It wasn't as straightforward as you might think." Lynn dipped her spoon into the mound of chocolate in her dish. "There was a lot of discussion. The money we were being offered was significant. While we have a healthy economy in Good Hope, the town's budgetary needs continue to grow, and no one on the board wants to increase taxes. Gladys believes the money would offset any loss in revenue as well as provide extra funding for other community projects."

"I tend to agree with Gladys." Fin took another lick of ice cream, more to give the comment time to sink in than out of hunger. "I bet news that a big film production was happening in Good Hope would be a huge tourist draw."

"That's what Gladys argued." Two lines formed between Lynn's brows. "I have to admit her being in favor of this particular project surprised me."

Fin wasn't surprised. Gladys was an actor. Of course she'd want a major film production in her town. Heck, she was probably hoping to snag a walk-on.

As they continued to stroll down the downtown sidewalk, Fin kept her tone casual. "Why was her support unexpected?"

"Gladys has been around a long time." Lynn's coral lips curved upward as she took the arm Steve offered. "The Twelve Nights, the Victorian home tour, those are staples of the December festivities. I thought Gladys would be more sentimental."

Fin exchanged a look with Jeremy. She wished they had a moment alone so she could ask if he agreed with Lynn's assessment. But he'd given her this opportunity, and Fin wasn't about to waste it. "Is that why you voted against it? Out of sentiment?"

Lynn slanted a surprised look in Fin's direction.

Clearly she hadn't expected her to pursue the discussion past a few questions.

"Since Fin has been living in LA, she's become very interested in the film industry." Jeremy smiled at Fin, and she recognized the deliberateness of the gesture. He was reminding Lynn, without saying the words, that they were a team. "In fact, I believe she's acquainted with Xander Tillman."

Fin wanted to slam her elbow into Jeremy's ribs. She settled for a smile.

It took her several seconds to realize Jeremy had brought up her relationship with Xander to protect her. When she returned to LA and her engagement to the director was announced, the connection would have been established.

Lynn seemed intrigued by Fin's connection with Xander. "Mr. Tillman appeared sincere in his desire to film here."

"He's convinced this is the perfect location." Jeremy tossed the comment out there before finishing off his cone.

Fin glanced at Jeremy.

His expression gave nothing away. "That's why it's back on the agenda. Since the board was evenly split and I've been approached by so many business owners who felt they weren't given a proper chance to be heard, I figured it deserved another look."

"Eliza won't change her vote." Lynn spoke with a surety that told Fin she'd been right to focus on the woman at her father's side. "I guess that leaves me."

"Is there a possibility you'll change your vote?" Her father finally spoke.

Fin shot him a grateful glance. With everyone participating, this appeared to be nothing more than a simple conversation between the four of them. As Lynn scooped up another spoonful of Rocky Road, Fin's heart stilled in watchful waiting.

Lynn Chapin had a spine of steel. Which was something Fin admired in a woman. But in this instance, she wished Lynn was a little more malleable.

She needed Lynn to see Xander's side. She needed her to change her vote. The clock was ticking. If the town board once again rejected the proposal, Jeremy's tiebreaking vote would be the only thing standing between losing Xander and her job.

Fin could shift her focus to convincing Jeremy but preferred not to do that unless absolutely necessary.

Much better—much simpler—if Lynn would reconsider.

"I like to believe I have an open mind." Lynn smiled at Steve. "Though I can be headstrong at times."

Fin's father flashed a smile and paused as they reached their vehicles. "Never noticed."

They exchanged looks that reminded Fin of two love-struck teens. When her father and Lynn turned to the car, Fin realized that other than learning Lynn's objections to the project, she hadn't accomplished much.

She decided to pursue the sentimental angle when Jeremy's hand tightened around her arm. Glancing up, she caught the barely perceptible shake of his head.

Fin almost pushed forward anyway. But her father had already stepped to his car to open the door, and Lynn was glancing at her wrist.

"I'm sorry to have to cut this short, but I'm watching my granddaughter this evening. David has a big project he's finishing up, and Camille has the night off."

Fin cocked her head. "Camille?"

"The nanny."

The next logical question would be to ask where was Whitney, but Fin didn't need to be warned to keep her mouth shut. She kept up on the local gossip and was aware Lynn's daughter-in-law spent a lot of time away from home.

"Have fun with your granddaughter." Fin tossed the rest of her cone into one of the high-tech solar trash cans the town was trying out in the downtown area. "We'll have to get together to discuss the All About Kids project."

"Absolutely." Lynn paused, hand on the top of the car. "How about I text you my availability? We'll find a time that works for both of us."

"Perfect." Fin and Jeremy remained at the curb while her father rounded the vehicle after closing Lynn's door.

Her dad, always the gentleman. He paused in front of Fin and gave her a quick hug. "It's good having you back. We'll have to do this again."

"I had fun." Despite what Xander had predicted, playing the "lame" game of mini golf and then enjoying an ice cream treat had been very enjoyable.

Could it be that she was a small-town girl at heart?

Fin nearly chuckled at the thought.

She and Jeremy remained on the sidewalk until her father's sedan disappeared from view.

Jeremy clapped a warm hand on her shoulder. "Well, Miss Mini Golf, I suppose it's time to head home."

Fin hesitated. She wasn't ready for the day to end. Then she reminded herself that she wouldn't be returning to an empty apartment. She'd be going home with Jeremy.

When Jeremy reached around her to open the passenger-side door—he was as much of a gentleman as her dad—she shot him a teasing smile. "On the way home we'll discuss payment."

He raised a brow.

"I won the game." Fin felt a surge of satisfaction.

Jeremy opened his mouth, then shut it. "Something tells me I should have clarified what you'd expect if you won."

Fin turned and rested her back against the car, feeling cheerful. "Yes. You definitely should have."

Chapter Sixteen

Jeremy supposed making dinner wasn't too high a price to pay. Not compared to the other penalties Fin might have extracted. She obviously wasn't aware that over the years he'd become quite proficient in the kitchen.

Before Fin had headed into the suite, he'd told her to prepare to be dazzled. She hadn't believed him.

"Something smells good." Ruby sauntered into the kitchen, her eyes clear and her cheeks nicely pink. The older woman lifted a brow. "Where's Delphinium?"

"In the bedroom, freshening up."

"Did you have fun golfing today?"

"We did." Jeremy turned from the skillet. "Fin mopped up the course with the rest of us."

"Did I hear my name?" Fin strolled into the room.

She'd changed from the cropped pants and polo shirt into a cotton dress the color of sunshine. Her hair, previously pulled back into some kind of knot, now hung loose to her shoulders.

Something in the way the dress was cut made him wonder if she was wearing a bra. Ignoring the fact that just the wondering had his body stirring, Jeremy lifted a wooden spoon in welcome. Then he stirred the contents of a large iron pot on the stove.

"Jeremy was just telling me that you, my dear, had a stellar day on the course." Ruby held out her arms and Fin moved in for a hug. "Congratulations."

Fin smiled and glanced at the stove. "What are we having?"

"Chicken and barley stew. Hearty. Healthy." Jeremy shot his grandmother a wink.

"Soups and stews were staples in my house growing up." Fin moved to the stove, appearing curious. "Look at all those vegetables."

"Because we were pressed for time, I used a package of frozen mixed vegetables." Jeremy glanced at his grandmother. "No additional sodium, so it's heart healthy."

"Is that bread I smell?"

Jeremy hid a smile. He remembered her love of carbs. "I have a corn-and-millet loaf on warm that Dinah made yesterday. The credit is all hers on the bread."

A look of amazement crossed Fin's face. "How, *why*, did you learn to cook like this?"

"My mother was determined I know more than how to nuke a freezer dinner. Grandma Ruby showed me that cooking, even for one, could be relaxing at the end of a busy day." He slanted a smile in his grandmother's direction.

"How about you, dear?" Ruby asked, reaching for a ladle.

Fin, who'd started setting the table, looked up. "What about me?"

Ruby inclined her head. "Do you do much cooking?"

"No." Her answer came quickly. "Most nights I work late. By the time I get home, I usually settle for a yogurt with some cheese and maybe a piece of fruit."

Ruby simply nodded, as if that lifestyle was something she understood rather than a completely foreign animal. "Do you enjoy cooking when you do have the time?"

"To tell you the truth, it's been so long since I prepared a meal for myself, I'm not sure." Fin placed a red napkin on the table and thought for a moment. "I enjoy baking with my sisters when I'm back in Good Hope for the holidays."

With experienced, precise movements, Ruby ladled the soup into square, white bowls. "Do you anticipate having that same busy lifestyle after the wedding?"

Jeremy's eyes met hers, warning her to take her time. It would be easy to get tripped up.

"Life here runs at a slower pace. It's one of Good Hope's most seductive charms." Fin smiled and sauntered to the stove. She opened the oven door and slid out the bread.

Not wanting to be outdone, Ruby placed the bowls of soup onto a tray.

Jeremy put a restraining hand on her arm. "You sit. Fin and I will put the food on the table."

Ruby smiled, her easy acquiescence taking him by surprise.

"You're already working together as a team." Ruby's gaze shifted to Fin. "That warms my heart."

Jeremy also hoped it took her mind off the question she'd posed to Fin that had been answered in generalities.

However, once they were seated at the table with the tantalizing aroma of soup and bread in the air, Ruby fixed a sharp-eyed gaze on Fin. "What is it you plan to do after the wedding?"

Fin, who'd cut off a small bite of the crunchy bread, lifted it to her lips and took a moment to chew, then followed with an iced tea chaser.

Ruby didn't fill the silence with inane chatter; she simply waited, stirring her soup as if the tantalizing mixture were still simmering on the stove.

"I've enjoyed my position at Entertainment Quest immensely." Fin kept her tone matter-of-fact.

Ruby cocked her head. "It's going to be difficult for you to leave it."

"It will. Every step in my career over the past ten years led me to this point." Fin's green eyes turned distant, as if she were looking back over the decade.

"What is it you like so much about this position?" The soup forgotten, Ruby leaned forward, obviously eager for details.

That was the thing about Ruby, Jeremy thought. His grandmother had an insatiable curiosity about practically everything. It was only one of the things that kept her young at heart.

Surprise flickered across Fin's face, almost if she'd never been asked that question before.

"I'm a development executive. The firm I work for focuses on book-to-screen adaptations." Fin leaned forward, seeming to warm to the topic. "One of my favorite parts of my job is identifying a project with potential. There's nothing better than pitching a story I love to studio executives. I haven't been around long enough to see one of mine make it all the way to production."

"How do you know what to look for?" Ruby must have decided the soup had been stirred enough, since she took her first taste and gave Jeremy a thumbs-up.

"I have to know what has appeal to audiences as well as what makes a good film script." Following Ruby's lead, Fin took her first spoonful of soup. Her eyes widened. She shifted her attention to Jeremy. "This is good. Really good."

"Naturally." He gave her a wink.

Fin took another spoonful. Sighed in pleasure.

"Your job sounds interesting." Ruby inclined her head. "Do you enjoy your coworkers?"

"They're very successful." The words came easily. "Talented women with a lot of industry knowledge."

Ruby took a sip of tea. "I don't believe that's what I asked."

"Shirleen, the head of the firm, is intense and focused. All in a good way," Fin hastened to add, as if her boss were out in the hall right now, listening to the conversation. "Ours is a highly competitive business. You can't risk offending the studios or high-profile directors."

For the first time Jeremy realized the outcome of Fin's trip to Good Hope had implications going beyond doing Xander a favor.

"You'll miss it." Ruby's comment was a statement, not a question.

"I will." Fin met Ruby's gaze, then shifted those warm, green eyes to settle on Jeremy. She reached over and covered his hand with hers, lacing their fingers together. "But I can honestly say right now there isn't any place I'd rather be than here with you and Jeremy."

Chapter Seventeen

"I hope nothing is wrong." Fin touched Lynn's arm.

"I'm sure it's nothing. Brynn has been rather . . . emotional lately." Lynn's wan smile appeared forced. "Some of it is probably because Mindy is a good friend and she's worried about her. Then, there are other circumstances . . ."

Fin gave Lynn's shoulder a supportive squeeze but didn't press. And she stood back while her father walked Lynn to the door and enfolded her in his arms for several heartbeats.

She was sorry to see Lynn leave her father's Labor Day barbecue. Not because Fin wanted to press the woman about Xander's proposal. She'd already done that earlier in the afternoon.

The strangest thing was, when Lynn finally seemed to warm to the idea—or at least appeared to be considering it more seriously—Fin found her own support for the project wavering.

It was difficult to imagine Christmas in Good Hope without the Twelve Nights celebrations or Floyd, dressed as Santa, delivering Giving Tree presents in his 1980s red maxivan. The Christmas stroll, the caroling, the lights at every business window . . .

Just thinking of it had Fin choking up.

"Everything okay?"

The light hand on her arm had Fin looking into Ami's green eyes.

"I should be asking you that question." Fin kept her tone light, knowing Ami was sensitive to the fact that after threatening to come early, Baby Cross was making her and Beck wait.

She knew her sister had become a champion curb walker and had turned into a spicy food aficionado. Any increased sexual activity, well, that was between Ami and Beck.

"I'm hanging in there." Ami patted her belly, which appeared lower than it had only a few days earlier. Her sister cocked her head. "Are you worried about Ruby?"

"Not at all. She's spending the day with Gladys and several other friends." Fin smiled. "With cards, dominos, and Chinese checkers on the agenda, it'll be a wild time."

Ami chuckled. "I love Ruby."

"She told me the other day she'd already bought my Christmas present." Fin's lips curved.

"What is it?" Ami's green eyes gleamed with curiosity.

Fin shook her head. "She wouldn't tell me. Said I'd have to wait until Christmas."

By then she'd be back in LA, and everyone in Good Hope—except for her family—would hate her. Ruby might even hate her. Fin's smile slipped.

She couldn't think of that now, wouldn't think of that now.

"What do you think of delaying Christmas?" Fin asked her sister.

When Ami hesitated, Fin realized this was the first time she'd asked a family member for their opinion on Xander's plan. Even though she'd heard half the town opposed the project, she'd assumed her family supported it.

Because that's what you wanted to believe.

"If the town board votes to approve, I think we should forget about all the activities until next year. I mean, we'll still have the church service and Floyd will still deliver the Giving Tree presents to needy families. But the Twelve Nights . . ." Ami chewed on her bottom lip, her green eyes serious. "It won't be the same in January."

"The money Good Hope would receive for the filming will go a long way toward strengthening the town coffers." Fin pulled out the argument that had seemed to impress the businesswoman part of Lynn Chapin.

"I know." Ami brushed back a strand of hair and sighed. "But I can't help thinking of Mom and Christmas the year before she died. For some in Good Hope, this will be their last Christmas."

That was an argument Fin didn't intend to touch. "I bet there's a lot of people who might enjoy having activities in January. Other than New Year's Day, it's a rather dull month."

Doubt blanketed Ami's face. "But will the events in January overshadow the Cherries' activities leading up to Valentine's Day? I don't know the answer, Fin."

"I don't know, either." A lump sat heavy in Fin's throat. "I'm not sure anymore how I feel about closing down the town in December. No caroling in the town square. No Christmas stroll. And, like you, it's difficult to imagine Good Hope without the Twelve Nights."

Ami patted her arm. "Now you understand why the town is divided."

"There are no easy answers, are there?"

"There may be," Ami conceded, "but I don't think I'm the one to find them. I'm exhausted from not sleeping well these last few nights and not thinking the best."

For the first time, Fin noticed the circles beneath her sister's eyes. Worry flooded her. "Is there anything I can do?"

"You've done it." Ami gripped her hand, her eyes moist. "Just by being here."

Stepping out onto the deck from the kitchen, Marigold stopped, her eyes taking in Fin's serious expression and Ami's tear-filled eyes. "What's wrong?"

"Nothing." Ami sniffed. "I'm just so h-happy to have all my sisters with me."

"Hoo-kay." Marigold, looking chic in all black, raked a hand through her tangled blonde curls.

Cade stepped from the hallway a second behind her, his hair looking as disheveled as hers. He gave her a swift kiss. "Time to beat the guys in horseshoes."

"What were you doing back there?" Fin asked.

"What do you think?" Marigold's eyes danced. "I was enjoying my man."

Fin rolled her eyes even as she fought a twinge of envy.

Marigold had spent years building a reputation as a top hair stylist in Chicago. Now she was building a name—and a life—in Good Hope, and doing it her way.

From everything Fin had heard, Marigold had all the business she wanted. And she had the man she loved . . .

All her sisters had found their princes. As had she, Fin reminded herself, glancing down at the diamond.

"Is this a private party? Or can anyone join?"

Fin lifted her gaze to see Hadley stepping into the backyard via the gate.

"I'm so happy you came." Ami practically squealed the words.

Ignoring the twinge of jealousy, Fin smiled and told herself that it was only expected that the two women had grown close. Hadley was Ami's second-in-command at the bakery. They saw each other nearly every day, while for the last ten years Fin had seen her sister only on holidays.

"I brought a box of apple doughnuts." Hadley set the bakery box on the glass-topped table still holding assorted salads, then her gaze narrowed on Ami. "You need to sit and put your feet up."

"We should all." Only when the words left Fin's mouth did she realize how demanding she sounded.

"I could sit." Prim strolled up the steps leading to the yard. "I just need a seat facing the yard. Just in case the boys decide croquet mallets would make good weapons."

For now the redheaded twins were playing the game under the supervision of their uncle Beck.

"I could use another Corona." Marigold slanted a glance at Hadley. "Can I get you one?"

Hadley hesitated. "If you're certain I'm not intruding."

Going with impulse, Fin looped her arm through Hadley's, surprising them both. "This is a perfect opportunity for us to get better acquainted."

Thirty minutes later, the women lounged on the deck. Beer had given way to mugs filled with cider. The bakery box that once held apple doughnuts dusted with cinnamon sugar now held only crumbs.

Fin dabbed at her lips with a napkin. "If I keep eating like that, I'm going to have to get a seat belt extender when I fly back to LA."

Surprise flickered across Hadley's face. "You're going back?"

"You know how it is when you move." Marigold waved a hand in the air. "So many details to finalize. I only moved back here from Chicago and it was an ordeal."

Fin shot her youngest sister a grateful smile.

Despite the very logical explanation, Hadley still appeared suspicious.

"I know none of you are really into gossip, but I heard some news yesterday." Marigold leaned forward, effectively diverting everyone's attention from Fin's return to California.

"What kind of news?" Ami took a sip of her cider, her eyes bright with interest.

Marigold glanced around the table, not speaking until she was assured everyone's eyes were on her.

She's always been such a drama queen, Fin thought with a fondness that surprised her. While she loved all of her sisters, she and Marigold had often clashed. But that was ancient history. She was discovering she really liked the woman her youngest sister had become.

"David Chapin and Whitney are separated." Marigold spoke in a dramatic voice worthy of any stage actress. "Rumor is she's left town and hired an attorney."

Hadley's mug dropped to the table with a thud, splashing cider. Though the pretty blonde recovered almost instantly, Fin saw the flash of shock in her eyes.

"I'm sorry." Hadley quickly mopped up the spill with her napkin, her cheeks now flushed.

Fin lifted her own mug to drink and studied Hadley over the rim. *Something is off here.*

"I wonder if that had something to do with Lynn rushing off." Concern covered Ami's face.

"Probably." Marigold sat back. "I can't say I'm surprised by the news. Whitney was gone more than she was home. Definitely not the recipe for a happy relationship."

Fin thought of Xander. "Lots of couples lead separate lives."

Marigold shot her a *get real* look.

"Yeah, and how many of those relationships last?" Marigold lifted a hand, thumb and forefinger pinched together. "Big fat zero."

Though Fin supposed she should argue the point, she kept silent.

"What about Brynn?" came Hadley's quiet question.

Fin set down her mug without taking a sip. "Brynn?"

"Their daughter." Tears were back in Ami's eyes. "She's the same age as the twins."

"She's eight," Hadley supplied, then flushed when all eyes turned to her. "She and her father come into the bakery a lot. The last time she was in, she mentioned she'd just turned eight."

"The kid is living with her father." Marigold sat back in her chair. "Whitney didn't want to be tied down by a child or a husband."

"Poor little peanut." Ami frowned. "I wonder if there's anything I can do . . ."

"You have enough on your plate," Fin told her. "You're going to have a little peanut of your own any day now."

A faint smile lifted Ami's lips.

"What's David going to do?" Marigold wondered aloud. "Who will watch her when he's working?"

"He works primarily from home." Hadley spoke absently, her corn-flower-blue eyes now dark. "They have a nanny, Camille."

"That's right." Marigold snapped her fingers. "Camille brought her to a couple of Seedlings meetings."

"Camille also came with Brynn to T-ball practice. I don't think I ever saw Whitney there," Prim added.

"A nanny isn't the same as a mother." Hadley's troubled gaze told Fin that the woman had some personal experience in the area.

Bad nanny?

At one of their many sisterly chocolate-and-wine get-togethers, Ami had once mentioned she thought Hadley might come from a privi-leged background. Not anything specific, just a few things the woman had let slip.

Fin thought of her boss. Shirleen had a nanny for her three kids. According to Shirl, there had never been any question of her staying home to care for them. In fact, with the last baby, Shirleen had been back on the job in two weeks.

The strange thing was, until Fin was back in Good Hope, that lifestyle hadn't even struck her as strange. She thought of Prim and

May and their two boys. They still had active and satisfying careers as accountants, but family came first.

It would be the same, she knew, for Beck and Ami.

And one day for Marigold and Cade.

Fin dropped a hand to her flat belly. One day she'd take the plunge, but she was finding it increasingly difficult to imagine a child, her child, with Xander's dark hair and eyes.

The only baby she could envision had blonde curls and vivid blue eyes.

Pain scraped across her heart, until she realized it was Hadley pushing back her chair. "I need to stop by the bakery and make sure I have everything ready for tomorrow."

"I'll come with—"

"No. You won't." Hadley motioned Ami back down with a stern expression that would do a drill sergeant proud. "I've got this. Your job is to rest."

"She's got too many curbs to walk," Marigold quipped.

When Hadley looked puzzled, Marigold just laughed. "We'll make sure she chills."

"Thank you." Hadley shifted her gaze to Fin and rose. "I appreciate the hospitality."

"I'm glad you stopped by." Fin stood. There had been too much talk of love and babies. There had also been a near slip when she'd mentioned returning to LA.

Hadley might have her secrets, but then so did she.

Fin glanced around the table. The men were busy pitching horseshoes. The twins were occupied hitting the ball—rather than each other—with colorful croquet mallets.

With Lynn gone and Hadley almost to the back gate, it was just her and her sisters. Could she find the courage to share what had happened in that hotel room in Milwaukee?

Ami winced and straightened. "This chair is murder on my back."

Prim sprang up. "I'll get you a kitchen chair."

Ami shifted again in her seat.

"Are you okay?" Fin reached over and touched her sister's hand.

"Just some back pain." Ami patted her stomach. "From carrying so much weight in front."

Prim returned with the chair.

"Thank you." Ami smiled and moved to the chair. "Much better."

Now, Fin told herself, *tell them now.* Her heart raced as she pushed the words she'd held so close to the tip of her tongue. "I—"

At the same time, Prim spoke. "I, well actually we—Max and I—have an announcement."

Fin shifted her gaze to her sister and saw the ivory skin spotted with freckles was paler than usual.

"I'm pregnant." Prim threw out her hands. "Nearly three months. The baby is due right around Fin's fake wedding date."

"Ohmigod." Ami squealed and jumped to her feet, crossing the distance to her sister. "I'm so happy for you and Max."

Marigold lifted her cup in a toast. "Big congrats."

"Our babies will be close." Prim hugged Ami, then turned to Marigold. "You and Cade better get busy so you can join the party."

"We're working on it," Marigold surprised everyone by saying.

"You are?" Ami's voice reflected her shock. "You never told me."

"You never asked." Marigold turned to Fin. "Are you and Xander going to try for a baby right away? I mean, you're not old, but you're not getting any younger, either."

"We haven't really talked about kids." Fin kept her voice casual, then leaned over and squeezed Prim's arm, meeting her gaze. "I'm so happy for you. Max must be over the moon."

"You should have seen his face when I told him." Prim's eyes turned misty. "We both teared up."

"Tell us all about it," Ami urged. "I want all the deets."

"I think I interrupted Fin." Prim cast an apologetic look in her direction.

Fin thought of the news she'd been about to share about what had happened during that long-ago weekend in Milwaukee, news that would likely bring everyone down rather than lift them up as Prim's news had done.

Even if she'd been desperate to share, there was no way she would say anything now. After all she'd endured, Prim deserved this time to celebrate with her sisters. And really, shouldn't she tell Jeremy before her sisters?

Not the time, Fin thought. Perhaps best never voiced. It was something to think about.

But not now.

"It wasn't important. I'd like to propose a toast to Prim, Max, and Baby Brody." Fin lifted her cider cup. "I'm beginning to realize the most important things in life are often the simplest. Here's to an easy pregnancy and many wonderful memories."

Chapter Eighteen

"I have to admit, when I returned to Good Hope, I never saw myself strolling through a corn maze with a reindeer dressed like a ballet dancer guarding the entrance." Fin fingered the animal's tulle skirt. "I'm betting Mindy is going to love her. I know I would have at that age."

"I hope so. In the past I haven't had the maze cut until the week before Halloween." Jeremy slanted her a sideways glance and smiled. It felt good to be with her. "A lot of the merchants wanted it ready in time for Septemberfest. Now, it can do double duty for the Wish Fulfilled party."

"This maze seems pretty big." Fin gestured wide. "How many acres?"

"Ten."

"A person could get lost in here." Fin touched one of the tall stalks on her right, her gaze focused down one of the endless rows of corn.

Intending to work from home, Jeremy had left the office early. When he'd discovered Fin sitting on the porch reading a book and his grandmother at her cardiac rehab session, he'd decided to play hooky. The promise of a walk through the corn maze had tempted Fin to play with him.

"Any progress with Lynn?" Dried stalks crackled under his feet, while overhead the sky was a brilliant blue.

"She says she's carefully considering the points I raised. She may change her position. She may not." Fin heaved a sigh. "I think I've pushed her as much as I can without becoming annoying."

"You've done your best. That's all anyone can ask." Jeremy paused at a crossroads and gestured. "Shall we go right? Or left?"

Fin started left, then changed course. Her lips lifted in a rueful smile. "Picking the right way is always difficult. Especially when both have merit."

"It's not always easy to know which way is best." Jeremy kept his tone conversational. "I know when the town board dropped the filming decision in my lap, I struggled."

"You did?" Fin's voice registered surprise. "I thought you were opposed from the beginning."

"Not entirely." When they reached yet another crossroads, he lifted a brow.

This time Fin turned left. As Jeremy wasn't in any hurry to end this outing, her choosing the long way suited him just fine.

"Like you said, there are good arguments both for and against." This was how it should be, he thought. How it had never been with anyone else. The ease of conversation. The give-and-take of opinions. The sexual pull.

Breathtakingly beautiful in simple shorts and top with her hair hanging loose around her face. Her red lips reminded him of ripe strawberries. Jeremy longed to kiss her, right here, right now, in the afternoon sun. He wanted to feel her lips soften under his mouth. To see her eyes close as she surrendered to sensation. To feel her soft curves mold against him.

But he held back, knowing the connection they were forging was important, too.

"In the end, it was the knowledge of all the locals and tourists who planned to celebrate Christmas in Good Hope that swayed my opinion." Their eyes met. "But I can tell you, the money Xander offered was tempting."

"My dad says you can never go wrong doing the right thing."

Jeremy kept his expression neutral. "Were you and Steve discussing something specific when that came up?"

Fin hesitated as they reached another decision point in the maze. When she once again turned to her left, Jeremy wondered if she was turned around or if she was deliberately choosing the longer path.

He caught up to her and took her hand.

Though she didn't pull away, she glanced down and then back up at him. "Is this a good idea?"

"It's a safety thing." Jeremy kept his expression solemn. "We remain together if we lose our way."

"It's easy to lose your way." Fin's murmur was so low he almost missed it.

Jeremy wondered if something had occurred during her dad's barbecue. She'd been unusually quiet ever since. "You and your sisters seemed to have a good time together on Monday."

"We always do." Instead of tensing, her lips curved, and the tiny pucker between her brows disappeared.

"If you ever want to have them over to Casa Rakes." Jeremy waved a hand. "Just remember, *mi casa es su casa*."

"Prim is pregnant." The words that burst from her lips appeared to startle her as much as they did him.

Jeremy stopped walking. "That's wonderful."

"It's very good news." Fin's eyes turned misty. "Max and Prim are thrilled. The baby is due sometime in March."

Jeremy fought a pang of envy. Would he ever know what it was like to be a father?

"Marigold let it slip that she and Cade are trying."

"They just got married."

"Apparently they don't want to wait." Fin lifted a hand, let it fall. "Ami is excited her child will have cousins around the same age."

The next logical question would be to ask when she and Xander planned to start a family.

Jeremy said nothing. Just the thought of any man putting hands on Fin set his blood to boiling.

"Look." Fin pointed.

A bird with a sharp beak and speckled wings sat atop one of the stalks, beady eyes fixed on them. Jeremy made a shooing motion with his hand. The starling, a bird with a penchant for attacking ripening fruit, merely cawed.

He noticed Fin hiding a smile as they resumed their stroll. What had they been talking about? Ah, yes. *Babies.*

"It must be hard." His cryptic comment left the words open to interpretation.

"You mean living so far away?" Fin continued without waiting for confirmation. "Now that both Prim and Marigold are back in Good Hope, I admit I do sometimes feel like I'm on the outside looking in."

"I was actually talking about them having babies."

"Yes, well." She glanced over at him, her expression giving nothing away. "Not every woman—or man—wants children."

"I suppose that's true."

Fin cocked her head. "Do you?"

"I always assumed I'd get married and have a family." Jeremy kept his voice as casual and offhand as hers. "What about you?"

She lifted a hand, waving away the question. "There's something I want to discuss with you. Something I need to tell you."

His heart stuttered at the raw emotion he saw in her eyes. Wanting to comfort, to soothe, Jeremy cupped her face in his hands and brushed a kiss across her warm, sweet mouth.

When she sighed, he folded her into his arms. They fit together perfectly.

"I've wanted to tell you this for the longest time."

The words, muffled against his shirtfront, had hope surging. Perhaps she wasn't leaving. Would she confess she'd never stopped loving him? Tell him being back in Good Hope had helped her see those old feelings had never died?

Jeremy rested his cheek against the top of Fin's sun-warmed hair. Despite time and distance, his love for her had never died.

"Take your time." Emotion made his voice husky. "You can tell me anything."

Fin tilted her head back, and Jeremy saw the question in her eyes.

In answer, he tucked a strand of hair behind her ear, his gaze unwavering. "Anything."

Their eye contact turned into a tangible connection between the two of them. But before she could speak, the moment was broken by a jarring ring.

"Ignore it."

Fin shook her head and reached into her pocket for her cell phone, her gaze never leaving his. "Ami has been having pains off and on. She could be having the baby."

Without glancing down, Fin hit "Accept."

"Gladys. Hello." Fin gave a little laugh, then stepped out of Jeremy's arms. "You think I sound odd? No, I'm fine. I thought you might be Ami."

Jeremy fought the urge to curse.

Fin bit her lip, glanced at him. "Yes. I have a moment."

Jeremy guided them out of the maze while Fin continued to listen to Gladys.

From the few remarks Fin got in, it appeared Gladys was attempting to nail down a "White Christmas" practice time. It was obvious—at least to him—Fin was doing her best to evade.

Though Fin might protest, Jeremy knew who'd win this round.

When the phone found its way back into Fin's pocket, he raised a brow. "When is the practice scheduled?"

Other than her twin nephews, Fin hadn't spent much time around children. She wasn't sure how to feel when Eliza announced that, because the Wish Fulfilled event was being held at Rakes Farm, Fin was to be the designated hostess for the event. Though there would be plenty of volunteers on hand, making sure Mindy had a magical time was Fin's responsibility.

Which was why, instead of dressing in red or green, Fin chose a fit-and-flare dress with a hot pink grid pattern. Everyone said pink was Mindy's favorite color. Fin jazzed up her simple dress by twisting a rectangular glittery scarf of the same color into a long, loose knot. A pair of sparkly, heeled sandals completed the outfit.

"You look as fresh and pretty as a strawberry parfait. Good enough to eat," Jeremy whispered in her ear as the truck carrying Mindy and her father pulled up.

Fin elbowed him. "You behave."

She focused on the Silverado. Katie Ruth had mentioned Owen preferred a low-key welcome to the event at the farm, so the guests waited in the barn for the guest of honor.

"Owen." Jeremy moved forward when the man stepped from the truck. "Good to see you."

After shaking hands, Jeremy angled his head toward her. "You remember Fin Bloom."

Fin would have recognized Owen anywhere. Same mop of sandy-brown hair and a face scattered with freckles. But the devilish twinkle in his hazel eyes was missing, and there were lines on his face that hadn't been there ten years ago.

"Hello, Delphinium." Owen smiled at Fin. "Congratulations on your engagement."

"Thank you." Fin followed him as he rounded the truck to open the door for Mindy.

His daughter was a slender child, about the same size as the twins. Maybe a bit smaller. Like Fin, she was dressed all in pink: a pretty tulle skirt with a clingy shirt and glittery cowboy boots. She could have been any bright-eyed little girl, except for the plain pink scarf covering a nearly bald head.

The child's eyes widened at the sight of Fin. She turned to her father. "She looks like a princess."

Owen smiled.

"I'm Fin Bloom, and I'm going to make sure you have a fabulous early Christmas." Fin stepped closer. "I love the way the boots flash when you walk."

Mindy grinned, showing a gap-toothed smile. She reached out and reverently touched Fin's scarf. "This is pretty."

Fin glanced again at the one covering the girl's head. Definitely nothing special. Not worthy of a little fashionista on her big day. "I know you're probably eager to explore the Christmas wonderland we have inside the barn, but I'd like you to come up to the house with me for a second."

Mindy blinked those big blue eyes. "Why?"

Leaning over, Fin whispered what she was planning in the child's ear. "Interested?"

Mindy eagerly nodded and started toward the house, cowboy boots flashing with each step.

Fin glanced at Owen's startled expression, then called out, "Ask your daddy if it's okay."

The child whirled. "Daddy, can I go with Fin to the house? Just for a few minutes. Please. It's super-duper important."

Any hesitation her father may have had melted at the pleading look in his daughter's eyes.

Fin patted Owen's arm and offered a reassuring smile. "Just give us five minutes."

When they returned, Mindy's scarf had been replaced by the glittery one that had hung around Fin's neck.

"This is a Heidi braid." Mindy touched the intricate coil that topped the scarf. "Fin has a friend who wears scarves all the time. And do you know what, Daddy?"

"What?"

"Her friend doesn't even have cancer."

Moisture filled Owen's eyes.

Once again Mindy lifted a hand to her scarf. "I can't wait to show this to Lia and Hannah and Brynn. They're my bestest friends."

"Well, they're waiting in the barn. So I think it's time we get this party started." Fin smiled at Mindy. "What do you think?"

That amazing gap-toothed smile flashed again. "Yes, please."

Fin gestured to Jeremy. Seconds later, as if by magic, the lights on the barn flashed on.

Mindy's eyes gleamed and she slipped her hand in Fin's. "Oooh. It's so beautiful."

An hour later the party was going strong. Mindy's friends had squealed when they'd seen her and, as predicted, pronounced her scarf "super cool."

Lindsay and Hadley manned the photo booth, which was currently doing a booming business, with kids going in as quickly as others went out. Not only would there be pictures taken inside the booth, but Izzie Deshler roamed the inside of the barn with her camera, taking candid shots.

In a distant corner, a temporary stage had been erected. The Triple Trio from the high school added to the festive atmosphere with a variety of Christmas carols.

Mindy and a couple of friends tumbled out of the photo booth, fake Santa beards askew, laughing. One of the girls must have said something about the pink tulle and fairy lights overhead, because all three looked up and beamed.

Fin's heart became a heavy, sweet mass in her chest. Mindy reminded her so much of herself at that age. A fashionista with a zest for life.

The child hadn't wanted to go to the Dells or even Disneyland. All she'd wished for was Christmas.

Fin realized if someone gave her a wish now, she wouldn't know what to say. She'd given up on wishes. The way she saw it, if you didn't wish, you couldn't be disappointed.

After the photo booth and a mini scavenger hunt, the children were herded to tables to decorate cupcakes, then write letters to Santa. Fin was staggered by all the wonderful toppings.

"It's like Willy Wonka, only there's more than chocolate." Marigold's eyes danced like a child's on Christmas morning. "I don't know what Katie Ruth was thinking, putting Anita in charge of the decorating. The piranha isn't nearly as nice as Willy, though I have to admit so far she's been good to the kids."

Fin opened her mouth to inform her sister that Anita had made all the cupcakes when Marigold gave a little wave.

"Anita gave me the stink eye." Marigold grinned. "Which means we must need more mini marshmallows."

Looking adorable as an elf, complete with pointy shoes and a hat, Marigold bounded off to refill the marshmallows.

"They're sure giving the children a lot of choices." Owen spoke from beside her. "It's like a candy store. Gumdrops, M&Ms, confetti sprinkles, mini marshmallows, and all those frosting flavors."

"We wanted it extra special for Mindy," Fin said simply.

"It's sure been a special day so far." Owen's voice thickened with emotion. "Eliza insisted we drive through the business district on our way here. All the Christmas lights were up and the holiday banners were on the light poles. People we didn't even know clapped and cheered when they spotted the truck."

Eliza had worked her magic, Fin thought with a smile. She wasn't surprised.

"Mindy hung out the window, waving." Owen cleared his throat. "When she got here, she turned shy. You giving her your scarf broke the ice. I'll see it gets back to you—"

"Oh, no, Owen." Fin's eyes met his. "The scarf is my Christmas gift to her."

Owen expelled a ragged breath. "Thank you."

"How's Mindy doing?" Fin asked as Jeremy joined them and slid an arm around her waist.

"Better." Some of the tension eased from Owen's face. "She's in a clinical trial and the doctor has been amazed by her response. I've been doing a whole lot of prayin' this drug combination continues to work."

Fin touched his arm. "I'll be adding my prayers to yours."

"Mine as well," Jeremy added.

They fell silent, watching the kids go crazy with the toppings. Fin had to hand it to Anita. Thanks to the help of about a dozen volunteers, she kept the kids in line without dousing their fun.

As Hadley bent over to help Brynn, Fin was struck that Hadley's hair color was nearly the same shade as the child's.

Once the cupcakes were decorated and devoured, the tables were cleared to allow the children to write letters to Santa. Ami sat beside Mindy, murmuring words of encouragement. Knowing the child was in good hands, Fin slipped outside to make sure all the corn maze volunteers were ready.

"I'm glad I caught up to you." Prim's gaze darted right, then left, as if making sure she wouldn't be overheard. "Do you know what's up with Dad?"

Fin had greeted her father when he arrived but hadn't seen him since. She'd assumed he was at one of the stations set up in the ten-acre maze. "What do you mean?"

Prim's hazel eyes were filled with worry. It was never a good sign when her normally unflappable sister looked ruffled.

"I spotted him in this tête-à-tête with Anita by the photo booth." Though no one was nearby, Prim kept her voice low. "They've been there since the cupcake decorating ended."

A sick feeling filled Fin's stomach. "That can't be good."

Prim pressed her lips together for a second. "That isn't all. I overheard them making plans to get together later tonight."

"What's got the two of you so stressed?" Marigold pulled off her elf hat, and blonde curls tumbled around her shoulders.

"If someone is messing with either of you, I'll haul 'em in." Cade whipped out his handcuffs but ruined the effect with a grin.

"You're a good brother-in-law." Prim patted his arm.

"Dad is with Anita." Fin saw no reason to sugarcoat. "Prim heard them making plans to get together tonight."

Marigold's eyes widened. "Shut the front door."

"That's all you can say?" Fin huffed.

"Oh, trust me, she can do much better." Cade shot his wife a teasing smile. "She's keeping it clean because this is a family-friendly event. Right, Goldilocks?"

Marigold stuck out her tongue, and laughing, Cade pulled her close.

Fin fought a pang of envy. Yep, her baby sister had found her prince.

But right now, she had more important things on her mind than prince envy. "What do you think is going on?"

"Have either of you seen Lynn?" Prim asked.

"We saw her a few minutes ago." Marigold exchanged a glance with her husband. "She looked pissed."

"Lynn is probably the most even-tempered person I know." Prim's brows pulled together in a worried frown.

"She knows he's with another woman." Marigold's tone brooked no argument. "A woman always knows."

Fin thought of Jessica and Xander. Yes, a woman knew.

Now Fin needed to figure out what she was going to do about it.

Chapter Nineteen

Fin preferred not to interfere in another person's life. Mainly because she didn't want their nose in her business. But this situation was different. She loved her father and wanted the best for him. While she could admit that Anita was attractive and smart, she'd never understood what her father saw in the woman Fin had once dubbed I-Need-a-Man and her sisters not-so-affectionately referred to as the piranha.

Still, Fin knew there had to be some good beneath Anita's sharp tongue and judgmental attitude. There had to be or her father wouldn't have been attracted to her.

"I'm mingling," Fin announced to no one in particular.

When everyone looked at her in surprise, she gestured with her left hand, the diamond winking in the lights. "I'll be checking out the photo booth."

Prim stepped forward. "I'll go with you."

Fin shook her head. "If Dad *is* with her, we don't want to look like we're ganging up on Anita."

"You're right." Prim exhaled a breath.

Marigold squeezed her arm. "You go, girl."

With her mind firmly focused on her mission, Fin entered the barn and strolled down the center aisle.

"Dad." Her heart gave a little skip when she saw he was alone. Like a prettily wrapped present with a bow on top, she'd just been handed the perfect opportunity. She wouldn't waste it. "I'm glad we ran into each other. I need to speak with you."

His smile disappeared. "Is something wrong?"

"Nonono. Everything is good." Fin hated to see the look of worry on his face. Hated even more knowing she'd put it there by her poorly chosen choice of words. Fin took his arm. "Walk with me."

Reaching the door leading outside, he followed her out into the bright sunshine.

"What's going on, Fin?" Steve kept his voice low, as if conscious of the people coming in and out of the barn.

"There's a gorgeous little spot I discovered past the flower beds that I want to show you."

"Don't you need to—?" Her father gestured with one hand to all the activity.

"My sisters are helping with the letters to Santa." Instead of taking the walkway to the house, Fin turned onto a path made of stepping stones. "And you have a few minutes before the kids descend on the maze and it turns crazy."

"I spotted Floyd when he arrived." Steve smiled. "If I didn't know it was him, I'd think Santa Claus really had dropped by."

"Mindy's going to love seeing him. She's really enjoying all this." Just thinking of the little girl brought a lump to her throat. She would think of Mindy later, Fin decided. Right now, her sisters were counting on her for answers.

"She's a sweet child." He glanced at Fin. "You know she and her dad live just down the street from me."

"I didn't realize that." Fin couldn't say she was surprised by the news. It seemed as if everyone in Good Hope was connected in one way or another.

"Jeremy has a beautiful place here."

Fin slanted a sideways glance as he paused to admire the chrysanthemums in glorious bloom at the side of the path. While there was an abundance of maroons and yellows, there were also some lovely peach-colored blossoms.

Her father's lips curved as he bent to get a better look at the peach ones. His silver wire-rimmed glasses and wiry gray hair gave him a scholarly look. As he'd grown older, his penchant for sweater vests made her think of Mister Rogers, a mainstay on nostalgia television when she was young.

Love for this kind, gentle man who'd always been her biggest champion had Fin's heart swelling. She blinked back tears. She didn't care if his relationship with Lynn went anywhere, she just wanted him with someone who'd make him happy.

He straightened and smiled. "Where is it you're taking me, Delphinium?"

"Not much farther." She took his hand, finding comfort in the warmth.

He still wore his wedding band, a circle of gold, worn to a dull shine. How had she not noticed that before? Of course, her trips home had always been brief and jam-packed with activities. Rarely had there been time to simply enjoy each other's company.

"I'm glad we've had this time together."

His fingers tightened around hers. "I am, too."

One more turn on the path and they reached their destination. Her father's eyes widened at the sight of a marble fountain with winding columns and two basins. Four curved stone benches encircled the fountain. Behind the benches were wildflowers in what appeared to be scattered disarray, but Fin recognized a pattern in the planting, in the way the purples and yellows and reds played off one another.

Steve turned toward her, his eyes wide as he took it all in. "What is this place?"

"I'm not sure." Fin lifted her hands, let them drop. "I found it by accident on one of my morning walks. I believe it's some kind of memorial garden."

"What makes you think that?"

"Look." She pointed to the manicured area between the benches and fountain. "See those stones? They have names and dates on them. Do you think people are buried here?"

Steve's gaze dropped to one of the round stones flush with the ground. *Edward J. Rakes*, it said, along with what appeared to be the year of his birth and death. "Eddie was Ruby's husband. I know for a fact that he's buried in the Good Hope cemetery. I was at the graveside service."

Fin stood close to her father as they read other names on other stones. "I've never seen anything like this."

"I haven't either, but I like it." Steve's expression softened. "It's a way to recognize those who were important to us."

"Don't you mean a way to remember?"

"Those we've loved deeply remain with us forever." Steve shoved his hands into his pockets, his gaze taking in the flowers, the gently sloping landscape, and the hundreds of cherry trees in the distance.

When his gaze settled expectantly on her, Fin knew she'd delayed long enough. The benches looked clean, but Fin wasn't in the mood to sit. She decided to casually mention her sisters had seen him with Anita by the photo booth and let the discussion flow from there.

"Are you and Anita getting back together?" Fin blurted, then suppressed a sigh.

So much for easing into it.

Steve's lids widened. She saw whatever he thought she was going to bring up, it wasn't this. "No. Why do you ask?"

"Several people saw you with Anita. You appeared to be having an intimate conversation." Actually, that had been more of Prim's impression, but Fin wanted to see her father's reaction to the comment.

His expression turned solemn. He pulled his hands from his pockets. "Nothing intimate about it. We were merely having a discussion."

"About what?"

Two frown lines appeared between her father's brows. "Do I ask you to tell me what you and Jeremy discuss in private?"

The gently spoken rebuke felt like a slap.

Fin lifted her chin. "No, but I'd hope if you were concerned, you'd tell me. That's what I'm doing," she said when he opened his mouth. "You let me know you were concerned about this fake engagement. I respected your honesty. I hope you afford me the same respect."

The tension she saw in the line of her father's jaw eased. "What has you concerned?"

"I don't want you to get back with her. I don't want to see you mess things up with Lynn."

Those gentle hazel eyes searched her face. "Did Lynn say something to you?"

A sinking feeling filled the pit of Fin's stomach. She shook her head. "I haven't spoken with her today. Someone said she looked upset. Then I heard you were with Anita and—"

"You added two and two and came up with five." Steve shook his head. "I'm not resuming a relationship with Anita. I simply wanted to speak with her about some concerns."

"What kind of concerns?" He might think it wasn't her business, but darn it, it was. He was her dad. If he was worried, she needed to know so she could make it right.

He paused for so long Fin wondered if he was going to answer. Then he took a breath. "I'm concerned about her behavior since I ended the relationship."

Fin wanted to say who cared about Anita, but it was obvious her father did care.

"What kinds of things has she been doing?"

"She's been doing a lot of partying." Steve hesitated. "Drinking to excess. Then there's her relationship with Adam Vogele."

"Being a cougar is practically a way of life in LA."

Steve shot her a sharp look, and Fin instantly regretted the flippant tone.

"I wanted Anita to know that I was concerned and make sure she knew that I'm here for her if she ever needs a friend."

"Seriously?"

"Her first husband, Richard, and I were friends. She was a friend of your mother's and of mine." The teacher in him was evident in the calm relaying of facts. "Just because I can't see us succeeding in a long-term relationship doesn't mean I no longer care about her welfare."

"I suppose that makes sense."

"Did you stop caring for Jeremy when you two broke up?"

Her head jerked up, but he continued. "Feelings, especially deep ones, don't disappear when a relationship ends. I'd hate to see Anita do something she might regret."

"Understood." It was almost time to end this conversation. But Fin had one more question. "What about Lynn?"

"I explained the situation to Lynn. She questioned my motives." Despite his nonchalance, Fin could see worry in the hazel depths. "Hopefully, once she has time to process, she'll understand."

"Is it worth it?" When her father's brows drew together, Fin realized additional explanation was necessary. "Is warning Anita worth the risk of pissing off Lynn?"

"If Lynn can't understand, she's not the woman I think she is." Steve rocked back on his heels. "Doing the right thing isn't always easy. In the end, it's the only honorable choice."

Fin nodded. "We better get back."

"What about you? How do you think the vote on the fifteenth will go?"

It was obvious by the change in topic he'd said all he was going to say about Anita and Lynn.

"I believe Lynn is open to changing her vote. But I can't be certain, which means I should double my efforts to convince Jeremy to go along. The problem is—" Fin bit her lip.

Her father offered an encouraging smile. "The problem is . . ."

Unlike some of her friends, Fin had always been able to count on her parents to be her sounding board. They'd always been ready to listen, available to give counsel without telling her what to do. Always supportive.

Except for the one time when she'd needed them most.

"Something is troubling you." The soothing tone mixed with the concern she now saw in his eyes—concern for her—was nearly her undoing. "Will you tell me about it?"

"It's everything," she blurted out. "It's my feelings for Jeremy when I'm engaged to another man. It's my promise to push an agenda I'm no longer sure I believe in. It's me not being sure who I am or what I want. It's that little girl in the barn who may not live to see another Christmas."

She whirled and started walking down the path. In several long strides he'd caught up with her. His strong fingers around her arm stopped her and had her turning to face him.

"I'm so confused, Daddy. And so very tired of all the lies." Then, she did something she hadn't done in years.

Fin burst into tears.

It felt to Fin as if she and Jeremy had turned some corner she hadn't known they'd been approaching. Laughing and teasing with him during the day and then sleeping only a short distance away from him at night—no wonder she'd cried all over her father yesterday.

Since the Wish Fulfilled event ended yesterday, she'd called Xander three times, needing to reassure herself of the connection between them. The last time he snapped.

"For God's sake, Fin. I don't need to know every little detail of your life."

Inhaling sharply, Fin stopped midsentence. She'd been in the process of telling him about Ami's latest doctor's appointment and the fact that her niece or nephew could make an appearance any moment. It wasn't as if she'd called during a time when she knew he'd be busy. Noon on a Sunday wasn't exactly prime time.

"I didn't realize you were so bored with me, Xander." There was a steel edge to her tone she didn't bother to hide.

"Not with you," he qualified, still sounding distracted. "But with your family. I barely know them. How can you possibly think I'd be interested in their lives?"

"You don't know them because you didn't choose to know them," Fin shot back. "One dinner was all I could get you to agree to attend."

"Why would I agree to more? A small-town schoolteacher? A cop? An accountant?" He gave a little laugh. "We don't have much in common."

Except me, Fin thought.

"From now on I'll contact you only when I have something to report."

As Xander continued to update her on what he'd been doing, Fin strolled to a glider under a large tree with leafy limbs and dropped down.

"Have you convinced Lynn Chapin to change her vote?" Xander's bluntness told Fin they'd chatted long enough. It was time to get down to business.

"I've spoken with her several times since you and I last talked."

"And?"

It was amazing how a single word could contain so much impatience.

"I believe she's considering changing her vote." Fin kept her voice even, not allowing it to reflect her own irritation.

The sound of a pen tapping against a hard surface sounded in her ear. "Considering isn't good enough. I need your assurance she'll vote for the proposal."

"You aren't going to get it. Not yet, anyway." Fin plowed ahead when he began to bluster. "If I push too hard, she'll dig in her heels. Lynn Chapin isn't a woman you can pressure."

She heard him grumble something under his breath.

"You should understand," Fin pointed out. "You're very much like that yourself."

He expelled a reluctant chuckle. "You know me so well."

Do I? Fin had begun to wonder. When he'd asked her to marry him, she'd seen herself as part of a Hollywood power couple. But had she ever truly seen Xander as a friend, a husband, the father of her children?

"Where are we with the mayor?" Xander changed tack. "If we can't count on this board member to switch her vote, you need to focus on convincing Rakes to vote our way."

"I spoke with him about the issue just today." Fin saw no need to mention she'd voiced her concerns about closing down the town. Xander would view that as the ultimate betrayal. "Jeremy is keeping an open mind."

"How are you two getting along?" Xander's abruptness had her bristling.

"Fine."

"Have you kissed him lately?"

Was all this bluster because he worried she and Jeremy might be getting too close? Or was he wanting to know so he could take a swipe at her for being disloyal?

235

It saddened Fin to realize she didn't know Xander well enough to know his motivation.

"You and I discussed the need for my engagement to Jeremy to appear real." Fin chose her words carefully. "So, the answer to your question is yes. I have kissed Jeremy when . . ." She hesitated for an imperceptible second. "Necessary."

"Good." The warm approval caught her off guard.

"Why good?"

"Odds are he's falling for you." Instead of distressed, Xander sounded pleased by the thought. "Men think with their dicks, Fin. If he's hot for you, he'll likely do whatever it takes to please you."

"You're not like that." The words popped out of her mouth before Fin could give them a second thought.

"You're right. I'm more pragmatic."

And calculating, Fin thought.

"Based on what you've said, it's time to up our game."

Fin rubbed her suddenly tight neck. "I don't understand what else I can do."

"Whatever is necessary to secure the mayor's vote."

"I've already done everything," Fin protested. "I've laid out the arguments. I've made it clear filming would be good for the community—"

"You weren't listening." Xander huffed out the accusation, annoyance mixing with impatience. "I said men think with their dicks. It's time to use that to your advantage."

Everything in Fin went cold. "Are you seriously suggesting I tease Jeremy with the promise of sex?"

"Whatever necessary, Fin." Xander's laugh held a harsh edge. "Sleep with him if you think it will change his mind. I've a lot riding on this film. I want that location secured."

I have. I want. Pragmatic. Calculating.

But hadn't she been the same? There had been no stars in her eyes. She'd seen their union as a practical one. "Is that why you proposed?"

He should have instantly responded. It would have made the denial that came more convincing. But he hesitated. "Certainly not. Why would you think that?"

"The timing, for one. The proposal came out of the blue."

"Nothing wrong with being spontaneous."

"There is something wrong with pimping out a woman you profess to love." Fin's stomach churned, forcing her to breathe through her mouth or be sick.

"That's not what I meant. You're putting words in my mouth."

The protest sounded weak. He knew it. More importantly, she knew it.

"I should never have accepted the ring."

"Sweetheart." Xander's voice grew soft and his tone turned persuasive. "You're making a big deal out of nothing. We make a good team. I realize I've put you in a tough position, but it was for us."

She tuned him out. The words meant nothing. There was only one person Xander Tillman cared about, and that was himself. Perhaps the realization should have made her sad. All Fin felt was relief.

"I'm not marrying you." Fin felt herself settle as the rightness of the decision washed over her.

"Relax. Enjoy this time with your family. I'll be in touch soon."

Before she could respond, the call ended.

Fin stared at the phone for a long moment before dropping it into her pocket. Moving to the dresser, she picked up the brush and, with teeth gritted, pulled it through her already smooth hair. The overhead light caught the stone and flashed.

Fin dropped the brush, then held out her left hand. She studied the stone, wondering how something so shiny could feel so heavy.

The mirror over the dresser captured her despair and reflected it back at her.

"He never loved you." She spoke calmly at her image. "And you never loved him."

There was power, she discovered, in speaking words aloud. In finally admitting what she hadn't been ready to accept. Turning her back on Xander felt an awful lot like turning her back on the life she'd built in California.

Not one and the same, she told herself as she slipped off the ring and set it on the dresser.

Chapter Twenty

"Delphinium." Ruby's voice sounded from the hall. "Gladys is here."

Fin hurried from the room. At the sounds of holiday music coming from the music room, her steps faltered.

You can do this, she told herself, forcing her feet to continue forward, one step at a time.

She stood in the doorway to the parlor for several seconds, absorbing the scene. Jeremy at the baby grand, fingers flying over the keys, Ruby and Gladys leaning over his shoulder as they sang along with a holiday classic.

Fin wasn't sure how long she'd stood there before Ruby glanced up. The older woman hurried across the room, hands outstretched. "There you are. There's our girl."

Gladys smiled broadly, her lips a festive purple. Then she frowned. "Where's your ring?"

Fin glanced down, then back up. "I took it off to wash my hands. I must have forgot to put it back on."

Jeremy rose from the piano bench and crossed to her. He brushed a kiss across her lips as if nothing was amiss.

"As long as it's safe." Ruby waved a hand, but a worried pucker had appeared between her brows.

Gladys clapped her hands. "Let's get started."

It became quickly apparent Gladys took directing this mini scene seriously. After spending several minutes reviewing what had happened in the story prior to this point, she instructed Fin where to stand in relation to Jeremy.

Panic rose to claw Fin's throat as Jeremy's fingers returned to the keys and he began to play the familiar song. She tried to focus on his rich voice with its perfect pitch and not think about when Gladys would signal her.

Fin opened her mouth to join in, but nothing came out. Her heart pounded like a bass drum against her ribs. Her skin turned clammy. She glanced helplessly at Jeremy, not sure she trusted her voice enough to speak.

Jeremy rose from the piano. "Fin and I are going to take a walk. We'll take this up again when we return."

When Gladys opened her mouth as if to protest, something she saw in Jeremy's eyes had her remaining silent.

"I made mango sun tea earlier," Ruby told her friend. "Why don't I pour everyone a glass?"

"Good idea." Jeremy kept his eyes focused on Fin. "We won't be long."

Fin didn't protest when he took her now-ice-cold hand and tugged her out of the room, then out the door. She barely felt the warmth of the sun on the clear, cloudless day, although she clung to his hand as if it were a life preserver in storm-tossed seas.

"You don't have any trouble singing hymns." Jeremy tossed the comment out there as they strode down the long lane toward the road.

"That's different." She'd finally found her voice, though it came out rough and scratchy.

"How?"

She shrugged.

They walked for another minute without speaking. "You mentioned once that you hadn't sang since high school."

Fin remained silent.

"Would this have something to do with the show choir competition in Milwaukee?"

The wings of a thousand hummingbirds beat against her throat. "Why would you ask that?"

"Eliza told me how you ditched the competition to go shopping." His blue eyes searched hers. "Something had to have happened. I know how much singing—and that competition—meant to you."

Tell him, a voice inside Fin urged. *This is your chance.*

But the words remained stuck inside. She couldn't force them past frozen lips.

"Did you give up singing as a penance of sorts, because you disappointed your friends?"

Some of the tension inside Fin eased at the realization that it was likely true, but not for the reason he thought. Singing and losing the baby in that hotel room had become linked in her mind.

Realizing he waited for an answer, she gave a jerky nod.

"I understand."

At her look of disbelief, a rueful smile tipped his lips.

"I experienced something very similar." He swung their clasped hands between them.

Some of the tension gripping Fin eased and she discovered she could breathe again. "Wh-what happened?"

"After you and I split, I didn't go fishing for years."

Fin inclined her head. "Why?"

His fingers tightened around hers.

"Fishing and you were linked. The thought of sitting on the bank without you was . . . painful. And I felt guilty over how it had ended between us." Jeremy cleared his throat. "But Max kept hounding me. One day I agreed just to shut him up. In time, it got easier. I was building new memories. Now the twins come with us, or Cade, or your dad, or all of them."

"You got over me."

He shook his head. "It got easier, but sometimes it's still difficult."

She squeezed his hand.

"Perhaps if you think of 'White Christmas' as a hymn, that might help you over the initial hurdle." He faced her then, running his hands up and down her arms as if to warm her. "I'll be right beside you, every step of the way. What do you think? Will you give the song another try?"

Before she'd finished nodding, his arms were around her. She pressed her head against his chest and accepted what her heart had always known. She'd never stopped loving this man.

They walked hand in hand to the music parlor. Jeremy had barely set his fingers on the keys when Fin's phone buzzed.

She was tempted to ignore it, but a tingle at the back of her neck had her pulling the phone from her pocket and checking the text. As she reread the message, her heart kicked into overdrive.

"Is there trouble?" Ruby rose and moved to her side.

Fin shook her head. A broad smile bloomed on her lips. "Ami's at the hospital having the baby."

Jeremy was already on his feet. "I'll get the car."

"I'm sorry, Gladys."

Fin's apology was immediately brushed aside by the older woman.

"Go." Ruby made a shooing gesture. "Text us pictures and give Ami and Beck our love."

Fin and Jeremy made it to the hospital in Sturgeon Bay in record time. Still, they were the last of the family to reach the labor and delivery waiting room. Even Cade, who'd been on duty today, had called in a deputy so he could be with Marigold.

"This could take hours." Prim leaned back against Max. "First labors are unpredictable."

Max planted a kiss on the top of her head. "Jackie White is picking up the boys from school. She said they can spend the night if need be."

"I won't leave until I know everything is okay with Ami and the baby," Prim told her husband.

"We're not going anywhere," Max assured her.

"I think we're all here for the duration." Steve absently sipped at the cup of coffee in his hand.

"How is Ami doing?" Fin glanced at Prim.

"Ninety percent effaced and dilated to six," Prim announced. "Oh, and her water broke on the way. That's the latest update from ten minutes ago."

Prim had been through this before so she knew the lingo. In this area, Fin was barely literate. "Is that good?"

Out of the corner of her eye, she saw Marigold pause in her conversation with Cade, also waiting for Prim's reply.

"It's excellent." Prim smiled. "Things are moving along, which is great, since they usually want the delivery within twenty-four hours of the water breaking."

In an attempt to calm herself, Fin took a breath and let it out. She told herself babies were born healthy and women made it through childbirth every day without any problems.

"Ami will be fine." The look in Jeremy's eyes was as steady as a clasp of his hand on her shoulder. "There's no need to worry."

"I can't seem to help myself." Fin's gaze lingered on her father, who'd begun to pace again. "He's worried, too."

Jeremy followed the direction of her gaze. "Let's see if we can get his mind on to something else."

Fin eyed her father. "The way he's pacing, I don't think we'll be able to get him to slow down enough to listen."

"Then we'll just have to keep up with him."

Fin's gaze lingered on Jeremy's face, and she felt the connection, this time deeper and stronger than before. Maybe because Xander was no longer between them. *Does he feel it too?* she wondered.

"Lynn."

Fin turned at the sound of Prim's welcome to see the blonde businesswoman enter the waiting room.

Dressed smartly in navy pants, a white silk shirt, and heels, Lynn looked every inch the head of the Chapin banking empire. Though her smile remained warm and friendly, Fin saw the falter when it settled on Steve.

It appeared the incident with Anita had left Lynn unsure of the reception she'd receive.

"I didn't want to intrude, but Ruby called me and—" Lynn stopped midsentence, as if realizing she was about to ramble. "I thought I'd stop and see how Ami is doing."

"All systems go," Prim announced. "Baby Cross is on the move."

"That's exciting." Lynn's smile appeared frozen on her lips. "Well, I think—"

Steve crossed the waiting room to her. "I'd like it if you'd stay and wait with me."

Lynn's clear blue eyes never left his as she spoke in a barely audible tone. "If you're sure that's what you want."

Fin held her breath.

"You're who I want." Her father's tone might be low, intended for Lynn's ears only, but standing close, Fin heard him clearly.

Lynn glanced at the cup Steve still held in his hand. "Do you have any more of that?"

Steve laughed. "I don't, but I'm acquainted with the vending machine down the hall."

He and Lynn were stopped in the doorway by Beck's appearance.

Fin rushed over along with the rest of the family to gather around him.

"Ami is well. We have a beautiful baby girl." Beck's soft southern drawl shook with emotion. "Her name is Sarah Rose. Eight pounds, two ounces, and twenty inches long."

Amid the chorus of congratulations and back slaps, Fin slipped in her question. "When can we see Ami?"

"Once they move her up to a room, she can have visitors." Beck, still dressed in delivery room scrubs, smiled wearily. "Her labor went fast, or at least that's what the doctor said. I don't know about Ami, but I feel as if I just pulled a double at the café."

"Congratulations." Steve stepped forward and extended his hand. When Beck clasped it, the older man smiled. "I'm honored that you and Ami chose to name the baby after Sarah."

Beck's gaze locked with his father-in-law's. A wealth of emotion passed between the two men. "I'll take good care of both of them."

"Sarah Rose Cross." Fin glanced at her sisters. "I like it."

"The name is perfect," Prim agreed.

"I'm relieved both of them are okay." When Marigold's voice shook, Fin realized she wasn't the only Bloom sister who'd been worried.

A heartbeat later, Fin found herself embraced in a sisterly group hug.

When Prim stepped back, her eyes held a decided sheen. "I'm happy we're together to share this special moment."

If not for Xander's request, Fin knew she'd likely be in LA, probably in a meeting. It might have been weeks before she could have arranged a long weekend back in Good Hope.

Prim lowered her voice, resting her hand on Fin's arm. "I hope you can be here when my baby is born."

Fin gave her sister another hug. "I hope so, too."

Jeremy had expected Fin's excited chatter when she'd hugged her sister and the tears that filled her eyes when she'd first held Sarah Rose in her arms. He hadn't expected her to turn quiet on the drive home.

Perhaps it was for the best his grandmother wouldn't be there when they got to the house. After he'd texted Ruby pictures of the baby, his grandmother had called to thank him. While she obtained all the pertinent details, Ruby mentioned Gladys had invited several friends over for an impromptu slumber party, including fondue and games.

When Jeremy was seized with the urge to remind her to take her medication and eat properly, he clamped his lips together. He was her grandson, he reminded himself, not her keeper.

As there was no real reason to rush home, he and Fin stopped to check out a new sushi bar in Sturgeon Bay. During the meal Jeremy thought she might mention what had caused her to miss the show choir competition, but Fin was in the mood to celebrate, so he gave her space.

It was only during the drive home she'd grown quiet.

When he unlocked the front door, he turned to her. "What do you say to a glass of champagne to celebrate?"

"I say it's a brilliant suggestion." Fin inclined her head. "Do you have any more bottles of Dom?"

When he returned moments later with a bottle and two glasses, he found her in the sitting area of their suite.

"I'll get a fire started." He set the bottle and glasses on a side table. "It's supposed to dip into the forties tonight."

Jeremy was conscious of her eyes on him while he lit the applewood logs that would soon fill the room with not only warmth but a fragrant scent.

Once the fire crackled, Jeremy splashed champagne into crystal flutes. He handed one to Fin before settling on the sofa beside her.

He clinked his glass against hers. "To Sarah Rose Cross."

"May she have a long and happy life." Fin took a sip, her expression turning pensive. "She was born at just the right time."

Jeremy lifted a brow.

"Ami and Beck are settled in their marriage. They wanted a baby." Fin's fingers gripped the glass. "Unlike the high school girls Lynn hopes to help with her All About Kids project. Neither they, nor their boyfriends, want a baby. It's not the right time."

"Sometimes," Jeremy chose his words carefully, "blessings come from the unexpected."

Fin's bark of laughter held no humor.

"I bet most pregnant high schoolers are probably wishing it—meaning the baby—would just go away." Fin cleared her throat, then took another sip of champagne. "I don't think I can do this."

Jeremy grabbed her hand and pulled her down when she tried to stand. "What's the matter, Finley? Won't you tell me what's got you tied in knots?"

She stared at him, her green eyes clouded. "After you hear what I have to say, you won't look at me the same way."

"Nothing you could say will change how I feel about you." He gripped her hands, squeezed tight. "I love you. I never stopped loving you."

Something that looked like pain flashed across Fin's face. She took a deep breath. "I was pregnant."

"You're"—Jeremy swallowed hard—"pregnant?"

"Not now." She shook her head. "Dear God, no. Not now. Back in high school."

Fin must have seen the questions in his eyes, or maybe she just wanted to get it all out, because she continued.

"I discovered I was pregnant around the time my mom was diagnosed with leukemia." She expelled a heavy breath. "When the first test was positive, I told myself it was an error. After taking five more tests, there was no doubt."

"You never said anything to me." His voice seemed to come from far away.

"It was a bad time." Fin rubbed her temple as if a headache threatened. "My mother was sick. Ami was out of control. Your parents appeared on the verge of separating."

All true, but none of that explained why he'd been kept in the dark. Nor did it explain what had happened to the baby.

His baby.

Jeremy swallowed past the dryness in his throat. "What happened?"

Fin took so long to answer he began to wonder if he was going to have to ask again.

Finally she spoke, but so softly he had to strain to hear. "The show choir competition."

He waited for more, his eyes never leaving hers.

"I miscarried in the hotel room." She closed her eyes for a few moments. When she opened them, they were flat and lifeless. "I slipped away from the group when they left for the auditorium and went back to the room. The cramps were horrible. Then it was done. Over. No more baby."

She swallowed convulsively. "I cleaned up the best I could. When the others got back, I told them I'd gone shopping. Eliza was furious. Heck, everyone was furious. We lost the competition."

Jeremy tried to make sense of the emotions pummeling him.

Focus on Fin, he told himself. He could figure out how he felt about all of this later.

He released her hands and pushed back a tendril of hair with one finger. "Why didn't you tell me?"

"You had so much going on," she began, then squirmed, swallowed. "There was nothing you could have done."

"I'd have been there for you." His voice shook despite his efforts to control it. "I can't imagine how alone you felt. I'm glad that at least you had your sisters for support."

Fin shook her head. "Ami was struggling with accepting our mom's illness. After the car accident, life in the Bloom family got even crazier."

"Wait. Are you telling me you told no one? Not me, not your sisters—"

"No one."

She'd been alone. She'd dealt with the loss all alone.

Jeremy didn't know whether to admire her courage or be pissed as hell.

"It was my"—when Jeremy found himself about to say *problem*, he changed directions—"baby, too."

Fin squared her shoulders and lifted her chin. "I prayed every night the tests were wrong and I would wake up not pregnant."

"The miscarriage wasn't your fault." He pulled her close and buried his face in her hair. "It wasn't anyone's fault."

When she flung her arms around his neck and began to cry, he felt tears slip down his cheeks.

Jeremy wasn't sure who he was crying for.

Maybe for Fin, for the young girl who'd gone through such hell alone.

Maybe for the baby they'd made together, who'd never had a chance to live.

And, maybe, a little for himself, for losing a child he'd never had a chance to know.

Chapter Twenty-One

Fin opened her eyes to sunlight streaming into the bedroom. She couldn't believe she'd slept all night. Maybe it was because she had Jeremy's warm body beside her, his arm slung over her in possession.

She'd been strung tight as a piano wire by the time she got ready for bed. When he'd crawled in beside her, as if he'd been doing it every night, Fin had slid over to make room.

Although it was impossible to be that close to Jeremy and not experience a sexual pull, last night had been about healing, not sex. Her confession had shocked him, yet he'd been incredibly understanding and kind.

He'd even said he loved her.

As emotions swirled inside her, Fin propped herself up on one elbow and watched the man she loved sleep. His chest rose and fell with deep, even breaths. Blond hair brushed his cheeks.

Xander was no longer between them. Since she'd arrived in Good Hope she'd used her California fiancé as a shield to keep Jeremy at arm's length. Now the shield was down and the only thing between them was her own fears.

"Why so serious?"

His deep voice, still gravelly with sleep, had her blinking, then gazing into a pair of vivid blue eyes. Eyes that somehow managed to look both sleepy and assessing.

"I was thinking about you. About doing this." Leaning close, she trailed a finger down his bristly jaw. "Yep. It's scratchy, just as I thought."

Before she could pull back, Jeremy captured her hand and brought it to his mouth, planting a moist kiss in the center of her palm.

Fin's breath quickened. "That's a nice good-morning kiss."

"It's a start." His eyes met hers and she saw the question. "I can do better."

Abruptly, she sat up, hugged her knees close.

He studied her. "You let me sleep with you."

"After the bombshell I laid on you, I guess I thought we both needed the closeness."

"Yeah, about that bombshell." Jeremy rubbed his jaw. "Do you ever . . ."

When the silence lengthened, Fin offered an encouraging smile.

He cleared his throat. "Do you ever wonder if the baby was a boy or a girl? Or what he or she would be like now?"

Last night she'd opened the door. It was only natural, now that he had time to process, he'd have questions.

"I find myself looking at kids walking down the street and thinking our child would be that age now." A familiar sense of melancholy washed over her. "If things had turned out differently, she—or he—would be a freshman in high school."

Jeremy was silent for several heartbeats. Then he expelled a ragged breath.

"We'd be cheering at sporting events or clapping way too loudly at theater productions. Because . . ." His throat moved convulsively as he swallowed. "Our child would have a great voice and excel at sports."

The image of them sitting together in a high school auditorium or bleachers—being *that* kind of parents—was so vivid it brought a smile to her lips . . . and an ache of yearning. Then Fin reined in the fancifulness and her smile faded. "We might not be together."

Sitting up, he linked his fingers with hers, his voice low and raspy. "We'd be together."

She gave a nervous-sounding laugh, and for a second she was that terrified high school junior again. "Your parents would have freaked out if I'd turned up pregnant at seventeen."

With his free hand, Jeremy brushed her hair back from her face. "They'd have gotten over the shock."

"Having one of their daughters pregnant in high school would have leveled my parents." Fin tried to pull her hand back, but he tightened his hold.

"Once they wrapped their brains around it, they'd have been okay. They knew how much I loved you." Jeremy stroked the side of their joined hands with his thumb. "How much you loved me."

Yes, they'd known how much she loved him.

Jeremy's gaze dropped to their linked fingers. "I don't believe I ever mentioned the time I stopped by your house. It was right after your mom got out of the hospital the first time."

Fin cocked her head. "Where was I?"

"I don't know. You and your sisters were out somewhere." When he looked up, the shadows playing in his eyes made them unreadable. "Your dad asked if I could hang around while he ran to the pharmacy. He didn't want to leave your mom alone."

"So you stayed with her."

"Of course."

Of course. Because Jeremy Rakes was that kind of guy, the strong, dependable sort. The kind of person a man—or woman—could count on.

"Your mom made me promise to take care of you. To see that you were happy." He hesitated for a moment. "I let you down."

The weary quality to his voice tugged at her heartstrings. To lighten the mood, she forced a teasing tone. "Hey, I think I've done okay with my life."

He didn't take the bait.

"I knew you were going through a lot with her being so sick and all. I didn't know about the baby." He dropped back on the pillow, his gaze focused on the ceiling. "You weren't acting right, but instead of delving deeper, instead of being supportive, I got angry and broke up with you."

"I pushed you away." The guilt was hers, not his. Fin stroked his arm in an attempt to soothe. "At first because I was afraid what I might reveal in your arms. Then because you reminded me of the loss. Which didn't make sense, because I—I hadn't wanted the baby."

"It was a part of you. A part of us." His expression turned brooding. "I should have been there for you. You should have let me be there for you."

"I handled it." Her tone was flat, matter-of-fact.

"You shouldn't have needed to handle it, not alone." He turned and his eyes met hers. "Grandpa Eddie used to say, 'A burden shared is a burden lifted.'"

Fin lifted her shoulders in a barely perceptible shrug.

"Will you tell your sisters?"

"Eventually." Fin thought of the joy currently infusing the Bloom family. "Not now. Not with Ami and Beck celebrating Sarah's birth and Prim and Max so excited about her pregnancy."

"Does Xander know?"

Startled surprise had her jerking back. "No. Why would he?"

"Well, he is the man you're going to marry. And our . . . the baby is an important part of your past."

"No to one." Fin expelled a long breath. "Yes to two."

He frowned. "You lost me."

"Yes to the second part of your statement." Fin's heart thudded heavily against her ribs. "The miscarriage is an important part of my past."

Something flickered in the backs of his eyes. "What about the first part?"

"I'm not going to marry Xander."

While Jeremy's gaze remained watchful, a spark flared in his eyes. "How do you feel about the engagement being over?"

"Relieved." Glancing down at her bare hand, Fin felt her heart lift. "He—"

"He's a Pompous Ass." Jeremy's warm hands slid beneath the hem of her pajama top. "Who never deserved you."

Sparks of electricity shot to her core at his touch. "What are you doing?"

"Getting reacquainted." As his hands roamed, he nuzzled the sensitive skin behind her ear.

"We need to—" Fin paused, not certain what she meant to say. Take it slow? No, definitely not that.

"I have condoms," he murmured between kisses. "In the dresser."

She was on the pill, so they'd be doubly protected. That knowledge should put to rest any unease. Then why, Fin wondered, did she feel as if she were teetering at the edge of a tall cliff? "Is—is this wise?"

"Yes." He looked up, his hair a tumble of waves, one lock falling rakishly across his forehead. "It's a reunion long overdue."

Her pulse became a swift, tripping beat.

"I've missed you, Finley," he murmured, twining the strands of her hair loosely around his fingers. Then taking the fingers of her hand, he kissed them, featherlight. "I'm going to make this good for you."

It was a vow. She heard the resolve in his voice and saw it in his eyes. Silently, she made the same promise.

A look of tenderness crossed his face. His smile was lopsided, his fingers not quite steady as they touched the curve of her cheek, trailed along the line of her jaw. When he finally kissed her, he took it slow, pressing his lips lightly to hers, teasingly, his mouth never pulling away.

Love fused with desire, so intertwined it was impossible to know where one ended and the other began. In that moment, Fin knew, wise or not, this was what she needed. *He* was what she needed. What she'd always need.

She tangled her fingers in his hair. It had never been like this with anyone else.

Sensation after sensation washed over her as his fingers stroked, brushed, lingered. When those wandering hands finally—blessedly—returned to her breasts, she groaned and cursed the fabric that separated them. Seconds later, her pajamas hit the floor.

Then his mouth replaced his hands and everything went hazy. Lost in sensation, Fin held on tight as the roller coaster began its ascent.

Fin reveled in the feel of the coiled strength of skin and muscle sliding under her fingers. When her fingers dipped beneath his waistband, his pajama bottoms joined hers on the floor.

She barely remembered him reaching for the condom, rolling it on, but she knew the moment he entered her. The feel of him was so familiar, so right.

Love hummed in her blood. As he continued to kiss, to touch, to caress, his stroking fingers sent shock waves of feeling through her body. From the glitter in Jeremy's eyes, she wasn't the only one having difficulty holding on to control.

Need became a carnal hunger.

Jeremy made a sound low in his throat, then caught her mouth in a hard, deep kiss. Her eyes met his. For a second everything stilled. In that moment, her heart simply overflowed.

"I love you, Finley." The declaration came out on a groan.

"Oh, Jeremy." His name came out on a tear as they crested the hill. The drop had her crying out again. But she wasn't alone. Not anymore. When she fell, he fell with her.

And, in his arms, nothing had ever felt so right.

Jeremy stepped out of the shower when a second, more forceful, knock sounded at the bedroom door. Giving Fin a quick kiss, he grabbed a towel. "Be right back."

Hurrying to the door, Jeremy eased it open a crack. At the sight of the sunny smile, he ratcheted down his irritation. "Good morning."

His grandmother's sharp-eyed gaze took in his bare shoulders then lingered on his damp hair.

"It's actually afternoon." The twinkle in her eyes had him shifting uncomfortably. "I wanted you to know I'm heading to cardiac rehab."

Jeremy blinked. "What time is it?"

"Nearly three." Ruby gave him a knowing smile. "Time flies when you're having fun."

Okay, it was clear his grandmother not only knew what he and Fin had been doing behind closed doors, but obviously approved.

"I'll be back around six."

"Have fun." He started to shut the door, but a strategically placed foot stopped it. Jeremy tilted his head. "Problem?"

"I know you're eager to get back to Delphinium, so let me say first that I'm sorry."

Keeping one hand firmly on the towel, Jeremy pushed back his wet hair with the other hand. "What about?"

"You have a visitor waiting for you in the parlor. I gave him a cup of coffee and a Danish." Ruby's brows pulled together in a troubled frown. "He was rather insistent on speaking with you."

"Who is it?"

"Kyle Kendrick."

Though he hadn't given his calendar much thought in recent hours, Jeremy didn't recall having a meeting scheduled with the contractor.

"I heard the shower and assumed you were ready for guests." Chagrin crossed Ruby's face. "I didn't realize that you and Delphinium were still . . . occupied."

"It's okay, Gram." Jeremy experienced a brief pang of regret at the thought of Fin, slick, wet, and waiting in the shower. "Tell him I'll be out in a few minutes."

He pushed the door shut and turned.

Fin stood two feet away, towel drying her hair. Naked. His body jumped to attention. Cat-green eyes met his. "Who is it you're meeting?"

"Kyle Kendrick." Casting one last longing glance at her, Jeremy moved to the closet and started pulling out clothes.

Instead of placing the towel around her body, Fin wrapped it around her hair, forming a turban. "What does he want?"

Fin sat on the bed in front of him, crossing one long leg over another.

His mouth went dry. He wanted her. Again.

In that moment, Jeremy knew he would never stop wanting her. Not just in his bed, but in his life.

"Did you blow off a meeting with him?"

"I don't think so. I hope not." But the question had him checking his phone's calendar. He frowned. "Nothing scheduled. I'm not sure why he's here. But Gram told him I'd meet with him, so—"

"No worries." Fin rose. "While you talk business, I'll get dressed and keep your grandmother company. I can't wait to hear all about Gladys's fondue party."

"She's not here."

"Of course she's here. She just interrupted our . . . shower."

"This place is a pit stop for her. She's off to cardiac rehab, where she'll probably meet a friend and head off somewhere else."

Fin's lips curved. "I want to be Grandma Ruby when I grow up."

"I like who you are just fine." Jeremy closed the distance between them and found himself intoxicated by the fresh citrus scent of her shampoo. Drops of moisture clung to her smooth skin, and he wished he had time to kiss each one.

"Take your time dressing." He slid his hands possessively up her sides, stopping just below her breasts. Out of time but unable to resist, he kissed her with a slow thoroughness that left her visibly trembling.

He started to step away when she grabbed his hand and pulled him back to her for a ferocious kiss.

He slid his arms around her. "Screw Kendrick."

But when his body pressed hard against hers, Fin gave him a little shove.

"Go." She laughed, but the desire in her eyes told a different story.

"Give me ten minutes." His gaze returned to her body, lingering on the luscious curves. "Don't rush getting dressed."

"Aye, aye, sir." The mock salute sent her large breasts swaying.

He blew out a breath. "You're not making this easy."

She shot him a cheeky smile. "What's the fun in easy?"

Jeremy strode down the hall, cursing his bad luck. If his grandmother had left for the gym a few minutes earlier, he'd be with Fin now. He'd never have answered the door, even if he'd heard the bell.

He found Kyle in the parlor, staring out the window. The man turned at the sound of his footsteps.

Standing a little over six feet, Kyle Kendrick had the tough build of a man who worked with his hands. Yet Jeremy knew Kyle not only worked for the company, but *ran* the company.

Kendrick Construction Inc. had its tentacles in all sorts of large commercial projects across the United States. Although Kyle looked to be in his early to midthirties, from what Jeremy had read, the man had been sharing management responsibilities with his father for nearly a decade.

"Sorry to keep you waiting." Jeremy crossed the room and held out his hand.

Jeremy noticed Kyle wore a suit. He wondered if a meeting had somehow missed making it onto his calendar. Until this moment, he'd never seen the contractor dressed in anything but jeans and work boots.

Kyle gripped Jeremy's hand, his gaze steady. "I hope I didn't interrupt anything."

"Not at all." Jeremy motioned for Kyle to take a seat, and when he did, Jeremy took the adjacent chair.

"Your admin said you'd taken the day off."

Jeremy hid a smile. Trust Dee Ann to cover for him. "What you have to say must be important to bring you all the way out here."

He didn't know what to think when Kyle jumped to his feet and began to pace.

Jeremy narrowed his gaze. Something was off here. But darn if he could figure it out. He clicked through the possibilities. Problems with subcontractors? Cost overruns?

Since the Good Hope Living Center was a private project, none of those things should impact the mayor's office.

Kyle gestured with one hand. "You have a nice place here."

"Thank you." Jeremy smiled, a sense of nostalgia mixing with pride. "Rakes Farm has been in my family for generations."

"I understand that sense of continuity. We have a horse farm in Kentucky that's been in our family for generations." The intense emotion in Kyle's voice left Jeremy puzzled. "Bloodlines mean a lot to the Kendricks."

When Jeremy said nothing, Kyle gave a nervous-sounding laugh. "You're probably wondering why I'm here."

Jeremy simply smiled and waited.

Kyle wiped his palms on his pants and once again began to pace. "Your parents don't live in Good Hope."

"They moved to Naples, Florida, several years ago." While Jeremy fervently hoped Kyle wouldn't take long to get to the point, he understood the value of small talk before getting down to business.

Kyle dropped back down in the chair and blew out a ragged breath. "My mother knows your father."

"Really?" Jeremy inclined his head. The conversation had just taken an interesting turn. "Did they go to college together?"

"Actually, they met in Fort Lauderdale during spring break between their junior and senior years in college."

Ed Rakes was the kind of guy who'd never met a stranger. And he was a man rarely forgotten. Even now, years after his parents had retired to the sunny south, people often asked after Jeremy's father.

"I'm sure you didn't drive all the way out here to tell me about a decades-old connection between our families." Jeremy tried to keep the impatience from his voice. It wasn't Kyle's fault he had Fin waiting—hopefully still naked—in the bedroom.

"I think you're my brother."

Jeremy jerked back. "Pardon?"

"We share the same father."

"You're mistaken." Jeremy wasn't sure what game Kyle Kendrick was playing, but he was shutting it down. "My parents have been married over thirty years. They've dated since they were freshmen in college."

"Except for a month their junior year." Kyle lifted his chin, his eyes clear and direct.

Jeremy went cold all over. "You've spoken with my father? He confirmed this?"

"No. Not yet." A muscle in Kyle's jaw jumped. "I wanted to speak with you first."

Jeremy pushed up from the chair, unable to sit any longer. He took a few steps, then whirled. "Why are you here? Why talk to me? If you believe there is some biological connection, go to the source."

"I've already confirmed my dad—ah, the father I grew up thinking was my dad—is not my biological father." Kyle scrubbed his face with his hands, looking bleak.

Bloodlines matter.

The words Kyle had spoken only moments earlier rang in Jeremy's ears.

"That still doesn't explain why you're telling me this instead of speaking with my father." The words came out more tersely than Jeremy had intended. But heck, if what this man was saying was true, his father had cheated on his mom.

Granted, they hadn't been married, or even engaged at that point, but they'd been a couple. Jeremy hadn't heard anything about a one-month breakup their junior year.

Kyle turned, blue eyes meeting blue eyes. "I want you to take a DNA test."

There was something about not only the color but the shape of the man's eyes that gave Jeremy pause. But he shoved the niggling thought aside. There had to be millions of people with blue eyes.

"Your hair is dark," Jeremy heard himself say. "Rakes have blond hair."

It was a comment that anyone with even an elementary knowledge of genetics would find ridiculous. But those eyes . . . the sick feeling in the pit of Jeremy's stomach told him this man could very well be his brother.

Growing up, Jeremy had wanted siblings. But after several miscarriages, his parents had quit trying. His mother laughingly insisted she'd gotten it right the first time.

Kyle reached down and lifted a manila envelope from his leather briefcase. "There's a DNA kit inside. All you have to do is swab the inside of your cheek and send it in."

Jeremy thought about that dark time in his parents' marriage. Had his father known he'd had another son? Or, if he'd cheated once, had he cheated again?

When Jeremy didn't reach out, Kyle lowered his hand.

"If it turns out we're brothers, then what?" Jeremy asked, his voice a throaty rasp. He cleared his throat.

"I'd like for us to get to know each other better. Maybe I could learn something about the Rakes family."

Jeremy clenched the top of an ornately carved throne chair. "What we possess?"

Kyle's dark brows pulled together in confusion. "I'm not sure what you mean."

Jeremy's hand swept the room filled with antiques. "My family has resources."

Anger flashed in Kyle's eyes. "I didn't come here looking for a hand-out. Kendricks have our own money."

"You're telling me you aren't a Kendrick." Jeremy spoke bluntly. "And bloodlines matter. I wonder, does your father still consider you his son? Now that he knows you don't share his blood?"

A muscle in Kyle's jaw jumped. He tossed the envelope at Jeremy, who let it fall untouched to the sofa.

"I can't force you to take the damn test." Kyle spoke through clenched teeth. "But I hope you'll consider it. Is there anything worse than not knowing the truth?"

Chapter Twenty-Two

When ten minutes stretched into twenty, Fin finally dressed. She opened the door to the suite, intending to see what was keeping Jeremy, when she heard the sound of raised male voices.

Instead of heading to the parlor, she made a beeline for the kitchen.

Ravenous after a night—and morning—of lovemaking, she decided to toss together some breakfast. Even though it was past midday, she was in the mood for eggs. Jeremy strolled in just as she was plating the eggs and bacon.

"I heard the front door slam and concluded the business meeting had come to an end." She frowned, taking in the tight set to his jaw and tense expression as she set the plates on the table. "What did Kyle want?"

Instead of answering, Jeremy dropped into a chair and took a long drink of the coffee she'd just poured. "God. I needed this."

Trying not to show her worry, Fin picked up a slice of bacon and nibbled. Jeremy was clearly unsettled by the conversation with Kendrick. That said a lot, considering Jeremy Rakes was one of the most unflappable guys she knew. "What brought him out here?"

Jeremy's fingers tightened around his cup. "He says he's my brother."

Fin dropped her bacon. "Seriously?"

"Actually, he's not positive. He *thinks* I am. He wants me to take a DNA test."

Fin forced herself to lift a fork and stab a bite of egg. If this guy was Jeremy's age or younger, that meant his father had engaged in an affair. Or it could be his mother had had a baby before they'd married and given it up . . .

There were lots of questions she wanted to ask, but she settled for the most direct. "Are you going to do the test?"

"I don't know." Jeremy's gaze dropped to his plate. "I wish he'd just talk to my father. Make him take the damn DNA test."

So, Fin thought, it was his father. "That sounds like a logical next step."

"It does." Jeremy's eyes were clouded. "But Kyle made it clear he wants to know for sure before he approaches my dad."

"Did your father have an . . . affair?"

"A fling with his mother over spring break in college." Jeremy blew out a breath. "Supposedly my parents were on a break from dating at the time."

"And his mother never told your dad she was pregnant?"

Jeremy's brows pulled together. "I guess I'm not sure what happened. I didn't ask. I was caught off guard."

"Did you ever . . . suspect . . . ?"

"That my father had cheated on my mom?" Jeremy blew out a breath. "No. But then again, I never suspected you were pregnant."

Fin jerked back her hand, her cheeks turning hot.

"I'm sorry, Fin. That came out all wrong." His tortured blue eyes met hers. "Forgive me."

"There's nothing to forgive." Shame flooded her.

Jeremy was cursing himself for not knowing she was pregnant when he could just as easily be cursing her for not telling him.

No more secrets, she promised.

Fin glanced at the food, which no longer held any appeal. "Let's get out of here."

"Where do you want to go?"

"Come with me to the hospital. It'll take your mind off it." Fin reached over and curved her fingers around his hand. "We can get better acquainted with my new niece."

Jeremy's gaze searched hers. "It's going to be difficult for both of us."

Fin blinked.

"Seeing the baby." He flipped their hands over and laced his fingers with hers. "We'll look at her and think of our child."

Our child.

For so long Fin had only thought of the baby she'd lost as hers. She hadn't really considered that the baby had been as much his.

"If you'd rather not go . . ."

"I want to go." His gaze met hers. "We're in this together, Finley. You're not alone anymore."

Instead of pulling into the hospital parking lot, Jeremy stopped in front of the house on Market Street.

"I'm glad I called for the room number before we drove all the way to Sturgeon Bay." Fin was out of the car before he had a chance to open her door. "I can't believe they sent her home so early."

"She and the baby must be doing well." Jeremy caught up to Fin, climbing the steps to the massive front porch together. "I never heard of anyone going home in twenty-four hours."

"I think that's some new insurance thing." The butterflies in Fin's stomach rose as one when Jeremy reached around her to ring the bell.

Too late they noticed the "Baby Sleeping. Please Don't Ring the Bell" sign.

"Oops." Fin grimaced. "We're starting off on a bad foot."

But when Beck opened the door, a pink-wrapped bundle in his arms and smile on his face, Fin relaxed.

She gestured to the sign, held in place by a pink gingham ribbon over the doorknob. "Sorry about the bell."

"No worries." With his free hand, Beck motioned them inside.

Fin had gotten used to seeing her brother-in-law dressed in suits or business-casual attire. Today, his long legs were encased in faded jeans. And his forest-green henley had clearly seen better days.

"Looking a bit worse for wear, Cross." Jeremy spoke in the mocking tone men reserved for close friends.

"I've been spit up on several times this morning," Beck said equitably. "Before the day is out, I'll probably be in pajamas."

"Where's Ami?" Fin glanced around.

"Upstairs taking care of some lady stuff." Beck gestured vaguely with one hand. "She'll be down in a minute."

Jeremy took her hand as they followed Beck into the parlor.

"Is that new?" Fin's gaze had been immediately drawn to an antique rocker.

"New to us." Beck gently jiggled the baby in his arms. "The piece actually dates back to the nineteenth century."

"It's lovely." Fin ran her hand across the ornate scalloped top of the chair.

"Would you like to hold her?" Beck asked Fin.

"Ah, sure." After exchanging a glance with Jeremy, Fin crossed to Beck and held out her arms.

Beck lifted his free hand, palm out, as if to keep her at bay. "You need to wash your hands."

"Oh, of course." That only made sense, Fin thought, as she stepped into the downstairs lavatory. When she returned to the parlor, she found the two men talking in low tones, the baby quiet in her father's arms.

"Before I hand her over, why don't you sit down." Beck may have phrased it as a suggestion, but he kept a tight hold on the baby. "Sitting while holding her can be a bit tricky."

Fin glanced at the rocker. "Should I sit there? Or—"

"I'd say the sofa," Beck gestured. "Ami will probably commandeer the rocker when she comes down."

Even as she sat, Fin's heart began to pound. She glanced at Jeremy, who still stood, hands in his pockets, rocking back on his boot heels.

He must have seen the SOS in her eyes, because he joined her on the sofa.

Beck shot Jeremy a sharp glance. "No touching the baby without washing your hands."

"You're going to want to hold her," Fin told him.

Without obvious reluctance, Jeremy rose. When he returned, Fin had Sarah Rose cradled in her arms.

"She's so tiny." Fin found herself mesmerized by the wisps of dark hair and rosebud mouth that moved even in sleep. She thought of the baby that had once grown inside her and knew, without a doubt, she'd have loved it.

"You're not wearing your engagement ring."

Fin was so focused on Sarah Rose it took several seconds for Beck's comment to register.

Her brother-in-law cast a speculative glance in Jeremy's direction.

"She wasn't wearing it yesterday, either," was all Jeremy said.

Beck refocused those sharp brown eyes on Fin. "Will this change in circumstance affect how long you remain in Good Hope?"

Fin was spared the need to respond when her sister entered the room. Like Beck, Ami was dressed for lounging at home in a pair of stretchy black pants and a jersey top with a scoop neck. Instead of shoes, her sister wore the UGG slippers Beck had given her for Christmas last year.

"You have a beautiful little girl, Ami." Fin glanced down at her niece and realized the butterflies were gone. "I'm happy for you and Beck."

Ami's eyes filled with tears. "Every time I look at her I can't help thinking how much Mom would have loved to meet her namesake."

"Mom knows." Fin met and held her sister's gaze. "She's right here with you, cheering you on. In the coming years she'll be that little voice in your head, reminding you of all the wonderful lessons she taught us that you and Beck will use in raising Sarah Rose."

Ami gave a watery smile. "I believe that's the nicest thing you've ever said to me."

"Mom never let us down." Fin gently stroked the top of Sarah's head with one finger. "She'd never leave you alone to navigate the parental waters."

"She didn't leave me alone. I have Beck." The glance Ami shot her husband was filled with love. "And I have you and my other sisters."

They stayed for another thirty minutes. When Sarah Rose began to fuss and Ami announced it was time for her feeding, Fin and Jeremy made their excuses and left.

"That wasn't as difficult as I thought it would be." Fin slanted a sideways glance at Jeremy and found him staring, a strange look in his eyes.

"What you said to Ami was really nice." He grinned. "Don't look so surprised. It was just what she needed to hear."

"I meant every word." When they reached the car, Fin put a hand on Jeremy's arm. "I feel like a walk. Do you feel like a walk?"

The butterfly swarm may have flown, but Fin had something to say and knew it would come easier on a walk.

"Sure." Jeremy stepped back to the sidewalk and held out his arm to her.

She took it. Instead of heading right, which would lead them to Main Street and the downtown shops, they turned left. Thankfully, when they passed Hill House, there was no sign of Eliza or any of the Cherries.

While most of the trees proudly strutted their fall colors, a few were bare, their leaves draped across the ground like skirts. The pleasant scent of fireplace smoke hung in the air.

Fin walked for nearly a block before speaking. "Beck brought up a good point."

Jeremy slanted a sideways glance. "Do you really want to talk about the importance of hand washing?"

Fin laughed. "He was a little anal about that."

"You don't know the half of it. When you were washing your hands, he asked me if you knew you should sing the ABCs while washing your hands."

She cocked her head.

"Apparently you need to take that amount of time to do an adequate job."

"My mother taught us to sing 'Yankee Doodle.'" Fin gave a little laugh. "I'd forgotten all about that until now."

Fin felt herself steady as they continued to walk. "I actually was referring to the part when Beck asked if the breakup with Xander would affect how long I stayed in Good Hope. I realized I hadn't gotten that far."

"You haven't had time." Jeremy's tone was light. "I kept you pretty busy this morning."

"I believe I gave as good as I got." She kept her tone equally light.

"Yes, you did." He leaned over and brushed a kiss against her hair.

When they reached the next intersection, Fin turned down a residential street filled with well-maintained cottages. Judging from the scooters and chalk on the sidewalk, they'd entered a family-friendly zone.

"If these homes were in LA, they'd bring a half million, easy."

Jeremy's gaze shifted from one of the homes, a Cape Cod–style story-and-a-half, back to Fin. He only shook his head. "Yet you still want to live there."

It may have been a statement, but Fin heard the question.

"My job is there." Fin waited for Jeremy to say something about her remaining in Good Hope. He'd said he loved her. Wouldn't asking her to stay be the next step? She found herself wishing he'd ask, then promptly banished the thought. "Of course, if I don't come through with this deal, that job may be gone."

"Seriously?"

"Shirleen, the owner and CEO, values her connections with industry professionals like Xander." Fin let out a breath. "I spoke with her. She's unhappy that I'm no longer with him, but she'll forgive my 'error in judgment' as long as I obtain the agreement to film here."

"I understand her wanting to please Xander, but quite honestly, you can only do so much." His brow furrowed. "Ultimately, you have no control over Lynn's vote. Or mine."

Xander thought I could control you with sex.

Just the thought of what her former fiancé had proposed had Fin's stomach churning.

Jeremy offered a distracted smile. "We should head back. I have some e-mails that need my attention."

"Same here. Only not e-mails." Fin waved a hand in the air. "I promised Lynn we'd get together to discuss the All About Kids project. I'll probably call her and set up a time to meet."

"What are you going to say when she notices you're not wearing the diamond?"

Fin lifted her chin. "I'm not putting it back on."

"That's not what I was suggesting." Jeremy took her hand, gave it a squeeze. "I just know people will ask. We need to be prepared."

He was right. People would notice and ask. Heck, Beck had noticed. Whatever they came up with, it'd have to be plausible. But Fin was done lying.

Fin thought for a moment. "I'll say that particular diamond never felt right. That while the stone was undeniably beautiful, the ring never reflected our feelings for each other."

Jeremy nodded approval.

As they walked in companionable silence for another block, Fin was reminded of the walks she'd often taken with her father. If something was troubling her, it would always come out during one of those nighttime strolls. Or when they were fishing.

"Do you ever think what you'd have done if you hadn't miscarried?"

Fin jolted at the softly spoken question. How many times was he going to want to discuss that horrible period in her life? Once again, she reminded herself that while she'd had years to come to grips with what had happened, Jeremy hadn't even had twenty-four hours to process.

"What would I have done?" Fin's gaze lingered on a church spire in the distance. "For a time, running away seemed a viable option."

Out of the corner of her eye, she caught his look of surprise. "Would you really have run?"

"Probably not." She sighed. "I didn't know what to do. My parents wouldn't have let me quit school. But my mom was in no shape to watch a baby. With all their medical bills, my parents couldn't have afforded to help with day care costs."

"Given time, I believe you'd have come to me." Jeremy's gaze met hers. "I'd have been there for you. Just like I'm here for you now."

She squeezed his hand. "I know."

For so long Fin had fought her own battles and made her own decisions. Leaning on anyone, even someone she loved, didn't come easy.

Still, she thought wistfully, there were times when it would be nice to lean . . . if only for a little while.

Chapter Twenty-Three

"Thanks for helping me." Mindy slipped her hand in Fin's. "I'm glad you came. It was so much fun."

When Marigold told Fin that the Seedlings group she and Cade oversaw was doing a unit on constructing games and could use an extra pair of hands, Fin had agreed to help. Jeremy was working late anyway, and Ruby had plans with friends.

With the vote scheduled for Friday and things still in limbo between her and Jeremy, between her and Shirleen, Fin needed to keep busy.

"I had fun, too." Fin smiled down at the girl, dressed in a fuzzy pink sweater and leggings with her flashy cowboy boots. The scarf she'd given Mindy last weekend covered her head.

"My daddy says you're going to marry the mayor and I'll get to see you a lot." Mindy glanced up at Fin, seeking confirmation.

Though they'd continued to make love, Jeremy hadn't mentioned marriage or said anything about her remaining in Good Hope. Not even after their rehearsal with Gladys yesterday, when they'd nailed the "White Christmas" duet and Gladys announced she'd like them to be her leads in the January production.

"You and I," Fin slung an arm around the girl's shoulders, "are buddies now. We won't lose touch."

"My mommy used to call me after she left." Mindy's lower lip began to tremble. "She doesn't anymore. She doesn't like me being sick. It makes her sad."

If Tessa Vaughn were standing in front of Fin, she'd punch her.

"I don't like having cancer," Mindy confided in a voice just above a whisper.

Out of my league, Fin thought.

"I'm sure your mother loves you." Fin kept her tone matter-of-fact. "I know your daddy does. His eyes light up whenever he sees you."

"But I want my mommy, too."

Sometimes we can't have what we want. The words were on the tip of Fin's tongue when she pulled them. True, but harsh. Too harsh.

"It's easy to think of all the things we want or stuff we can't have at the moment." *Or ever,* Fin thought. "Have you heard of a gratitude jar?"

Mindy shook her head, curiosity driving the shadows from her eyes.

"My sister Ami keeps one. Each day you write on a scrap of paper one thing you're grateful for, then you put it in the jar." Fin touched the girl's shoulder, and they stepped aside to let David and Brynn past. Though the architect smiled, his eyes were hooded, and sadness filled the depths. "Whenever you're feeling sad, you pull out some of the scraps of paper and read them. It's a count-your-blessings kind of thing."

Mindy's forehead wrinkled. "I think I understand."

Out of the corner of her eye, Fin saw Owen at the end of the long hall, waiting just inside the doorway. She'd heard him mention to Prim that he might be a few minutes late picking up Mindy, and Fin had promised to keep his daughter company.

"Like tonight, you might be grateful you got to make up a new game, or maybe you're grateful for your friends, or even for the pretty blue sky." Fin kept her tone light and smiled down at the child. "It doesn't have to be anything big."

A determined glint filled Mindy's baby blues. "I know what I'm going to write."

Fin wasn't going to ask, then decided this wasn't a wish. "What is it?"

"Not what, who." Mindy flung her arms around Fin and squeezed tight. "I'm happy I have you."

"What a little sweetheart." Ruby dabbed at her eyes with a linen hand-kerchief when Fin relayed the story. "My heart breaks for her."

"I saw that you and she had connected at the Wish Fulfilled party, but I didn't realize the extent of the bond that had formed." Jeremy splashed more wine into Fin's glass.

When Fin had arrived home—or rather at Jeremy's home—she'd found him and his grandmother on the terrace. Ruby appeared to be enjoying her cup of herbal tea, but after Fin's close encounter of the Mindy kind, it was the bottle of Shiraz that beckoned.

"There's just something about her," Fin mused, taking another sip. "In so many ways Mindy reminds me of myself at that age. She comes across as supremely confident but she feels things deeply."

Ruby exchanged a glance with Jeremy. "It sounds as if you handled her questions quite well."

"I don't know about that." Fin stared down into her glass. "I didn't want to dash her hopes about her mom, so I redirected."

Jeremy sat back, his fingers wrapped around the wineglass, "Tessa may come back."

Fin shook her head. "She doesn't even call anymore, but Mindy still hopes and wishes. That's a dead-end street."

Ruby lifted her teacup, her gaze curious. "Why do you say that?"

"She's setting herself up for disappointment." Fin gave a harsh laugh. "Think about it. If you don't wish, if you don't hope, you can't be disappointed."

Looking startled, Jeremy frowned. "Do you really—?"

The phone Fin had tossed on the table cut him off when it began to vibrate and ring. She scooped it up.

"No, you're not interrupting." *My dad,* she mouthed. Her smile disappeared. A roaring filled her ears as he relayed details. "Yes, I understand. Thanks for letting me know."

Fin dropped her hand to the table, the phone slipping from her grasp. She closed her eyes for a second.

How could this be? Mindy had *skipped* down the hall to her father only hours before.

"What is it?" Jeremy reached forward, covering her hand with his. "Is it Ami? The baby?"

Fin heard the panic in his voice and fought for composure.

"It's Mindy. She had a seizure. Dad saw the ambulance pull up. They've taken her to the hospital." Fin raked a hand through her hair. "Apparently she wasn't doing as well as Owen thought."

Jeremy was already on his feet. "Let's go."

She looked up in surprise. "Where?"

"To the hospital. She'll want to see you."

"She might already be dead." Though Fin spoke calmly, the noose around her heart tightened painfully.

I can't do this, Fin thought. *I won't do this.*

Shock whitened Jeremy's face. "Is that what your dad said?"

"No, but it's clear this won't end well."

Ruby's worried gaze shifted from her to Jeremy.

"I can't do this, Jeremy." Fin lifted her glass, her voice cool and detached. "I'm going back to LA. Things are simpler there. Everything stays on the surface. That's how I like it."

"Fin." His tone was as gentle as a caress. "Let's take a walk and talk this out. I'll call the hospital and see—"

"No." She shook her head as panic rose to choke her. "Can't go there. Won't go there."

"Don't shut me out." His voice rose, but with visible effort, he pulled it back down. "I'm here for you. Tell me what you're feeling."

"Mindy isn't mine. She's nothing to me." Saying the words felt like a betrayal, but Fin wouldn't take them back. She'd already lost one child. She couldn't bear losing another.

Getting close to Mindy had been a mistake.

Wishing for more with Jeremy, that had been a mistake, too.

Fin pushed back her chair with a clatter and rushed into the house.

When Jeremy rose to follow, Ruby grabbed his arm.

"Let her go, son. She's got some hard things she needs to work out in her own head." Her eyes softened. "She'll be back."

Jeremy dropped back into his chair, exhaled a ragged breath. "You're only saying that because you think Rakes marry their first love."

"I'm saying that because Delphinium loves you."

Jeremy knew Fin loved him. But he also realized she'd built a wall around her heart after the death of their child. She'd opened it a little to let him in, but could she open it wide enough to allow herself to experience all the pleasures—and pains—of a life together?

That was the million-dollar question.

At the stop sign where the country road intersected with the highway, Fin took a moment to send Jeremy a text.

I won't be home tonight

The second she hit Send, she wished she could pull back the message. Though she believed she'd done the right thing in notifying him—she wouldn't want him or Ruby to worry—Rakes Farm wasn't her home.

It had started to feel that way, Fin admitted as she turned onto Highway 42, in a way that nothing had since she'd left her family home at eighteen. But she couldn't stay in Good Hope. Her experience with Jeremy—and with Mindy—had helped her see the truth.

Fin had spent years giving love a wide berth. She'd refused to lay herself open to hurt and disappointment. And she'd been happy. Relatively happy, anyway.

But even an engagement ring on her hand hadn't been enough to keep her heart from opening to Jeremy. And Mindy, well, the little fashionista with the gap-toothed smile and pink cowboy boots had somehow slipped under her defenses when she wasn't looking.

Where had any of it got her? She was miserable.

It was time to return to California.

But when Fin drove by the hospital in Sturgeon Bay, instead of continuing down the highway that would lead her out of Door County, she turned into the parking lot.

She wasn't certain how long she'd been sitting in the car when the door opened and Eliza slid into the passenger seat.

Fin frowned. "What are you doing?"

"Well, I wasn't looking for you, if that's what you're thinking."

"That'd have been hard to do, since I didn't know myself that I was headed here until I parked the car." Fin gathered her courage. "Mindy?"

"Laughing and charming the nurses."

Fin blinked. "Are you serious?"

"They're releasing her in the morning. The doctor made a change in her medication that should take care of any future seizures. They're only keeping her overnight as a precaution."

Fin expelled a heavy sigh. "The cancer is worse."

"No." Eliza reached over and touched Fin's arm. "Not at all. That wasn't the impression I got, anyway."

Tears slipped down Fin's cheeks. She turned her head quickly, hoping Eliza hadn't noticed.

"You and I are a lot alike, Delphinium. We act as if we don't care when we do."

Fin swiped at her cheeks.

"Face your demons, Fin. I have." Eliza's voice turned uncharacteristically gentle. "I had to face the fact that Jeremy doesn't love me. That he loves you."

Fin turned in her seat to face the woman. "Perhaps after I'm gone he'll—"

Eliza gave her head a decided shake. "I'm not about to go down that road. That would be just another lie I'd be telling myself. It's one thing to wish for something that can never be and quite another not to allow yourself to wish at all."

This was the strangest conversation, Fin thought. If she couldn't smell the scent of Eliza's perfume and see her face barely a foot away, she'd think she was dreaming. "I don't understand."

"I believe you do. For you, happiness *is* within reach. Think about what you want, then take that step. Otherwise you'll spend the rest of your life wondering what might have been if you'd just had the guts to try." Eliza pushed open the car door but remained seated. "The vote is Friday. Will I see you there?"

Fin shrugged. "I don't know."

"Fair enough." Eliza stepped from the vehicle but leaned back in, one hand resting on the doorframe. "Mindy's been asking for you."

Eliza shut the door and strolled off without a backward glance. Even before she'd disappeared from sight, Fin began to cry.

"I was so happy you called last night. Do you realize how long it's been since we've done this?" Steve moved his line slightly, teasing the fish with the plump worm.

After leaving the hospital, Fin had called her dad from the Sweet Dreams Motel, asking if he'd be interested in a "date" after his last class. "You and I used to do a lot of fishing."

"We did." Steve reclined back in the green-and-white woven lawn chair that matched the one he'd brought along for her. "I try to get out here as much as I can. With Max or Jeremy or the twins. Though when Callum and Connor come, we don't get much fishing done."

"I've been replaced." Fin wondered how her tone could be so light when her heart was so heavy.

Her father touched her arm, waited until she met his hazel eyes. "No one replaces my Delphinium."

"You have other children. You don't need me."

Fin winced. God, she sounded pathetic.

"Is that why you stopped coming back as often?" His gaze searched hers. "You thought you didn't matter?"

The softly spoken question surprised her. She realized she'd expected him to argue, to insist he needed her just as much as her siblings. Her palms turned slick on her bamboo pole.

"I believe your sisters are happy with the paths they've chosen." Steve cleared his throat. "That makes me happy."

Fin nodded, keeping her gaze focused on the smooth water.

"What does happiness look like for you?" Her father's voice remained conversational. "An important job title? A house at the beach? A husband who is a big-time Hollywood director?"

His tone held no judgment, only curiosity.

"No Hollywood director for me." Fin lifted her hand and wiggled her bare ring finger. "I broke it off with Xander."

"I'm glad." Her father nodded in greeting to an older man and his grandson who passed by with a string of fish. "He wasn't the right man for you."

"How can you say that?" A brittle smile formed on her lips. "You barely knew him."

"All the times you asked, he never came home with you. That told me that you—and what you wanted—weren't his priority." Steve lifted a brow.

"You're right. I wasn't a priority."

Once again, they sat in silence for several long moments.

"Are you happy, sweetheart?"

During the past few weeks she'd been happy—and more content—than she'd been in a long time. Instead of answering, she lifted her shoulder in a slight shrug and returned her attention to the water.

"What about Jeremy?"

"He thinks I won't open up and let myself feel." She jerked the pole, the sudden movement effectively scaring off any interested fish. "He says he'll be there for me. I don't lean. Not on anyone."

She lifted her chin.

"There isn't anything wrong with leaning, honey. We all do it at times." Steve touched his fingers to the side of her face, giving Fin no choice but to look at him. "It's a sign of trust, a way of receiving strength from each other."

"I also keep secrets." Fin swallowed against the lump rising in her throat. "From Jeremy. From you and Mom. From my sisters."

Steve set down his pole. "What kind of secrets?"

For a second Fin was tempted to give an answer that would satisfy him without saying anything at all. His life was finally on track. He had Lynn and his teaching and his grandchildren. Anita was out of the picture. Her dad didn't need more drama in his life.

But Fin was tired of the lies. "I was pregnant in high school. I had a miscarriage."

Clearly stunned, her father's eyes widened. Then, without a word, he took the pole from her hands and wrapped his arms around her, holding her tight.

Fin laid her head against the warmth of his shirt and let the words spill out.

"I'm sorry you had to go through such an emotional time alone." He stroked her hair. "I can't imagine how hard that was for you."

She sniffled, wished for a tissue. In answer, he pulled a perfectly folded handkerchief from his shirt pocket and handed it to her.

He continued to stroke her hair with those large, gentle hands while she dabbed her eyes, then blew her nose.

"I must look a mess."

"You were a brave girl."

Startled, Fin blinked.

"You thought about everyone's feelings but your own. You bore all the heartache and pain and fear in silence." His lips twisted in a wry smile. "That doesn't surprise me."

"It doesn't?"

"You've been like that since you were a little girl. Never wanting to add to anyone's burden."

Fin gave a hiccupping laugh. "I don't think that's how most people would describe me."

"They don't really know you." He took her hands in his. "You're so like your mother."

She lifted a hand in protest. "Mom and Ami—"

"—had a lot of common interests. But in terms of personality, it's you who favors your mother." Steve shook his head, his lips curving slightly. "Sarah didn't like to lean, either. It caused some arguments."

"Really?"

He nodded, his eyes distant with memories. "When you love someone, you want to be there for them. If they don't tell you when they're hurting or when they need something, it makes a person—well, in my case it made me feel as if Sarah didn't trust me. That she didn't think she could count on me. That I wasn't strong enough to handle it, whatever *it* was. Yet your mom thought she was looking out for me."

Steve met her gaze. "If you think about it, it's a kind of well-meaning arrogance."

Fin couldn't hide her surprise. She couldn't recall her father ever saying an unkind word about her mother. "But you and Mom had a good marriage and were happy together."

"We were very happy. In a marriage, there's a give-and-take." His eyes turned misty. "There's growth. Or there should be. A husband and wife learn to work together, to understand and respect each other's needs. Your mother and I struggled—oh, especially in those early years—but we learned."

"It's probably too late for me and Jeremy."

"It's never too late if you love each other." He cupped her cheek with the palm of one large hand. "One of those things your mother and I discovered was that sometimes—actually, most of the time—hurts can be healed if you start off with the two most powerful words in any relationship."

Fin inclined her head. "What words would those be?"

"I'm sorry."

Chapter Twenty-Four

All the seats in the board chambers were filled by the time Eliza arrived. As there were still fifteen minutes before the meeting would start, she was in no hurry to take her seat on the dais at the front. Turning on her heel, she strode down the corridor and ran into Jeremy locking up his office.

He looked tired, she thought, as he so rarely did.

She kept her tone light. "Ready for the big vote?"

His thoughtful gaze settled on her. "Do you think it'll come to me breaking another tie?"

"Hard to say. Lynn has been wavering, but she told me this afternoon, unless something drastic is brought up at the meeting, none of the arguments have caused her to change her vote."

Jeremy swore.

Eliza arched a brow. "Problem?"

"If the board ties and I vote against Xander's proposition, I'll be putting Fin out of a job." He swiped a hand through his hair. "I want her to stay because this is what she wants, because I'm what she wants, not because she has nowhere else to go. It's probably a moot point anyway. I don't think she's ready to invest in a relationship, with me or anyone."

"You're wrong."

His gaze sharpened. "About?"

"She loves you, Jeremy. All you have to do is look at her to see it." Eliza gave a little laugh. "As far as being ready to invest in relationships, I spoke with Owen yesterday. He told me Fin went to see Mindy in the hospital."

"Really?" The bald hope in his eyes humbled her.

Would she ever find anyone who would love her that much?

"Don't stress about the board vote." She patted his shoulder. "Lynn is only one member. There are three others who will be voting."

Before he could ask any questions, Eliza hurried down the shiny linoleum hallway, a woman with a mission. If she had to vote for that blasted proposition to spare Jeremy from being put in the middle, she'd do it.

He'd been there for her all those years ago. She'd be there for him now.

The meeting began on time, with three merchants and two citizens lining up to comment.

Eliza blinked when Fin arrived, looking chic—but professional—in a red linen dress and heels. She took her place at the end of the line queued behind the microphone.

"Did you know Fin planned to speak?" Lynn whispered, covering the microphone on the table before them with her hand.

Eliza shook her head, then glanced at Jeremy, who appeared equally startled. She listened to all of the comments with only half an ear, anticipation humming in her blood.

"Delphinium Bloom." As per protocol, Fin identified herself when she stepped to the microphone.

She was an excellent public speaker, Eliza realized, as Fin gave an impassioned speech about community and all that made Good Hope a wonderful place to live.

"Recently, an early Christmas was held for one of our junior citizens, Mindy Vaughn. Mindy was offered a chance to wish for anything. She could have gone anywhere, done anything, yet she wished to celebrate Christmas in Good Hope. I understand her wish. No place is more special than Good Hope during that time of year when we all come together in a spirit of giving and love." Fin's eyes strayed to Jeremy. "If I've learned anything in my years away from here, it's that family and community are what's important in life. I urge the board to vote against the proposition currently before them. Even if it's only for one year, it's a time the citizens of Good Hope will never get back. In this time of global uncertainty and tension, we need more than ever to hold tight to those traditions that bind us—and bring us—together. Thank you."

The board voted three to one against the proposition. Gladys told Eliza that Fin's eloquent speech had caused her not only to change her vote but to redouble her efforts to get Fin back on the community theater stage where she belonged.

Eliza smiled when she saw Jeremy stride after Fin once the meeting adjourned.

As it should be, Eliza told herself.

Though most weren't aware of the fact, she really did like happy endings.

Fin took the long way out of the courthouse to avoid the crowds leaving the boardroom. The hallway that exited out the south door was deserted, the only sound the click of her heels on the shiny linoleum.

By the time the footsteps registered, it was too late. Fin gasped when someone grabbed from behind and spun her around. Ready to fight, she jerked from the man's grasp. Then she saw his face. "Xander."

"What the hell was that all about?"

Though she couldn't recall ever seeing him quite so angry, Fin refused to be cowed. "It was a public forum. I gave my opinion."

He jabbed a finger at her. "You did it to get back at me."

"This wasn't about you, Xander." Fin kept her tone level.

"I don't believe you. Let me tell you now, Shirleen isn't going to keep you on. Not after this stunt." A muscle in Xander's jaw jumped. "You're going to regret this. When you have time to think about all you've given up, you're going to have nothing but regrets."

Fin knew he believed what he was saying. She also knew he was wrong.

"Hollywood is all about pursuing your dreams, but I've spent the past ten years telling myself not to wish, not to dream. All because I feared being hurt. That plan may have kept my heart safe, but it wasn't living. I want more." Fin touched his arm. "I don't regret my time in LA or with you, because those roads led me back to Good Hope. This is where I belong."

"I heard shouting." Jeremy moved to stand between her and Xander. "Is everything okay?"

"I had to have been blind." Xander gave a humorless chuckle. "For her, it's always been you."

Xander shook his head, his gaze now on Fin. "I'm done wasting time on this backward town."

"One second, please," Fin called out when he turned to go. She stepped around Jeremy and moved to Xander. Pulling the diamond from her bag, she held it up for a second, then dropped the ring into Xander's suit pocket. She surprised herself—and him—when she brushed a kiss across his cheek. "Have a good life. I wish you much success."

Xander stared at her for a long moment. "We could have been so good together."

Jeremy waited until Xander was out of sight before he stepped close, trailing a finger up Fin's bare arm, leaving gooseflesh in its wake. "Is what he said true?"

Fin swallowed against the dryness in her throat. "He said a lot of things."

He took a half step forward, eliminating the space between them. Placing two fingers under her chin, Jeremy tipped her head back. "That for you, it's always been me?"

Her heart stuttered as love swamped her.

No more lies.

No more running.

"Always." Fin wrapped her arms around his neck and her lips found his. "Forever."

Epilogue

Sarah Rose Bloom's first Christmas party, held the afternoon of Christmas Day at her family home, included laughter and conversation and a platter of lavender cookies with rosewater icing. The cookies had been her grandmother's favorite and were a staple of any Bloom gathering.

"These look amazing." Fin took a bite and her eyes widened. She whirled, her shocked gaze focusing on Ami. "You found the secret ingredient."

The cookies, ones Ami and their mother had made countless times for every family occasion, had no written recipe. There hadn't been a need. Ami and her mother often joked they could make them in their sleep.

Except once Sarah had passed away, try as she might, Ami couldn't recall the one ingredient that made their recipe special.

"It was the strangest thing." Ami's eyes turned soft as she gazed at her daughter, gurgling, in Beck's arms. "Sarah Rose was with me in the kitchen while I set out the ingredients. I found myself automatically reaching for orange zest."

"Circle of life." Fin got so caught up visiting with Ami that it took a second for her to realize Jeremy was no longer at her side.

"Our engagement was a con," Fin heard him tell his grandmother when she approached the kitchen. "It was our way of getting you to agree to the surgery."

From her position in the hall, Fin watched Ruby lift the teapot from the burner. "I wondered when you were going to come clean."

"You knew?"

"I knew all along you and Delphinium were conning me. Because I was conning you." Ruby's voice held a smile. "When I spotted the diamond on her finger I saw a way to get the two of you back together. Quick thinking for an old lady with a bad ticker."

Jeremy shook his head and laughed.

Leaving them to their mutual confessions, Fin wandered back down the hall to the parlor and convinced her brother-in-law to part with his daughter.

Love stirred as Fin gazed down at the baby with her tuft of dark hair and chubby cheeks. She thought of Ami's vision . . . or had it been a wish? Regardless, it had come true.

Maybe one day she and Jeremy would have another child . . . Fin found her gaze drawn to the curtains at the large window. Through the lace she saw snow continued to fall.

"I'm dreaming of a White Christmas . . ." Fin sang softly and watched Sarah Rose's eyes grow wide.

She'd reached the refrain when Jeremy returned from the kitchen with his grandmother. He sat down beside her on the sofa and added his voice to hers. Everyone quickly joined in.

Sarah Rose waved her chubby arms, her eyes as bright as the star at the top of the tree.

When the song concluded, Fin glanced around the room. At her father and Lynn, at Marigold and Cade, at Prim and Max—at the twins playing with little cars by the tree—and at Ami and Beck, gazing proudly at their beautiful Sarah Rose. Then finally at the man who sat beside her, his arm draped around her shoulders.

Whenever his gaze settled on her, the star that sat atop the tree seemed to shine extra bright.

Star light, star bright, first star I see tonight . . .

The nursery rhyme had her lips curving. Fin didn't have to wish tonight. She had what she wanted.

Jeremy rose to his feet. "Come outside with me for a minute."

Before Fin could push to her feet, Beck plucked Sarah Rose from her arms.

"It's difficult to get up while holding a baby." Beck's arms tightened protectively around his little girl.

Fin shook her head. "I pity any boy that comes sniffing around her when she's sixteen."

Beck grinned and gestured with his head toward Jeremy. "You watch. He'll be the same way."

Of that, Fin had no doubt. It was a comforting thought.

She and Jeremy grabbed their coats before stepping outside.

"I love being out here where the snow is falling and everything is so still." Fin moved to stand beside Jeremy at the porch rail. "It's been a wonderful Christmas."

"Having family around keeps you grounded." He looked at her. "You and I are lucky that way. We know who we are, where we came from, and where we're going."

"Are you thinking about Kyle?"

He nodded. "Do you think I should do the DNA test?"

Knowing Jeremy as she did, Fin knew he'd eventually agree to take the test. She slipped her arm through his. "You have time to decide. We've had a lot to deal with the last couple of months. We need to be kind to ourselves and, for now, soak in the love that surrounds us."

That brought a smile to his lips. "When did you become such a philosopher?"

"When? Hmmm." Bringing a finger to her lips, Fin thought for a moment. Then, looping her arms around Jeremy's neck, she pulled him close. "I guess when I realized that with you in my life, I have everything I need. I couldn't wish for anything more."

ABOUT the AUTHOR

Cindy Kirk's passion for words started at an early age. At sixteen, she wrote in her diary: "I don't know what I would do if I couldn't be a writer." Her writing life soon began after taking a class at a local community college. Once her daughter went off to college, Kirk returned to her passion in earnest and jumped straight into composing book-length fiction.

An incurable romantic and eternal optimist, Kirk creates characters who grow and learn from their mistakes while achieving happy endings in the process. She loves reading and writing romance novels because she believes in the undeniable power of love and the promise of happily ever after. She lives in Nebraska with her high-school-sweetheart husband and their two dogs.